Mitch cursed under his breath. "Look, I really have about a dozen things to get done—"

"Say you *do* have to make an arrest," she cut in. "You'll have to work with a federal prosecutor, testify in court…. The Park Service will pay for all that."

"*So?* What's it got to do with you seeing the crime scene? It's goddamn silly if you ask me."

Anne kept her expression neutral. "I'm the one making the call here. Now, is it a long way?"

"Oh," he answered, his jaw tight, "it's just exactly opposite of where we were going." He could have sworn she was studying him. He stared straight ahead, not wanting to meet her eyes. Something about this woman who attracted him was… He searched his mind but couldn't come up with a word to describe her. *Confusing,* maybe.

Dear Reader,

The Anasazi Indians have always fascinated us. Since we're originally from the East Coast, neither of us had heard of them before moving to Aspen. Over the years, we've read everything we could get our hands on about these ancient North Americans, and we've traveled to Chaco Canyon, Mesa Verde and other ruins in the area. We wrote a Superromance novel years ago called *West of the Sun,* which was about the Anasazi, and we wrote another about counterfeit pottery entitled *Firecloud.* In *The Ranger and the Widow* our tale is about both.

Canyonlands National Park, the setting for our story, is a place of wonder. Everything we tell you about it—from the colors, the rocks, to the arches and spires—is true, only multiplied a hundred times in real life. And just off the road, everywhere, are thousand-year-old Anasazi ruins. Amazing!

The problem of moki poaching—looting ruins for valuable artifacts—which can be both innocent and deliberate, is very serious. There are strict federal laws against it, but there aren't enough rangers to police any of the huge parks. And the profits from selling artifacts are truly enormous, as the characters in our story well know.

We hope that all our readers are inspired to travel to the remarkable Canyonlands to see the glory of the park and the ruins for themselves.

Sincerely yours,

Molly and Carla

THE RANGER
AND
THE WIDOW
Lynn
Erickson

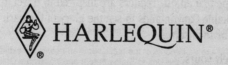

HARLEQUIN®

TORONTO • NEW YORK • LONDON
AMSTERDAM • PARIS • SYDNEY • HAMBURG
STOCKHOLM • ATHENS • TOKYO • MILAN • MADRID
PRAGUE • WARSAW • BUDAPEST • AUCKLAND

This book is dedicated to Audrey—friend, fan,
expert source on Canyonlands National Park and
our intrepid typist.

ISBN 0-373-70897-1

THE RANGER AND THE WIDOW

Visit us at www.romance.net

Printed in U.S.A.

The landscape everywhere, away from the river, is of rock—
cliffs of rock; tables of rock; plateaus of rock; terraces of
rock; crags of rock—ten thousand strangely carved forms.
Rocks everywhere, and no vegetation; no soil; no sand.
In long, gentle curves, the river winds about these rocks.
—John Wesley Powell, 1869

PROLOGUE

OVER 300 MILLION YEARS ago the Great Basin of North America was covered by a warm primeval sea, in alternate cycles shallow and deep, as the land, groaning and cracking, thrust upward, then dropped. Water evaporated and mineral sediment accumulated. Debris from erosion added dark shale striations; limestone added white.

Then the sea retreated, losing its last battle, and left a broad river delta with streams that deposited further layers.

The river dried up and desert took over, thousands of square miles of red sand dunes, blowing and shifting in the moaning wind, empty and sterile, hardening into fiery sandstone.

Desert gave way to streams and lakes, eroding the soft rock, leaving massive vertical cliffs.

The mighty Green and Colorado rivers formed, and their inexorable forces stripped away more layers, sculpting the land. They are still sculpting it today, although in the brief span of mankind this is not evident.

Man has been there for only the narrowest band on the yardstick of time, venturing into the twisting red canyons, living and dying, a puny creature.

The land endures: brilliantly colored rock, cliffs,

canyons, arches, spires, mesas carved by water and wind and the age. A land of grand vistas and narrow crevices.

Canyonlands.

CHAPTER ONE

THE SKY WAS BEGINNING to darken as the two men in separate trucks reached the hanging tree deep in the red-rock wasteland of Canyonlands National Park.

The wiry man got out of his pickup and gestured to the other man as he pulled up alongside, his tires raising plumes of dust. When the second man hesitated, the wiry one gestured again, nodding toward the hump beneath a tarp in the bed of his vehicle.

"No." The second man shook his head vehemently. "I can't...touch him."

"I need your help."

"Do you have to do this? He's...the kid's already...dead."

"It's gotta be done."

"Why?"

The wiry man's lip curled up at a corner. "Blame it on the Anasazi," he said. "It's what their spirits want."

"No. I won't help. You're...sick."

The wiry man turned away. "Go on home, then. I'll handle this myself."

The second man did not delay. He put his truck in gear and sped off down the dried-up riverbed, while the first man pulled a cigarette out of the pack in his breast pocket, lit it between cupped hands, took a couple of drags, then faced up to his chore.

The body was heavy with the exaggerated weight-
iness of death. He had to half drag it out of the back
of the truck and across the uneven ground to the
gnarled tree. Once he had the noose fashioned and the
loose end over a limb, the job was easier—he only
had to hoist the deadweight up until the young man's
feet were dangling above the ground, wrap the end of
the rope around the tree and snug it down.

He stood for a moment, smoking, admiring his
handiwork. The body turned slowly in the slight
breeze that was beginning to glide along the floor of
the canyon. The immense sky above was brilliant
mauve and orange and pink, as only a desert sunset
could be, and the shadows were long by now. The
body's counterpart on the ground twisted eerily, elon-
gated.

Damn arrogant pup, the wiry man thought, *coming
here and trying to ruin everything. Just got what you
deserved.*

The canyon was washed in purple by the time the
man took a last look at the student archaeologist's
corpse, checked the ground for anything he might
have left, then climbed into his truck and drove off,
confident the night wind would erase both sets of tire
tracks.

He was always careful, and a helluva lot smarter
than the handful of park rangers whose responsibility
it was to patrol the huge area. He never left a clue
that could tie him to any of the criminal activities he
pursued on federal land.

But he had overlooked something, something he'd
missed in the dead student's pocket, small and seemingly insignificant, but conversely something so crucial it would cast new light on the history of mankind
in North America.

CHAPTER TWO

CHIEF PARK RANGER Jim Mitchell—Mitch—had to get past Martha, and it wasn't going to be easy.

"Look, Martha, I have to learn my way around this park," he said patiently.

"There's work on your desk." His secretary nodded toward a growing stack of files.

"It can wait. This is more important. I'll be back by noon."

"The schedules and the budget have to be done, and you need to call about the plumbing in the visitors' bathroom, and—"

"It's Sunday," he pointed out.

She gave up, but not without a disapproving frown, and Mitch gratefully made it past her and out into the early-morning brightness. He drew in a deep breath of the champagne-dry air, settled his National Park Service straw Stetson on his head, adjusted the holstered gun on his belt and climbed into his white Bronco, with its distinctive green stripe. *Free,* he thought, *free at last.*

He drove along the dirt road well beyond the paved tourist circuit, heading south toward the area he'd passed last week that he wanted to explore. The need to know the park was becoming an obsession with him. An obsession and a labor of love. He couldn't get over the fact that he'd left Washington and his

Secret Service job six months ago, figuring his life was pretty much over. And then he'd found it had just begun.

The sun slanted in the rear window of the Bronco, warming his back. The windows were open, and the sage-scented morning air blew in.

He followed Lavender Canyon for a time, then turned off onto a dry streambed that served as a road in the summer, steering around a boulder some ancient flood had deposited. Amazing country. For a city boy, even more amazing. He'd read everything he could get his hands on once he knew where he'd be stationed, and he'd learned about the desert Southwest, with its geological wonders and priceless Anasazi archaeological sites.

He'd never heard of the Anasazi before undertaking his research. They sure weren't mentioned in school curriculum in the East. But they had built great stone cities over a thousand years ago, before disappearing during a long drought period.

The Anasazi hadn't vanished, of course—they'd migrated to where water could be found, the Rio Grande Valley, and they were still around, now called Hopi Indians, or Zuni or Tewa.

Funny, how he'd ended up here. It had started on the worst day of his life. He'd been on duty during a vice presidential campaign tour, when an attempt was made on the candidate's life. Mitch was caught in the cross fire while shoving the vice president out of danger, and he'd been shot. Had his femur shattered. He'd survived, but he still limped. Sure, he'd been a hero; but unable to function at a hundred percent anymore, he'd been given his choice of less sensitive federal jobs.

Chief ranger of Canyonlands National Park, Needles District. The damn park in southeastern Utah was so huge it had three entirely separate districts, each with its own staff and visitor centers. They were so far apart, on often impassable dirt roads, that the distance between them could amount to hundreds of miles.

"Whoa, there," Mitch said out loud as a rattlesnake slithered sideways across the dry wash in front of his wheels.

Snakes, lizards, a few mule deer, shy desert bighorn sheep, cacti, stunted trees, saltbush, galleta. Pack rats and scorpions. It was a hard land, but the sheer number of species that thrived on it despite the intense heat and dryness continuously astonished Mitch.

He kept trying to get his daughter, Brooke, interested in the park, but the fourteen-year-old disdained any mention of it.

"I hate this place," she wailed. "It's so far from everything. All my friends. The malls. There's nothing to do here, Dad, nothing!"

"But, Brooke, it's so beautiful. You can hike or fish or camp out."

Brooke inevitably rolled her eyes. "Like I really want to do those *cool* things."

The boringly repetitive conversation had been going on all summer.

Mitch groaned. Maybe it'd be better when they moved into Moab for school in the fall once the tourist season ended. Moab wasn't exactly Washington, but it was the biggest town for a long, long ways.

Then again, maybe his ex-wife, Denise, would want to take Brooke back. Denise, remarried, with a new baby, lived in Las Vegas, Nevada now. Well,

Vegas was a city, he supposed, but he'd prefer Brooke to stay here with him.

Brooke was back at the staff housing this Sunday morning. He hoped she found something to do with herself. She baby-sat a lot for the younger children of other park employees, but she'd so far refused to work in the Visitor Center, even though she'd been asked to help the interpretive division with its children's campfire program.

The heat was already scorching as Mitch turned up a canyon that drew his interest. Although he tried to get out to new areas of the Needles District, it'd take a lifetime to travel every square inch of it. He passed a tumble of adobe bricks under a rock overhang. There was no official sign this far off the beaten track, but he knew he'd come to an Anasazi ruin, one of their small settlements, consisting of some grain silos, perhaps, or a ceremonial pit dug into the earth, known as a kiva. Scratched onto the rock face were pictures—petroglyphs—native animals, symbolic markings, a hunchback figure that he recognized instantly as Kokopelli, the ancient god of fertility and mischief, or so archaeologists and anthropologists believed. In this rendition, Kokopelli wasn't playing a flute, though he was often depicted with one. He also usually had a hump on his back—some researchers thought it was really a backpack, and Kokopelli was a trader, wandering up from the Aztecs in Mexico with his wares.

Fascinating.

Mitch had many duties—he was basically on the job twenty-four hours a day. He was traffic cop, medic, information giver, rescuer, fireman and protector of federal land. Part of his job involved this very ruin, this simple jumble of collapsed sandstone bricks. There were thousands, if not millions, of these sites in the Southwest, many of them in Canyonlands, most of them in the Needles District. Some still contained valuable artifacts, pots, sandals, weapons, tools. Very few skeletons, though—the Anasazi did not bury their dead near their settlements. The history of a bygone civilization lay in these ruins, and strict laws had been passed to protect the sites.

A big part of Mitch's job was to thwart the destruction of these sites and the theft of the artifacts. Sometimes the thieves were innocents: a tourist family who found a potsherd with a colorful design on it and decided to take it home.

But mostly the thieves were not innocent; they were determined, organized, knowledgeable men.

Moki poachers. That's what the Hopi called them. Those who stole from the dead. Grave looters.

Mitch found his new job immensely satisfying. He'd been unsure when he'd accepted the appointment, wondering whether such a drastic change would work for him. He still carried a gun as head of the protection division of the Needles District, but he'd never used it. Probably never would.

He drove past the small ruin, and continued up the dry wash. He hadn't been here before, and he was trying to picture in his mind where he was. He'd studied the topographical maps of the park, but the land was so cut and folded over upon itself, so twisted and scoured, that it was confusing.

The Bronco groaned and bumped along in four-wheel-drive. The temperature would hit a hundred on this August day, he was thinking. Not a cloud was in sight. The sapphire-blue sky arced from horizon to horizon.

It would rain soon, he'd been told. In late summer when the monsoon arrived. For the Indians, July was the beginning of their year—to celebrate the coming of the rain. Well, it was August now, but no rain had fallen since early June. It was late this year.

He let himself sink into the new feelings he'd been having lately while out in the far reaches of the park, alone, just him and the rattlers and Indian rice grass. He'd been trying to put a name to the feeling, and he'd finally succeeded. He was drawn to the land. It held a mystical quality for him, as if when he left the Visitor Center he entered a new realm, an almost eerie place, one where he was always on the verge of seeing, experiencing, something strange and magical.

He was uncomfortable admitting that to himself. It was embarrassing. He'd certainly never admit it to a living soul, not even Brooke. So he kept the feeling inside, a curious bit of whimsy that he'd never have thought he was capable of.

He knew what his staff thought of him. His ex-wife, Denise, had voiced it often enough. "The strong silent type," she'd said. "Mr. Tough Guy. Hide those feelings, Mitch. For God's sakes, don't let anyone know you're human."

He tried to imagine what Denise would say if he told her how profoundly this land affected him. She'd laugh. Oh, yeah, she'd get a kick out of that.

He wondered, as he so often did, if Brooke would be better off with her mother and the new husband. He tormented himself with it. Was he being selfish? Was Brooke truly better off in Canyonlands?

Mitch slowed the truck to navigate a narrow, sharp-angled curve in the little-used road, downshifting, easing his tires over the loose rock. He was concentrating on not getting stuck, shifting again as he negotiated the curve, when he saw it.

First, his eye caught the motion of the birds flapping upward. He thought for a split second the wind had scattered leaves, but there was no wind, just the faintest of breezes. And there were no leaves. Then he thought his eyes were playing tricks on him, or that the shimmering heat was creating an illusion.

He jammed on the brakes and squinted. There was something, a figure hunched in an old twisted scrub-oak tree. He decided it was a joke. Someone, off in this remote corner of the park, was playing a joke and had hung a life-size figure of Kokopelli in the old dead tree.

He took off his sunglasses, squinted again, and stared at the figure that was backlit by the sun.

Sure, it was a prank, he was thinking. Then the figure began to stir in the barely perceptible breeze, and Mitch's breath halted in his lungs.

It was a body. A *human* goddamn body.

As he stared, disbelieving, details isolated themselves: dead branch, a rope hanging from it, the noose around the body's neck, the clothes—tattered—mutilation by animals evident.

A goddamn human body.

A *lynching*.

Out here? In Canyonlands?

He put the Bronco in park and got out, his heart pounding against his rib cage, his brain grinding into gear as he approached the tree.

No, he cautioned himself, halting. He wasn't approaching a corpse; he was about to tread all over the crime scene, and if he'd learned nothing else in his training with the Secret Service, he'd learned that the integrity of a crime scene had to be protected.

His radio.

Mitch backtracked to the Bronco and tried to call Martha. Nothing. Static. The rock walls of the steep canyon were cutting off communication. There was only one thing he could do—scramble up the canyon wall to call from the hilltop.

Sweating, his leg twinging, he managed to climb to the top and his secretary.

"Martha, listen carefully. I've found a dead body. I'm somewhere near Lavender Canyon."

"What?" Martha squawked.

"I'm going to want the sheriff and his forensic team from Moab. Martha, do you read me?"

"Say it again, Mitch. Over."

"There's a dead body hanging from a tree."

"An accident? Do I send in a helicopter, the medics?"

"It was no accident, Martha. Inform the sheriff. Tell him I'll be waiting. We don't need helicopters. The man's already dead." Then he gave her map coordinates. "Have you got it?"

"Yes, sir, yes, I'll call right away. Over and out."

He scrambled back down to the canyon floor, took a swig of water from his bottle and went to work. It'd be hours before the sheriff got there, and he wasn't about to sit around waiting.

He had a camera, a Polaroid, which he carried to document crimes in the park. *Lesser* crimes up to this point.

He took two cartridges of film from every angle, filmed the half-smudged-out tire tracks, the body, animal tracks mixed with human footprints, barely discernible flat-soled cowboy boots. He was careful not to step on any marks on the ground that might be vital later to his investigation.

And all the time his heart beat an angry tattoo and his mouth was dry. A murder. Under *his* jurisdiction.

Finally, he approached the body. It was a young man—that much he could tell. But there had been the animals, and God only knows what other disturbances to the crime scene, and Mitch realized that between the animals and the elements, collecting any useful forensic evidence from the corpse was going to be damn hard. Carefully, he cut the body down and, with equal care, he covered it with a new tarp he carried in the back of the Bronco.

Just as he was pulling the tarp over the face he froze.

Mitch *knew* this young man.

He was one of Chick Draco's archaeological students who'd been working this summer at the Red Canyon dig.

Oh, boy, was the shit going to hit the fan. An innocent young student. Ah, God, what a tragedy.

How had it happened? Why? Who? Who could have done this?

He noticed two things at the same time then: a bullet hole in the side of the head. Small caliber, he registered. No exit wound. And a piece of pottery, which must have fallen out of a pocket when Mitch had lowered the body to the ground.

He picked up the piece gingerly, by the edges. It was maybe two inches by three inches, and black. A shiny black, with some raised lines on it—the outline of part of a face, an ear, an eye. He placed the potsherd in the back of his Bronco.

He was sitting in the truck, doors open to catch the breeze, when the sheriff arrived with two deputies. After Sheriff Ted Warner looked the scene over, Mitch thumbed his Stetson back on his head and blew out a breath. "I realize the park is my territory," he said to Warner, "but I'd like the use of your forensic men and your pull with the state lab in Salt Lake City. We simply aren't equipped for this."

"No problem, glad to lend a hand. Both my boys here are trained."

"Thanks," Mitch said.

After that it was the usual: the deputies crawling over the area, collecting dust and fibers—some unusual fibers on the boy's shorts—and asking a hundred questions of Mitch, taking pages of notes, snapping two more rolls of film.

Then one of the deputies pulled the dead man's wallet out of his back pocket, held it by the corner, and opened it. "Zachary Sterner," he called out. "Address is 135 Central Park West, New York City."

"Damn," Sheriff Warner said, "some New York rich kid. There'll be hell to pay over this."

The coroner arrived last, as per procedure, and made his on-site examination. When Mitch asked if the kid had been killed here, the coroner shook his head. "Can't say till I have the body back at the office, but my educated guess is no, the young man was shot somewhere else, then brought to this spot."

"How soon before you'll have a full report?"

"Couple days. I'll fax it right over as soon as it's ready."

Sheriff Warner was still going off on what a mess

this murder was going to create. "Damn rich kid," the sheriff muttered over and over. "What a zoo we're going to have in town."

WARNER DIDN'T KNOW how right he was. The next twenty-four hours were a frenzy of phone calls and questions and conferences with the park rangers and the San Juan County law-enforcement officers. The media began showing up before dawn the next morning, first in Moab and then swarming all over the park.

It turned out that the dead student's father was a major presidential campaign contributor, a big player behind the scenes, a personal friend of the president.

The story hit the airwaves by that night, with videotapes of Canyonlands, of the hanging tree. Halfbaked theories abounded, and Mitch was bombarded with orders from Washington to solve this crime yesterday.

The media men and women pursued Mitch, one of them even sneaking up the private road to the staff housing near the Visitor Center. Despite Mitch's having changed into jeans and a plain shirt, the reporter still recognized him. "*That* James Mitchell. You're the guy who took the bullet for the veep. Holy cow. How about an interview? An exclusive?"

Mitch pulled himself up to his full six-foot-two and gave the young man a hard look. "No interview, nothing. And you're trespassing. Now, get yourself on out of here before I haul your butt in."

It wasn't just Mitch who was hounded, but the entire Needles District staff. All forty-five of them, their numbered swelled by the twenty temporary summer workers, were under strict orders to remain silent.

Brooke only had one thing to say about the entire affair: "You cut down a dead body! How *could* you? It's so gross, Dad."

Once the media were under control—more or less—Mitch turned to the one chore he'd been putting off. He had to talk to Chick Draco.

Mitch liked Chick—the quintessential absent-minded professor, a renowned authority on ancient Native American cultures—a lot. Chick was obsessed with his research, loved the kids who came to work with him in the summer and was hopeless at pursuing grant money.

Brooke in tow, Mitch walked down the row of staff housing to knock on Chick's door.

Ellen Draco let them in.

"Is Chick here?' Mitch asked.

"Yes. Oh, he'll be so glad to see you, Mitch. He's been having a terrible time. Just awful."

"I can imagine."

Chick came out from the bedroom. A tall, shambling man, he looked drawn, his pale eyes red-rimmed, his straight, fair hair flopping over his forehead, unkempt.

"I'm so sorry," was about all Mitch could say.

"We all are." The archaeologist ran a hand across his face. "I can't believe it. Zachary was such a smart kid—brilliant, really. And he's gone, just like that. And in such a…hideous way. I simply can't take it in."

"How are the rest of the crew?"

"They're stunned, shocked. I'm trying to keep them from hearing the gory details. Some of them are terrified. I know you stationed a ranger out at the dig…just in case—but I've still had parents calling me all day. God, it's awful."

Ellen patted her husband's arm, and then she took Brooke into the kitchen to get everyone drinks.

"You realize—" Mitch lowered his voice "—that I'm going to have to interview every student out there."

"Oh, no…"

"I'm afraid so. And soon."

Chick shook his head dispiritedly.

"I'll try to get to them all myself, but the ones I can't, I'll have someone…considerate conduct the interview."

"The students are already so upset."

"I know," Mitch said. "I'm sorry."

"Do you have any idea, any idea at all, who did this?"

"Not yet. But I've asked for the sheriff's help. I hope I'll make an arrest soon."

"I should have been stricter," Chick said plaintively. "Kept those kids in camp every second of the day."

"They're grown men and women," Mitch was quick to point out. "You aren't running a day care."

But Chick only shook his head. "Why? Why?"

"We don't know. But we will. The killer wanted to make a point. The death was staged. The noose, the tree—it's as if he was warning someone off."

"Hanging—what an awful way to die," Chick whispered.

"Zachary wasn't killed by the hanging. Didn't they tell you?"

"What?" Chick raised his head.

"He was shot first, then hung from that tree. It was a definite message."

Chick stared at him, horrified.

Ellen came in with glasses of wine, Brooke following with her Coke. Mitch hoped they hadn't heard the conversation. It was too ugly.

They sat in silence for a time, and Mitch let his eyes rove over the books that lined the walls of the Dracos' modest summer apartment. Thick archaeological tomes with photographs of Chick on digs all over the Southwest and potsherds scattered about, dusty pieces of ancient pottery that he collected.

Potsherds.

"Damn, I just remembered something," Mitch said. "Let me get it. I'd like you to take a look."

"What is it?" Chick asked.

But Mitch was already half out the door. "Back in a second," he said over his shoulder.

He found the piece of pottery lying in the back of his Bronco, which was parked in front of his own apartment. He wrapped it in his handkerchief and headed back to the Dracos'.

"Here," he said, unfolding the handkerchief, holding his hand out to Chick. "It fell out of Zachary's pocket. I should have sent it off to the lab for testing, but frankly, I forgot I had it. What do you think?"

Chick glanced at the piece.

"Well, what do you think? Could it be important? I mean, as evidence?"

The archaeologist shook his head. "Black on black, a glossy slip. A human figure. The Anasazi never made anything like this."

"Oh."

"A nice piece, very pretty but unexceptional."

"Could it be from your Red Canyon dig?"

"No, we're finding Mimbres-style black-and-orange geometric stuff, nothing like this."

"Where could he have picked it up?"

Chick shrugged. "Pottery shards in an area of possibly five million sites are a dime a dozen. But it's more likely from a trash can behind a curio shop in Moab. Let me hang on to it for a while. I'll ask my kids out at Red Canyon."

"Sure, but then I want to get it up to the lab in Salt Lake." Mitch rose to leave. "Well, we better be going. I hope this is cleared up soon."

"Oh, so do we," Ellen said. "Thanks so much for stopping by."

Chick followed them out to the parking lot in front of the adobe staff apartments. "I'll put this in my truck so I won't forget it," he said, opening the door of his dusty pickup and setting it inside, and Mitch and Brooke left then, walking back to their own apartment.

As soon as they were out of earshot, Brooke said, "You are *so* embarrassing, Dad."

"Oh, yeah? And what did I do now?"

"All that stuff about a stupid piece of pottery. He *told* you it was nothing."

"I have to ask these questions, honey. It's my job."

"Well you don't have to ask like ten times." And she rolled her eyes.

He shut up. No point getting into it with her. Still, the potsherd had been in the dead student's pocket, and Mitch wanted to know why.

CHAPTER THREE

THE VIEWS FROM David Draco's aerie were dizzying, views that spanned the Sonoran Desert, Arizona's Valley of the Sun. He stood on the sweeping terrace below his swimming pool and adobe house, which was set into the sandstone cliff as if a part of the rock itself, and watched the sun set over Phoenix and Scottsdale, his views reaching south to Mesa and Tempe and west to Sun City.

It took a lot of money to afford those views and David Draco, art-gallery owner and philanthropist, had money. And a political future, if he wanted it. It was said that if the native son were so inclined, he'd be a shoo-in at the next gubernatorial election.

In David's favor, of course, were his wealth and good looks. At sixty-two, he still had a full head of hair, shockingly white against his tan skin and light-blue eyes. He was in excellent health. Tall and lean and fit. And he was charming, a good listener, careful with his words. He'd once heard that you never regretted something you didn't say, and he lived by that motto.

He donated to charities, at least twenty of them, and had personally funded two of his nephew's archaeological digs when government grant money had been tight. He was a friend to the Native American art community, and a friend to Arizona. He was, however, not politically motivated; there was still too much money to be made in the buying and selling of southwestern Native American art or, more precisely, the illegal procurement and selling of ancient artifacts.

David turned away from the magnificent desert sunset and looked up toward his house, where his nephew Chick was standing by the swimming pool, engaged in conversation with David's young wife.

David sipped on his cocktail and observed the couple: Chick, the typical archaeologist, whose head was buried in the sand, often literally; and Claire, David's picture-perfect, twenty-eight-year-old blond wife. As he studied them, Claire put her hand on Chick's arm and shook her head, no doubt commiserating with him on the death of his young student. Chick had attended the funeral in New York that very morning before stopping over in Phoenix on the way back to the Utah dig.

Naïve jumped to David's mind. Claire was youthfully naïve about the source of David's wealth, and Chick, though a decade older than Claire, simply refused to comprehend that the world turned on money and power, and the endowments and grants that funded his work in the desert were intricately woven from that same fabric. Chick was naïve, all right, and so obsessed by his work that he couldn't see the forest for the trees. Yet Chick's work was absolutely vital. It was, after all, the very core of the Draco family business.

"Come join us, darling," Claire invited, and she raised her cocktail glass. "Can I get you another? Chick is ready."

"Ah, yes, sure, I'll be right there," David replied,

"I just have a quick call to make." Even from where he stood on the lower terrace he could see her pout. He adored that pout. He adored everything about the former Miss Arizona beauty queen.

He didn't sit when he dialed the Utah number on his cell phone. And he made sure he was well out of earshot of his family. His back to the lower terrace wall, he waited while the phone rang several times, and then finally the voice of his artifact supplier came on.

"Yeah?"

There was no mistaking that voice. "It's me," David said.

"Yes? Me who?"

"You know exactly who." David's handsome, perfectly tanned face grew tight.

His supplier laughed. "Thought I might be hearin' from you."

"I just have one question," David said. "Was it necessary?"

"Was *what* necessary?"

"Don't play games with me. The student. Chick's student. Wasn't there some other way?"

"Nope. Kid saw everything."

"Everything?"

"Yup. And I couldn't let him go blabbing, now could I?"

David's frown deepened. If only that boy hadn't been so well connected. His family wasn't going to just let this go. The bullet was bad enough. But hanging him? And after he was already dead?

"Your methods stink," David said. "You should have consulted me first. My God..."

"I'm calling the shots here," the supplier said.

"I'm the one who risks my neck day in and day out so you can live like a goddamn king."

"You're very well compensated. Don't give me that crap."

"Whatever."

"I want you to get things under control from here on out. Is that clear? If we're to continue doing business, I want to be in on every decision."

There was a pause. "Sure," the man finally said.

They finished their conversation shortly, and David switched off the cell phone. He was still troubled. The man was making stupid mistakes that could so easily be avoided. Hell, the student's death could have been made to look like an accident. None of this was necessary.

"David!" Claire called. "Enough business. Your poor nephew is feeling neglected, aren't you, Chick?"

"Be right along," David called back. But instead of joining his wife and nephew immediately, he sought out Paul Kasper, his right-hand man and bodyguard, and spoke to him in front of the garage, where Paul had been parking the cars for the night.

"Look, Paul," he said, "I know this is not part of your duties, but I need you to drive up to Utah and talk to my man there."

The ex-Navy SEAL nodded. "Sure, Mr. Draco. Just tell me what you have to have done."

"I want to apply a little pressure. I want him to remember who's the boss in this arrangement."

"I understand."

"If you have to get a bit physical, then do so. This man understands that sort of thing better than he does verbal instruction."

"Of course, sir."

David nodded, then began to walk away, but suddenly he turned back to his bodyguard. "Be careful, though, Paul, you hear? He's no pushover."

"Got it, sir, no problem," the two-hundred-pound young man said.

"Good, good," David replied, and finally he joined his family by the pool.

Claire handed him a fresh drink and pecked him on the cheek. She smelled as fresh and dry as the desert, sweet fresh, and David experienced that familiar tightening in his groin. If Nephew Chick wasn't around...

"Well, Chick," he said, "you've had a distressing day. The funeral this morning, the long flight—it's a lot. Let's sit by the pool and relax and maybe you can forget about things for a few minutes."

"It was pretty awful, David. These past couple days..."

"I know, I know. Now, sit and tell me all about the Red Canyon dig. Come on, sit right beside Claire here. And how is your lovely wife, Ellen?"

"Yes," Claire said, patting the seat next to her on a cushioned lounge. "And those adorable children of yours. Tell us everything and let's forget this dreadful business of the student for a while. The police will handle it. Tell him, David. The police will find that horrible murderer, won't they?"

"Of course they will," David said, careful not to meet Chick's glance. "They always get their man."

CHAPTER FOUR

ANNE WINSLOW TOOK the rental agreement, the car keys and Utah road map from the agent, hoisted her briefcase strap over her shoulder, then paused. "Are you sure this map is adequate to get me to Canyonlands?" she asked the agent.

The woman smiled indulgently. "There're only a handful of highways in Utah, Ms. Winslow, you'll do fine with that. This isn't Washington, D.C."

"No, it's not," Anne agreed, and she forced a polite smile, a rare smile nowadays, and headed out of the Salt Lake City airport terminal to locate the rental car.

The agent had been accurate; finding the two-lane highway heading south toward a dot on the map called Moab was easy.

As an undercover field investigator with the Justice Department in Washington, Anne had been to most states, but never to Utah. Never, really, to the sparsely populated desert Southwest. The land was a revelation. The flat, seemingly endless expanse of the Great Salt Lake to the west, the spiny Rocky Mountains jutting up to the east, some still snowcapped despite the summer heat. What really struck her was all the openness, the *space*. No towns, nothing but high desert and twisted mountains as far as the eye could see.

She didn't know whether to feel lost and alone in the immensity of the land, or liberated by its possibilities.

The colors were new to her eye. Striated rocks of red, ocher, orange, umber, and dazzling blue summer sky.

Clear, sharp, *dry*, she mused as she drove, and despite herself a flicker of interest stirred in her belly. It had been a long time since she'd felt anything. At thirty-five, single, Anne felt old beyond her time, used up, disillusioned. *Bitter*. The truth was she didn't care about this assignment, didn't allow herself to feel a thing for the dead son of the major campaign contributor or that this special assignment had come directly through the Oval Office.

The attorney general herself had briefed Anne just yesterday afternoon. "Look, this Sterner guy gives so much money to the campaign this is a special favor. The president wants this case solved, Agent Winslow. But it can't look like the feds are butting in. You know, the usual routine. Your assignment is to preserve the integrity of the evidence in case it ever gets to court. We have to depend on the local guys to solve the murder, but they make mistakes, the kind you wouldn't. You following me?"

"Absolutely."

"You will keep an eye on everything and everyone. You will report back to me. You'll have to use your own judgment about stepping in—only do it if absolutely necessary. You will, in other words, be walking on eggshells."

The attorney general gave her a tired smile. "That's why *you're* going to Utah, Agent Winslow, and not a man. But I'll deny I ever said that."

"Yes, ma'am."

"*Discreet* is the key word here. Your cover story is detailed in that folder—the police reports and dossiers on the people involved are included." She'd handed Anne a packet. "You'll want to read up on Mitchell, the chief ranger. Interesting guy."

"Mitchell?"

"James Mitchell, ex Secret Service."

"Oh, *that* Mitchell." Then Anne had glanced at the name on the airline ticket. Her name. She'd raised a brow.

"It's all right," the attorney general had said. "If anyone checks, you're covered."

"I understand." Anne had nodded and stood. She knew her job. She'd been at the Justice Department for nine years, ever since graduating from George Washington University with a degree in criminology.

She was smart, and had a good nose for investigative work, a sort of sixth sense when it came to truth and lies. The trouble was that she no longer had any real interest in her work. Sometimes she thought she'd be better off alone, living like a hermit somewhere far from civilization. She just was not fit company.

"Discretion, Agent, please," the attorney general had emphasized once more, and Anne had left the office at Justice, gotten in her car and driven home to the D.C. suburb of Arlington. To her one-room apartment and her cat, Yoda, who was now staying with a neighbor. Here in the strange land of rock and river and sky, her life in the East seemed a million miles away.

It took half the afternoon to reach the town of Moab in southeastern Utah. She drove down out of the high desert into a valley flanked by enormous folded red rocks, down to the broad Colorado River, where signs announced the town's tourist attractions: Scenic Helicopter Flights, River Rafting, Mountain Biking Trails.

Cruising along Moab's main street, she was struck by the festive atmosphere, and she immediately felt out of place, overdressed.

Men and women and children filled the streets. Tourists. Shorts-clad people with long, lean tanned legs, wearing hiking boots and baseball caps and sunglasses; people in tight black bicycling shorts, helmets and those odd-looking bicycling shoes. Tons of bicycles on the streets, lots of bicycle shops. Huge numbers of vehicles—RVs with grandparents resting nearby, Jeeps and sport-utility vans carrying either kayaks or bicycles on roof racks, motorcycles. Crowds everywhere, everyone unfolding tourist maps of the area, sipping on bottled water or licking ice-cream cones. Here Anne was in her city clothes—beige linen suit, functional beige pumps, even hose.

She thought about the few things she'd packed. Had she even brought shorts? Slacks? She'd packed so quickly, more concerned about reading the files given her and making sure she left extra cat food for Yoda than she was about her clothes. But then, Anne thought, four years had gone by since she'd given a damn what she looked like. She wasn't here to impress people with her "outdoor" attire. She was here to try to get to the bottom of a very strange murder.

"Discreet," the attorney general had said, and Anne sure knew that drill: don't get in the face of the local authorities. To that end, a formal letter had been sent ahead, introducing her as National Park Service field accountant Anne Winslow, assigned to the park to evaluate its annual budget and to make cost-cutting recommendations. Anne Winslow, numbers cruncher.

She found the National Park Service headquarters with no trouble. It was a typical government building, without personality. Windows, doors, a parking lot, an American flag. Off to the east she could still see those tall mountains topped with snow, even though Moab itself was hot as hell.

She got her briefcase from the backseat and headed toward the building. She hadn't even entered it yet, but she knew that everyone inside was going to resent her. That, of course, was the idea. Smoke and mirrors. The staff would be so busy trying to impress the budget lady that hopefully no one would discover her real assignment.

At the reception counter Anne set down her briefcase and announced that she was there to see Chief Ranger James Mitchell.

"You're the, ah, lady from Washington?" the young female ranger said, eyeing Anne's attire.

"Yes. Is he in?"

"I'll, ah, ring him. If you'll just take a seat by the door?"

"Fine," Anne said, and she wondered how long he'd keep her waiting.

Even before Mitchell appeared, Anne was prepared. From his file she knew the man who'd discovered the body was not only retired Secret Service but a hero. Hell, everyone in Washington was aware he'd been shot in the line of duty.

What she hadn't been prepared for was the limp. It was barely discernible, but nonetheless present when he crossed the lobby to greet her.

A wonder he hadn't been killed, went through her

mind—and there they were, those tears burning behind her eyes. All she had to do was think of death or hear the word and her control fled.

With effort, she stood and shook his hand. "Anne Winslow," she began, "I've been sent to evaluate the park's—"

But he cut her off. "I know who you are, Ms. Winslow. I'm Chief Ranger James Mitchell. I go by Mitch."

"Right," she said. "And I'm Anne, if that makes it easier."

He nodded. "If you'll follow me…?"

"Sure," she said.

Mitchell—Mitch, he'd said—was everything she had expected from his dossier. Close-cropped medium-brown hair just tipped with gray, a tall man, quite trim and in good shape, with a guarded expression that most likely had come from his years with the Secret Service.

He wore the standard NPS uniform—gray shirt, gray pants—with an NPS patch on his left shoulder, a gold badge above his left pocket and a gold name tag on his right pocket. And a holster hung from his belt. A gun. She hadn't been prepared for that.

He led her to an untidy room and gestured for her to sit. "This isn't my office. I'm just borrowing it," he said. "I spend most of my time in the park. The Needles District. I apologize for the informality."

"No problem," she said.

She noticed that he unconsciously rubbed his thigh—had he developed the habit since his injury?

"I'll be getting back to Needles as soon as I can. We're pathetically shorthanded."

The resentment in his voice was not lost on her.

"Well, yes," she replied, sitting opposite him, "that is a common complaint during the busy tourist months. All the parks have the same complaint, Mr.— Mitch, that is."

"I'm sure they do."

She had expected a hard edge to him. What she hadn't discerned from a Secret Service file photo was the bedrock integrity that emanated from him, and the space around him that buffered him from the world. His manner spoke of inner strength and a sober watchfulness. She would have said he was an attractive man, except that he had removed so much of himself from his interaction with her that she really couldn't say. Had this happened since he was shot? Or was she reading too much into his demeanor? Maybe he was merely annoyed at her presence and giving her a cool reception.

None of that mattered, though; what mattered was her real assignment. She'd have to be careful. Her initial read of him was that Mitch was nobody's fool.

And she had to have this man on her side. "So you're the James Mitchell everyone's heard of."

"And what James Mitchell is that?"

"The one who saved the vice president's life. You're a hero." She tried her best to smile at him, but she was afraid he'd know it was false.

"A hero. Listen, Anne, I was doing my job, that's all. Any agent would have done the same."

"Perhaps, but you're the one who did it, and you'll have to take the glory."

His dark-blue eyes fixed on hers. "Believe me, I'm no more a hero than you are."

"I'm just an accountant."

"And you do the job you're trained for, right?"

"Right." *Liar,* she thought, and she met his gaze squarely, and that was when it happened—a hot rush in her belly as their eyes held for a heartbeat too long.

She was so shocked, so caught off guard by her physical reaction, that it took her a moment to recover. She smoothed her linen skirt over her knees, avoiding his sharp eyes. My God, she couldn't remember the last time she'd had a reaction to a man.

Flustered, praying he hadn't noticed, she let out a breath, smiled and said, "I'd like to get going first thing in the morning."

"Sure. Where would you like to begin? All the bookkeeping files are kept right here in—"

"Actually," she interrupted, "I'd like to tour the park itself. I need to get a feel for exactly what it is I'm dealing with."

"Tour the park," he said, half under his breath. "Do you have any idea how *large* the park is?"

"I have a vague idea. I assume I'll have a much better picture after I've seen it." Another false smile.

He made a noncommittal sound and then stood. "I suppose I'm to be the tour guide," he said dryly.

"If it wouldn't be an imposition." What she couldn't say was that she knew he was the man who'd discovered the student's body, the man heading up the murder investigation. Her guide *had* to be Mitch.

She rose and hoisted the strap of her briefcase over her shoulder. "Eight o'clock tomorrow, then?"

"Seven would be better."

"Seven, it is. Here?"

"No. Actually I've arranged for you to stay in the park, in the staff housing." He opened a desk drawer and took out a map. "Just follow the route I've marked and stop by the Visitor Center. My secretary,

Martha, will have a key ready for you. She's made sure there are some groceries in the place.''

"And how far is it to the, ah, Needles District?''

"I'm afraid it's still a seventy-mile drive.''

"What?'' Anne glanced up immediately from the map.

"I'm afraid so. Like I told you, it's big out here, Anne. I'd show you the way to the Needles District myself, but I have to stop by the sheriff's. You'll probably hear about it, if you haven't already, but we had a homicide in the park the other day.''

"Oh, really?''

"Yes. Doesn't happen often.''

"How alarming.'' She tried to show mild interest. "And have you made an arrest or anything?''

"Frankly,'' he said, "no.''

"Gosh,'' she said, "that's too bad. But I'm sure you will.''

"Let's hope so.''

He escorted her out then, even walked her to her rented car and pointed out the route again on the map he'd given her. She knew he was trying to be polite. *Don't tick off the budget lady from Washington.* But she could sense that edge in him, almost see the annoyance in those eyes behind the mirrored sunglasses, and she knew he'd much prefer that someone else had this assignment, anyone but him.

Too bad. "See you at seven? The, ah, Visitor Center?''

"Seven sharp,'' he said, and he left her there, walking with that slight limp to a NPS white-and-green Ford Bronco. Presumably, he was going to see the San Juan County sheriff. How very much easier her job would be if she could have tagged along. But she couldn't—she was merely a lowly accountant.

She started the car, flipped the air conditioner to high and thought, *seventy more miles.*

What bothered her wasn't the long drive she still faced. She pulled out of the parking lot, turned south on the two-chlane road and recalled with frightening clarity that crazy rush of heat in her stomach when he'd leveled those eyes on her.

That shouldn't have happened. She shouldn't have let it happen. What on earth had come over her, anyway? It had only been a year since Lyle… Twelve short months. She wasn't ready. She never wanted a man again, not unless it was Lyle. And that was impossible. Lyle was dead.

JERRY HAWKINS LEANED his shovel against a crumbling sandstone wall and pulled a cigarette from a pack in the breast pocket of his faded plaid shirt.

He struck a match on his thumbnail, his ropy muscles flexing under his torn-off sleeves, lit the cigarette and blew out a stream of smoke. He eyed his cousin. "Take a break, Harv," Jerry called.

"Thought you'd never ask." Harvey Hawkins laid aside his shovel and joined his cousin Jerry by the kiva pit in the ruin where they'd been digging for the past two months.

Harv fetched the water bottle from the backpack and took a long drink. "Man, is it a hot one," he breathed. "We could get twice the work done in half the time if we waited till September. I don't see why we…"

"No can do," Jerry said.

"I only meant that this ruin has waited a real long time. What's the hurry?"

"Money, that's what," Jerry reminded him.

"Yeah, money."

"We can't be digging around here too long. There's a time limit. Remember?" He had to keep the goal dangling in front of Harv, like a carrot before a horse, or Harv would lose interest. Poor man, not too well endowed in the brain area. But he *was* Jerry's cousin.

"Check that area on the next level, will you?" Jerry said.

Harv wandered off into the shadowed maze of ancient sandstone rooms that Jerry himself had named the New Ruin. Of the dozens of Native American sites he'd looted in his forty-two years, of the hundreds that the Hawkins family had robbed of artifacts since settling in this territory over a hundred years before, no one had named a ruin. But then, no one in the infamous Hawkins clan had come across one like this.

Jerry had not yet gotten the tree-ring and carbon-dating results back from his pal at the Utah lab where he'd sent samples, but he'd known from the beginning that this site was extraordinary.

The ruin had confused him—its stonework and pottery were more advanced than anything he'd seen before. Yet he guessed it was very old, perhaps even older than the Anasazi or Mogollon or Mimbres people who'd lived here in the first millennium A.D.

Jerry Hawkins was rarely surprised, but New Ruin surprised him. Harv had no idea what he was unearthing, but Jerry did. By God, he knew.

He'd known since first stumbling across the site in

a hidden crack below a mesa that was cut by a rare, still-flowing stream. It had something unique about it. This entirely new tribe of Indians had erected beautifully chiseled sandstone walls to form a maze of rooms on the floor and up a wall of a hidden canyon. They'd fashioned T-shaped doorways and created art on their walls and on their earthen jars and pots and plates the likes of which Jerry had never seen. Remnants of their sandals and clothing were exquisitely woven, and they'd cultivated the valley—irrigated and planted corn and squash and beans. There was turquoise jewelry and carved wooden headdresses and many signs of an intricately structured society within its walls.

These Ancient Ones had clearly held religious ceremonies. And, astounding to Jerry, they'd buried their dead near their dwellings, and buried them with their prized possessions: pottery, jewelry, feathers, shells from ancient inland seas, carved deer-bone scrapers, stone tools, even carved bone toys for the children.

Jerry had noticed none of this at first. He'd stood at the site, his jaw open as Harv looked at him curiously, and he saw only the intricate stone and mortar work of the walls. But he knew. He just knew. And he knew that he'd been led to this site. *Him*. Jerry Hawkins. Led here by the Anasazi themselves, their spirits beckoning him to discover their secret and priceless treasures.

Now he took a long last drag on his cigarette and stubbed it out on the ground, then replaced it in the pack in his pocket, and he felt the presence of their spirits keenly, as keenly as he had that first day two months ago. Yes. They had led him here.

"We gonna be out of here before dark?" Harv's

voice intruded on his pondering. "I'd sure like a beer or two in Moab before I head home."

"Yeah, whatever," Jerry said.

"What about the rangers? I mean, should we wait till dark?"

"Nah," Jerry said, "screw 'em. They're too busy with the stupid tourists to mess with us right now. It's safe to haul a load out."

"I hope so. I keep thinking maybe they took on extra help. I mean after the dead student and all."

"Quit worrying."

"Shame about that kid, though. I mean, he didn't really *do* anything."

"He stumbled across this place is what he did. It was his bad luck we happened to be here." Then Jerry laughed, the cords in his neck standing out. "Actually, it was our *good* luck we discovered him before he could tell anyone. The punk would have ruined everything."

Harv picked up his shovel. "I only wish that student, well, you know... It's like a bad omen, Jerry. I mean, you remember that King Tut guy? That curse on his tomb? Maybe this is too big for us. One guy is already dead," Harv whispered, his brown eyes widening. "And man, here he turns out to be the son of a 500 guy..."

"A *Fortune* 500 guy," Jerry corrected.

"Yeah, and a friend of the president."

"The guy gives the party money is all. Lots of people gave campaign money. You worry too damn much. Now, let's get that room over there finished, and for God's sake, Harv, don't leave a sign that you've been digging."

"I'm real careful."

"Yeah, sure you are. It's like cleaning up after a bull in a china shop when you get done."

They both went back to work while the light was good. Jerry forgot Harv completely when he unearthed a particularly lovely pot, a black-on-black with scored antelope chasing themselves around the wide bowl as if at a dead gallop for eternity. This one would bring a fortune, there was barely a chip on it.

"Oh, baby, you are a keeper," Jerry said, touching the surface of the ancient pot with reverence. When Chick Draco "discovered" New Ruin and archaeologists swarmed the site, sending all the artifacts to museums, this baby would be worth a bundle. Maybe Jerry wouldn't even cut David Draco in on the deal.

He stared at the treasure, carefully dusting a little more dirt from its base. "Friggin' beautiful," he said, and finally he placed the pot on a sandstone wall, where the late-afternoon sun warmed it for the first time in countless centuries. Jerry cocked his head and studied the pot for a moment, his gaze transfixed by the leaping antelope, which were so vibrant it was as though the sun were giving them new life.

Silently, in a personal ritual, he thanked the long-dead potter for his skill, and that was when he felt the eyes on his back.

He spun around. Had to be Harv. But Harv was nowhere in sight. Suddenly, the hairs on his neck stood up. He knew who it was. As always, they were watching.

CHAPTER FIVE

MITCH LEANED AGAINST the U-shaped bar in Moab, one shoe on the brass footrail, an elbow resting casually on the polished mahogany counter. A barely touched beer sat before him.

In the long mirror behind the top-shelf liquor bottles and cash register, he could see through a neon beer sign the Hawkins boys: the brains of the family, Jerry, and his not-so-clever cousin, Harv. They were in full swing this evening—four beers and three empty shot glasses in front of them, Jerry regaling the bartender with some cock-and-bull story about how his ancestors were the first to discover Canyonlands and myriad Anasazi ruins, and how those same *generous* ancestors had laid claim to the land, only to donate it all to the federal government in the early 1920s.

Mitch wanted to laugh, but everyone at the locals' hangout knew Jerry was full of it, so why stir things up?

Mitch was not at the Rivers Saloon by accident or because he was thirsty. It was getting late, the sun had set and he needed to head back to the park and fix dinner for Brooke, who'd been baby-sitting but should be done within the hour.

And he *had* been headed home after his stopover at the sheriff's office, where he had checked on the progress of the Utah Bureau of Investigation, which was running ballistic tests on the slug taken from the student's head wound. They were also scheduled to ID some fibers found on the boy's clothes and dirt taken from beneath his fingernails, which would hopefully give the authorities a clue where he'd been in the park that day. Of course, the sheriff had informed Mitch, the test results would take some time, despite the requested rush order.

But, driving past the saloon, Mitch had spotted Jerry's battered red pickup in the parking lot by the river, and on a whim—or was it an intuition?—he'd pulled in.

"Another beer?" the bartender asked, making his rounds.

Mitch shook his head. "I still have to drive to Needles. One will do it. Thanks, anyway."

And that was when Jerry's eyes met his in the mirror. "Hey, let me buy one for the ranger here. The dude's a national hero, after all," Jerry said, loud enough for the whole bar to hear.

Mitch leaned forward and smiled thinly. "Thanks, but I'm out of here."

"Oh, come on," Jerry persisted, tucking his long, mouse-colored hair behind his ears, his weathered face drawn into a smirk. "Cops won't stop one of their own, especially a hero. Let me buy you that drink, pal."

Again, Mitch shook his head. "Some other time, Hawkins."

"Oh, so the man knows me," Jerry said.

"You've been pointed out to me once or twice."

"You mean I'm practically as famous as you? Wow." He turned to his cousin. "Harv, this is that guy they keep talking about, Chief Ranger Mitchell, right?''

Harv reached around another customer and insisted on shaking Mitch's hand. "That was something, man, when you caught that bullet. We all thought it was pretty damn cool, you know?''

Before Mitch could reply, Jerry punched his cousin in the shoulder and said, "Shut up, will ya, Harv? You're embarrassing the hero.''

Mitch nodded and kept the smile on his lips. "Say, Jerry," he said, "didn't I see your truck down in the park the other day? I think it was the same day that kid was killed. Was it Saturday?''

A sudden tense hush fell over the bar. But Mitch didn't care. He'd spoken deliberately. It was no secret in these parts that if anyone knew of illegal activities in the park it was Jerry Hawkins. Mitch would give his left arm for a search warrant to go into Hawkins's home and look for a small-caliber handgun. But no judge on earth would issue a warrant on Mitch's hunch.

From what he had gleaned in his short time at Canyonlands, everyone in a five-hundred-mile radius knew the Hawkinses were the prime looters of artifacts. What bothered him, what had prompted him to stop at the saloon in the first place, was that piece of broken pottery, the shard he'd found by the student's body. That, coupled with the brutal manner in which the student had been strung up, smacked of Hawkins family involvement. To Mitch, it wasn't that big a stretch: death, pottery, the Hawkinses. But when Mitch had mentioned that train of thought to the sheriff, Warner had been skeptical, saying nothing seemed to be adding up on this bizarre case. And maybe the sheriff was right. Still, putting a couple screws to Jerry Hawkins wouldn't hurt.

"Let's see," Jerry was musing, "Saturday. Um, Saturday. Nah, I was home, doing my laundry. It was really stacking up, you know?"

Mitch felt his jaw tighten. He finished his beer, his eyes riveted on Jerry over the rim of the glass. When he set his glass down, pushed a dollar toward the bartender and settled his hat back on his head, he paused. "Gosh, Jerry," he said, "you wouldn't have someone to alibi you during the rinse cycle, would you?" Then, without waiting for Hawkins to reply, he strode out of the bar, hoping his damn limp wasn't too pronounced.

"Hell," he muttered as he climbed into the Bronco, unsure who had won that crossing of swords. He didn't regret the verbal scuffle, though, not for a minute. Something about Hawkins back there, something in his demeanor, something behind those shrewd dark eyes, told Mitch he'd struck a nerve.

He pulled out onto Highway 191 and drove south, aware that he was running awfully late and that Brooke had been on such an emotional roller coaster this summer he never knew just how she was going to react to anything he said or did. Then there was that budget lady from Washington, who couldn't simply sit down in an empty office in Moab and do her damn job. No. Ms. Anne Winslow just had to see the park. And *he* had to be the tour guide. He still had those students to interview, twelve of them....

An image of Anne flew into his head as he followed the sweeping curve of the road past Kane Springs camping area. A pretty woman. Not exactly beautiful, but undeniably attractive, with a nice nose, a generous mouth and wide hazel eyes, her light-brown hair worn just below her ears, parted to one side. He recalled, unbidden, that it had fallen softly over a cheek when she'd reached for something in her briefcase.

She had a good figure under those city clothes of hers. A little flat chested, maybe, but great legs, long and smooth looking, nicely curved calves and ankles. Heck, everyone at headquarters had noticed her legs, Mitch recalled.

But her eyes... Despite their striking hazel color and the dark fringe of her lashes, something was missing, as if the light behind them had dimmed. He hated to think the cause was her job, although maybe it was. Maybe the Park Service was cutting down the main office staff, too. God knows, they were plenty stingy with the parks themselves. Which, of course, didn't bode well for Canyonlands. He sure as hell hoped she wasn't trying to save a dime here in an effort to keep her job. That would be just great.

Mitch frowned. He had to meet her at seven in the morning. Probably spend the entire day showing her around, and even then they'd barely cover a tenth of the Needles District—never mind the two other districts: the Maze and the Island in the Sky.

How long was she going to be here?

Mitch's thoughts circled and came back to Brooke and dinner, then that shard he'd found at the murder scene. Chick Draco had considered it nothing special, maybe even junk pottery. Yet the feeling persisted that somehow the kid's death and the shard were linked. And whenever Mitch thought about Native American pottery in the park, he thought about the Hawkins clan and their blatant moki poaching.

The shard. And he'd left it with Chick. *Evidence.* Hell, he should have logged it in. That was basic crime-scene management he'd learned years ago at Quantico when he'd been in training for the Secret Service. Okay, so his years on guard detail had left him rusty in the area of crime, but still…

Angry with himself, Mitch turned onto the Needles District road and headed toward the Outpost, where he could grab a couple of things for dinner. Maybe he'd phone Brooke from there and see if she needed anything special.

The shard popped into mind again and he cussed out loud. He had to get it back from Chick. "Stupid, stupid," he muttered. He'd broken the simplest of rules. Like a rookie. Well, he wasn't going to let it go on. He was going to goddamn fix his dumb mistake.

THE SUN HAD NOT YET RISEN over the canyon wall that guarded the Red Canyon dig when Chick Draco and his twelve summer students formed a circle around the rim of the kiva, clasping hands.

To an onlooker, the scene might have appeared ridiculous, the rite of a New Age cult, but to Chick and the young men and women, their ritual seemed fitting in light of the death of one of their own. The kiva was the core of Anasazi spiritualism, where their religious ceremonies were held and where the mystical was possible. This gathering felt right.

Chick had made the decision to hold this ceremony after he'd returned from the funeral in New York and the stopover in Scottsdale. Frankly, he'd told his wife last night, he didn't know what else to do for his still shocked and confused protégés.

Chick said a few words first. "The funeral was beautiful," he whispered, "and I felt you were all there with Zach. He's laid to rest beneath a lovely oak tree, next to his grandparents and their grandparents. It was...comforting. I'll miss him terribly, though."

A minute of silence followed; then one of the students cleared her throat and spoke. "Zach was such a character. When I first met him in June, he put this rubber rattlesnake in my sleeping bag. God, it was such a stupid prank for a twenty-three-year-old. I was furious but he was laughing so hard, well, it was catchy, and I had to smile. He was always doing stuff like that. I'll...I'll miss him so much." Her voice broke then and trailed away into the new silence.

"Goodbye, Zach," someone else murmured.

Several others spoke, still clasping hands in the circle, their heads bowed toward the dark opening of the kiva.

"He's in God's hands now," one of the male students said.

"Amen," came another voice.

"We will all miss you, Zach. It wasn't...fair. It's not fair to die so young."

Then Chick spoke again as the early rays of sun spilled over the rim of the canyon and fell on their faces and backs, before slipping gently into the mouth of the kiva. "Goodbye for now, Zach. You were loved."

Slowly, the group let go of hands and drifted away in twos and threes, the new day awaiting them with uncertainty and promise.

MITCH WAS ALWAYS PUNCTUAL. When he'd said "Seven o'clock at the Visitor Center" he'd meant it.

But that was before Brooke had gotten out of bed on the wrong side.

She stomped into the kitchen. "I'm going to spend the day in Moab and you have to drive me, Dad," she announced at 6:45.

Coffee mug in hand, Mitch blew out a frustrated breath. "I told you last night, honey, I have to play tour guide to this lady from Washington. I'm meeting her, in fact—" he checked the wall clock "—in fifteen minutes."

He saw his daughter's face, so like his own but feminine, the bloom of youth in her eyes and skin and willowy frame, and knew he'd already lost the battle.

"I *hate* it here," the fourteen-year-old said, and her voice carried out the open windows of their adobe apartment, shattering the silence.

He flinched. "What do you want me to do, Brooke—screw up my job?"

"I don't care what you do. You have to drive me to Moab. You *have* to. I'll die here. All my new friends live in town. All of them. How am I supposed to start school there with everybody thinking I'm a nerd? It's not fair. I hate it here."

Mitch thought quickly. It *wasn't* fair. She had a point. "Look," he said, "I'll, ah, check with Martha and see if she isn't making a trip into town. Okay? I'll call you from the Visitor Center."

"What if she isn't going in?"

"I'll think of something else. One of the rangers will be making the trip."

"*When?* I won't wait till noon. I'll hitchhike."

"No, you *won't*. I'll take care of it. But before I

go—'' he looked again at the clock ''—we better get something straight here.''

Brooke's lower lip quivered.

''I don't want you and those new friends of yours to try anything funny. You know what I'm getting at?''

Silence.

Damn, this was hard. ''I'm talking drugs and sex, kiddo. I'd be a pretty bad father if I didn't voice my concerns.''

She really lost it then. She screamed that she'd never done those things and he was a jerk and she hated him.

And that was the way Mitch left for the Visitor Center. It was nearly a quarter after the hour when he pulled into the rangers' parking, his jaw locked. He'd heard and read about raising a teen and how hard it could be. *But until you experience it yourself,* he acknowledged, *you haven't got a clue.*

He strode into the center, saw Martha stocking the display rack of park maps, and he caught her nod toward the big plate-glass window, where budget-lady Anne Winslow was waiting, her back to him, her shoulders as rigid as steel.

Damn.

'''Morning,'' he said as he walked up, his leg bothering him today.

She pivoted. ''You said seven.''

''Yes, I did. I apologize. Family stuff.''

''I see,'' she said, her tone cool, her eyes assessing. ''I hope there won't be any more delays. I have a schedule, too.''

And that was when Mitch cornered Martha and all but begged her to run Brooke into Moab. ''And call

her right away, will you? Let her know when you'll
pick her up.''

"No prob, Boss," Martha said. "I have to make a
run in today anyway."

"And find out how she's getting home, will you?"

"No problem."

"Oh, and pull Joe Staghorn off his regular route
and tell him to drive out to Red Canyon and begin
the student interviews." Mitch ticked off a list of
questions he wanted answered.

"This came in early this morning," Martha said,
handing him a set of faxes.

"The coroner's report? Why didn't you tell me?"
He took the papers.

"You didn't give me a chance, boss."

"Okay, thanks," he said, and started reading.
Somewhere in the back of his mind he knew Anne
was waiting for him, but this report was important.

He got the gist of it rapidly: .22-caliber bullet and
yes, the body had been moved, the time of death was
at least twelve hours before he'd found the body.
Then he had to toss the report on his desk and leave
to meet Anne.

"See you later," he said to Martha on his way past.

"Go on, placate the budget lady," Martha said; she
gazed out to the parking lot, where Anne waited for
him. "Nice outfit she's wearing, huh?"

Mitch hadn't noticed at first, but when he got outside and eyed Anne's attire, he felt his blood sim-
mering. Was she kidding? Linen slacks, a silk blouse,
sandals?

He marched up to where she awaited him by the
passenger door of his Bronco. With cold reserve, his
sunglasses dangling from a finger, his eyes moved

down her form. "We're going to stop at your apartment next door and you're going to change into decent backcountry clothes, or you aren't going anywhere with me," he ground out.

She started to say something, her eyes shooting sparks at him, but then she seemed to catch herself. "Okay," she said, "fine. I'll see what I brought."

It didn't take her long to change. Mitch assumed the khaki shorts and walking shoes—no socks—she reappeared in must have been her only choice. She'd switched blouses, but was still wearing a silky-looking thing, off-white—one of those sleeveless scoop-neck jobs that his wife used to wear under a blazer.

Mitch was resting against the fender of the Bronco, arms folded stiffly, when she came out. "Better," he said, inspecting her, "but you're going to fry. Your arms and legs..." With skin as pale and smooth as hers, he found himself thinking, she'd burn in fifteen minutes out here.

"I guess I'm pretty city-white," she admitted.

"Uh-huh." He unfolded himself, opened the glove compartment and handed her a tube of sunscreen. "Here. I had to learn the hard way." Then he watched as she slathered the stuff on her arms and legs, propping each foot up on the running board of the vehicle as she applied the cream.

He leaned past her when she was done, put the tube back in its place and saw the extra pair of sunglasses he kept. He got them out. "Try these. I'm sure they're too big, but it gets bright as hell out in the desert, and you'll be glad you've got them."

Anne took the glasses, put them on and peered at herself in the side mirror. "They're fine. Thanks."

He nodded. "Let's get going. I want to run in to the Outpost and grab some sandwiches before we take off. Okay?" He started the engine.

"Fine," she said.

"There's water in the back. We recommend a gallon per person a day in the summer."

"A gallon?"

"By the end of the day," he said, "you'll be a believer."

After the Outpost, Mitch made a run to Big Spring Canyon Overlook on the single paved road in the park. He stopped at Slickrock Foot Trail and Pothole Point on the way, doing his job, which was, for the most part, seeing to the safety of the visitors and protecting the federal lands for the millions who would come in the future.

As he drove, occasionally halting to speak to a tourist about a camping permit or to give directions, he was aware of Anne's interest while she looked out the open window on her side of the Bronco.

Good, she was getting more into her guided tour. Yesterday she'd seemed… He thought back. There'd been no light in her eyes. Pretty hazel eyes, but distant.

Well, this place would cure whatever ailed her. No one could be unaffected by this majestic land. He never tired of it. Figured he never would, because it could take the rest of his life to explore the entire region, and even then he knew he could never see it all.

At the overlook they both got out while Mitch wrote up a report from a young man and woman on bikes who said their tent was stolen from a campsite at Squaw Flats last night. He told them to check at headquarters when they left the park, but the odds of recovering the tent were not great.

Anne waited at the overlook, her hands resting on a rail as she scanned the twisted red land below and the distant sandstone spires of eroded rock.

"It's something, huh?" he found himself saying.

"Lovely." She stared at the view, not saying another word. Then she turned to him. "I haven't seen anything like this. Ever."

"I believe that."

"It's like this all over the park? Hundreds of square miles of this?"

"The land changes, but it's never less impressive. That's why I'm here, I guess. Somebody's got to keep this place safe for humanity."

"I'm beginning to see what you mean."

"Will they understand this in Washington? Do they get it?"

She took the borrowed sunglasses off and met his gaze. "Probably not."

He shook his head in exasperation.

"I can try," she said, "to convince them."

"Yeah, you do that."

They retraced the in route, veered onto a graded dirt road that led past Elephant Hill and deep into the park, where many of the foot trails and archaeological sites were located. Mitch stopped often, checking with the fewer and fewer tourists they came across as they put distance between themselves and civilization. He heard about an elderly hiker with a sprained back who'd made it out to a four-wheel-drive road with the help of friends, then caught a lift to Moab. Someone else stopped Mitch and told him about a dead mule deer near Druid Arch.

"Shot?" Mitch asked, but the camper didn't know.

"I take it you have fines for that sort of thing," Anne said as they headed on.

"You bet," Mitch said, his gaze on her for a minute. "But you have to catch them."

"Like catching the person who killed that student?" she said.

"A lot like that."

"Any new word on the murder?" she asked mildly. Mitch frowned. "Nope."

"I heard you were the one who found the body."

"Where'd you hear that?" he asked quickly.

"Oh, your secretary, Martha, told me last night when I stopped by to get my key."

"She's got a big mouth," he muttered.

"But you actually found the body?"

"Yeah, I did."

"That must have been awful."

"It always is."

"Mmm," she said.

He could have sworn she studied his profile as he drove—studied it for too long—but he stared straight ahead, not wanting to meet her eyes. Somehow he felt that might be dangerous, too intimate. Something about this woman was... He searched his mind but couldn't come up with a word to describe her. *Confusing*, maybe.

Eventually he had to say something to break the taut atmosphere between them.

"Speaking of the murder," he began, "I really should be checking on a few things today." *Such as the shard I left with Chick*, Mitch thought. "It's pretty hard to run an investigation while I'm..."

"Driving the budget lady around?"

"Something like that."

"But you have other rangers under your command, don't you?"

"Of course."

She was full of questions all morning. As they passed an Anasazi ruin, she suddenly wanted to know how one scientist got a permit to dig in the park and another didn't, how students were selected to work at a dig for the summer. Mitch explained what he could, which really wasn't much.

"Permits to excavate a ruin come from an entirely different department," he said. "And then there are the Native Americans themselves. They have a big say in who digs where and how the artifacts are to be handled."

As if to punctuate their discussion about the thousands of Anasazi ruins located in the park boundaries, Mitch happened across an entire family in the act of looting, their four-wheel-drive parked right next to the sign forbidding any disturbance or removal of artifacts at the site. The fines were even listed right there.

He pulled up alongside their SUV and parked. "I can't believe how goddamn bold these people can be," he grated out.

"Maybe they really didn't see the sign," Anne suggested.

But he shook his head. "Oh, they'll *say* they didn't see it, all right—they always do. But look at them... Shovels, buckets, the works. They know. They probably do this every summer."

"And they can't be stopped?"

Mitch moved abruptly around to her. "Not with the pitiful handful of rangers the government hires to protect the land,'' he said pointedly. ''Budget, you know.''

That silenced her.

This time Mitch did write the people up and handed them a court summons to appear in Moab in October or pay a hefty fine. Sometimes he let people off if he believed they were ignorant of the laws. But this family... He ought to introduce them to the Hawkins clan, he mused as he handed the father the ticket and summons.

''You figure just because you wear a gun you can intimidate people?'' the man asked. ''Well, these are federal lands, buddy, and I own them just as much as anyone. I pay my taxes.''

''Yes, sir,'' Mitch said, his voice even; he wasn't about to rise to the bait. He did, however, take a hard look at the collection of potsherds the family had put together. ''I'm going to have to confiscate these,'' he said. ''But you can ask the judge for them back, though, and explain how you pay your taxes.''

The man cursed.

As they were driving away, Anne inquired, ''How do you keep your cool like that?''

''I didn't keep my cool at all.''

''I thought you did that very...professionally.''

''Thanks,'' he said dryly.

He drove to the picnic ground at Newspaper Rock for lunch. There, looming above the cottonwood trees that surrounded the area, was a cliff face full of ancient petroglyphs. Situated right off the main road near the park entrance, the site was one of the most popular in the area. She might as well see it.

They climbed down from the Bronco, and he pulled the sandwiches and water bottles out, then set them on a picnic table. He sure as hell wasn't going to spout the history of the place until she asked. *If* she asked.

"What is this place called?" she finally said.

"Newspaper Rock. Ham or turkey?"

"What? Oh, turkey, please."

She took a bite, swallowed. "Newspaper Rock. I like that. Who did all those pictures?"

"The Anasazi, and whoever else traveled this way for the past two thousand years. Since before Christ was born."

"Like kids carving their initials into a tree?" she wondered. "Or are those real messages up there?"

"I don't know."

"There are feet, and hands and animals. Bighorn sheep, deer, men on horseback. Wow, so some are newer pictures." She took her sandwich and walked up to the rock face to study it. Then she turned around. "I like this. Kind of like the want ads."

Mitch only shrugged, scrutinizing her when she turned back to the rock paintings. Budget lady and numbers cruncher, ostensibly a boring career, a dull person. Yet he sensed more to Anne, a lot more.

One foot propped up on the bench as he chewed on the sandwich, he watched her move along the wall, and again he thought what a nice figure she had. A good, attractive face, pretty eyes, beautiful skin and a nice shape. Why wasn't she into a more active job with the Park Service? She was obviously intelligent, and she'd let him see a sense of humor, but then there was that dark side, those moments when she seemed to turn inward as if seeking a safe harbor the outside world didn't offer.

He was curious despite the million other things on

his mind. Had some guy abused her? He couldn't see that, though. She was too self-assured to put up with that. Still... Ms. Winslow was keeping *something* from him. He knew it.

At one point she faced him abruptly. Without saying anything, she pointed at an ancient outline of a hand painted on the rock face, then she smiled and shook her head. Mitch couldn't help the tightening in his groin. She looked very young and vulnerable, her guard lowered. Yeah, budget-lady Winslow could get to a guy when she was herself. Not that he had time for this. Still, he was flesh and blood, and it had been real long since he'd been with a woman.

She finally returned to the table and sat across from him, tucking a strand of honey-colored hair behind her ear. He noticed then the sun flush on her skin, and her nose was turning pink. The sunscreen was not powerful enough. He frowned, got up and found the tube of zinc oxide in the glove compartment in the Bronco. If this total sunblock didn't work, nothing would.

"What's that?" she asked suspiciously.

"Zinc oxide. Your nose is burning."

"What?" She put a finger up and felt the bridge of her nose. "Is it really?"

"Yes, this stuff is even better than sunscreen."

He swiped his finger across the sticky white cream, reached over and wiped it on her nose.

"Is it rubbed in?" she asked.

He almost smiled. "It doesn't rub in. It just sits there. A big white blob."

"You're kidding."

She finished her sandwich and swung her legs around so she could study the petroglyphs again.

"Some of them are beautiful," she said, almost wistfully.

"There are much more beautiful ones elsewhere."

"Will you show them to me?"

He shrugged. When in God's name was he going to find the time for *that?*

"So, you really feel you can live here, out in this remoteness?" she eventually asked.

"Sure."

"You don't miss the people, the city?"

"Plenty of people around here. Too many this time of year."

"Mmm. Sometimes I wish…" She trailed off, and again he saw her retreat inward, to her safe harbor. He would have asked what the hell was with her, but it wasn't his place. And besides, he thought, packing up their litter, he didn't really care.

CHAPTER SIX

DAVID DRACO GREETED HIS clients in his Fifth Avenue art gallery in Scottsdale and led them to his private office. The man, Uri, a Russian stationed with the diplomatic corps in Los Angeles, had money. But his wife, Magda, a former Hungarian beauty queen, was the one with taste.

She stopped several times in the gallery to exclaim over some of the fine art on display.

"Oh, Uri, this is exquisite!" Her blond head tilted to one side as she studied a painting by one of the hot new southwestern artists.

"Very pretty," Uri acknowledged.

David nodded. "The artist is highly sought-after. It's difficult to even keep her work in stock."

They socialized in Uri's broken English while his wife moved from western painting to Indian pottery, from bronze statuettes to kachina dolls to pricey turquoise-and-silver jewelry. David was aware this was all preliminary chitchat and Uri, whom he'd always believed to be in the Russian Mafia, was there solely to purchase something for his wife that couldn't be found in a Scottsdale gallery. Or any gallery in the Southwest, for that matter. This couple wanted an illegally obtained artifact, something they could either sell back in Moscow or exhibit in their private collection.

"Shall we go to my office now?" David suggested.

He showed them two extraordinary Anasazi pots that dated to 1200 A.D. The woman was impressed, extolling the condition of the pots and clinging to her husband's arm.

"Darling, they are so fabulous. But which one should I choose?"

Indulgent, Uri said, "Maybe we take both."

David sat behind his desk, fingers steepled under his chin, and smiled charmingly while the woman tried to come to a decision. Though either pot would cost them in excess of thirty thousand dollars, price was not an issue. It rarely was with any of David's special, backroom clientele.

He waited patiently for the moment he was certain she was going to make a decision and then he cleared his throat. "Before you choose," David said, "I should tell you that in a couple of weeks I expect to have several very, very special pieces."

The woman's interest sharpened. "Yes?"

David bowed his head. "I'm having some tests run on a few of the potsherds from a particular ruin, so I hesitate to mention a date at this time, but I do expect these pieces will predate any known Anasazi site by several hundred years. The discovery of this site is nothing short of astounding," he added.

"I'm thrilled," the woman crooned. "Oh, Uri, can you imagine? I'll be the envy of my friends." Then she turned to David and frowned. "But how will anyone know how special the pieces are, Mr. Draco? I've read of no new discovery. How is this possible?"

"The discovery of the ruin has not even been announced yet," he said. "I only mentioned it because you have been very good and, I might add, discriminating clients, and I'd like you to have a shot at one of the pieces.''

The woman was hooked, as David had known she would be, and Uri could do nothing but spread his big hands and acquiesce. "You will call us in L.A. when a piece becomes available?''

''Of course.''

''And you will keep your very best piece for me?'' the woman pouted.

''As always,'' David said.

She purchased one of the pots David had initially shown her, but then, he had been sure of that, too. As he drove home that afternoon in the blazing Arizona sun with the air-conditioning blasting in his BMW, he felt good about the exchange with the Russian and his Hungarian wife. Now, if he could just keep Hawkins in line. Of course, David's bodyguard, Paul, was on his way to do just that—to *remind* Hawkins who was boss. Too much was at stake to have it all come crashing down around their ears now.

ONLY THROUGH SHEER LUCK did Anne see it. She was gazing at the spectacularly striated canyon walls as Mitch drove, when a movement caught her eye. It was as if someone had taken her head and swiveled it to point out something important. Then, in a split second her brain registered what it was, adrenaline surged in her veins, she gave a strangled yell. Mitch stomped on the brakes. The vehicle skidded, throwing Anne forward against her seat belt.

Bouncing, crashing down the canyon wall, a huge boulder leaped at them. Dust plumed behind it, and the ground shook as it hit the canyon floor. It stopped in front of the Bronco, almost touching the bumper.

"Goddamn," Mitch panted, his voice thick with the aftereffect of fear. "We could have been killed."

Anne's heart was banging against her ribs. She drew in a deep breath. "Does this happen often?" she managed to whisper.

"It never happens," he muttered, then got out of the Bronco and stood there, hands on hips, and stared up at the canyon wall.

She needed a minute to collect herself before joining him by the boulder. Her knees were shaky, as though turned to liquid. "Do you think another one might come down? Shouldn't we get out of here?" she asked.

But he was shaking his head. "No. I'm pretty sure this was an isolated incident. What I can't figure—" he began, then stopped.

"What?"

"It's probably nothing."

"I still want to hear."

"This just doesn't happen. Not unless the ground is saturated. Late winter, early spring, okay. But not as dry as it's been."

"Are you implying something?"

"No," he said, a frown etched on his brow. "I'm only stating a fact. This is a big park, Anne. With millions of spots like this one. Why did that boulder choose to give way at this exact moment in time? A coincidence?"

"What else could it be?"

"I don't know," he said half under his breath, and then he caught himself, and turned his attention to her. "God, I didn't even think... Are you all right? That was as close as it comes. You want to head back?"

"Certainly not. I still have my job to do." *If only he knew,* she thought.

He cocked his head and eyed her. A certain degree of respect showed in his gaze. "You know, you're pretty tough. You have nine lives, like a cat?"

"Only one," she said quietly, "like everybody else."

Back in the Bronco, he put the vehicle in reverse, then steered around the boulder.

"We come out near the river up ahead, then there's a road back to the Visitor Center," he said. "I still need to check on a couple of campsites, and then we can…"

"I'd like to see the spot where the murder occurred," she said abruptly.

"You *what?* That can't be a part of your job. I don't—"

"Oh, but it could have an effect on the budget."

"I don't see how."

"Well," she pivoted in her seat and stared at him "time, as they say, is money. The investigation takes time, and the Park Service is paying for that time."

Mitch cursed under his breath. "Look, I really have about a dozen things to get done back at the Visitor Center. I don't see why—"

"Say you *do* make an arrest," she cut in. "You'll have to put the whole case together, work with a federal prosecutor, testify in court…"

"So?"

"The Park Service is paying for all that."

"*So?* What's it got to do with seeing the crime scene? It's goddamn silly, if you ask me."

Anne kept her expression in neutral. "I'm the one making the call here. Now, is it a long way?"

"Oh," he said, his jaw tight, "it's just exactly opposite of where we were going."

"Well then," Anne said, "we better get started, hadn't we?" She clicked the seat-belt tongue into the buckle and gave him a smile. Was she flirting with this man? Impossible, in view of the whole situation—her job, the lies she was telling—and his valuable time. This wasn't a joke.

And yet... Somehow she was enjoying herself, which was ridiculous. She hadn't enjoyed a thing, nothing, for four years, ever since her husband Lyle had been diagnosed with cancer.

What was happening to her?

She gave Mitch a sidelong glance and there it was again—that sudden warmth bubbling up in her belly. She was bludgeoned by guilt—there had never been anyone but Lyle, and now his precious memory—and still she felt insanely alive. It had to be the park, the rare beauty of Canyonlands.

'You sure, you really *sure* you want to make this trip?" Mitch was saying.

"Yes." She licked dry lips. "Yes, I'm sure."

It took a long time to reach the site where Zachary Sterner had been found. The spot was isolated. No campers or bicyclists or hikers, no vehicles, no signs of humanity whatsoever. At last, at the opening that marked the canyon's ancient beginning, they came to the grotesquely gnarled tree—the hanging tree.

Mitch stopped the Bronco. "There it is." He nodded.

A thousand police procedural questions came to mind, but she didn't dare ask a single one. Instead, she said, "Can I get out and walk around, or will I mess up some evidence?"

"Nothing left to mess up. Everyone's been here and gone."

She exited the vehicle and moved closer to the dead tree. The sun burned down on her, hotter here on the canyon floor. The heat made her feel weak, and it was hard to concentrate. She forced herself to think. Had the body been brought here from outside of the park? By whom? Why? What kind of sicko would transport a dead body to this remote place and leave it hanging in a tree? As a warning? To whom?

And *why?* If they could figure out *why,* they'd have an idea where to look for *who.*

"Ugly," she heard Mitch say beside her.

"Yes." She turned to him. "And you found the body. It must have been…"

"It hasn't been my best week."

"Did you know the victim?"

"Only as one of the kids working on the Red Canyon dig."

"But isn't it odd that no one has any idea why the boy was killed? I mean, usually there's a motive. Well, in movies and books, anyway."

"Yes, it's odd, but I'm sure we'll figure it out. If and when I get back to work on the case," he added bluntly.

Anne ignored his sarcasm. "You must have a couple of ideas, though."

"Ideas?"

"On the motive."

He shot her a curious glance.

"Such as," she persisted, "a robbery, random violence?"

Mitch said nothing; he just stared at her.

"Or a fight over a woman," she went on. "Now,

I'm sure I've read that murder is almost always a family thing, but it's hard to imagine a family member coming all the way here to shoot the young man and then *hang* him. That would just be too crazy, don't you think?''

Mitch still remained silent, and she pretended to fiddle with the borrowed sunglasses while he stared at her. The bureaucratic infighting that caused one government agency to keep information from another was plain dumb, she mused. What could it possibly hurt if Mitch here, an honest, hardworking guy, knew she'd been sent to keep an eye on the investigation, even help solve it if possible? He'd probably be glad for the help.

But no. This was, if anything, a case for the FBI, yet no one had called them in. The president, in an effort to placate his friend, had asked for some assistance from his appointee, the attorney general. So here she, Anne Winslow, was, walking on eggshells, trying to appease everyone while keeping up this bogus cover story that only served to inconvenience everyone. *God.*

''I will find the killer,'' Mitch said, but he was talking to himself.

And then Anne reflected aloud, too. ''It has to be hell for the parents.''

''Yeah,'' Mitch said, ''I can't even contemplate it. If anything happened to my daughter…''

''You have a daughter?''

''Yes. Brooke. She's fourteen.''

Of course Anne was already aware of that from his file. She was also aware he was divorced and that his ex-wife's name was Denise.

''And your wife?'' she asked.

"I'm divorced." Flatly.

"I see."

And now, was he going to ask her if *she* had children, if *she* was divorced? If he did, she was afraid she'd tear up, and she couldn't let him see that. To prevent the possibility, she abruptly walked away from him toward the tree and stood staring at it.

Why *here?*

What had Zachary Sterner done that had so enraged or threatened someone that he had to be murdered...twice?

"The only evidence was the rope—which you can buy in any hardware store—and tire tracks—which were smudged over. Whoever did it was smart."

"Cruel," she said, and she felt an involuntary shudder go through her.

"Cruel, yes."

"Let's get out of here," she said suddenly, and she started walking swiftly back to the Bronco.

She watched him approach through the dusty windshield, a tall man, even more imposing in the straw Stetson and uniform. Even though he was from the East, from Washington like her, he fit in out here.

And then she noticed his limp again. Odd, how you forgot about it. She was struck by the notion that his halting stride was only an annoyance to him. She would have thought he'd have worn his infirmity like a badge of merit considering the heroic circumstances of his injury. But he didn't seem to pay any attention to it. Curious.

An interesting man, she had to admit. Wounded in the line of duty, starting over, taking on a new career, a new life. Why, he could have retired on his pension, with full honors and a disability allowance.

If only she had the courage to start over, the will. It was too hard, though, her loss still too fresh in her mind. Suddenly, she envied Jim Mitchell.

"Have you seen enough?" he was asking. "Got a whole bunch of budget ideas to jot in your notebook?"

"There's no need to be sarcastic. I can't make budget suggestions if I don't know how things work. Now I have a sense of how remote this spot is. How *big* the whole park is. Maybe my recommendations will be favorable to the annual budgeting for Canyonlands."

He turned on the engine and then pinned her with a glare. "Why do I doubt that?"

"Such a skeptic. Really, Mitch, you have no idea what I do."

"Which brings me to the question," he said, his eyes still on her rigorously, "just how long *does* a budget review take?"

"Oh," she said, "as long as it takes. So, shall we go?"

The drive back to the Visitor Center was long and slow, the Bronco bucking along the rough sandy track. She noted that he handled the four-wheel-drive vehicle well and wondered where he'd learned to do that. Certainly not in Beltway traffic. The sun was lower in the western sky, and sometimes they were plunged deep into shadows, cast by sheer rock walls. Then they'd emerge into the full light of day, and the far-off spires and humps of red rock would be illuminated in brilliant bands of light.

Yes, the land was beautiful, she had to admit, strangely afraid to allow herself to feel it, to feel anything pleasurable. As if she were somehow cheating.

"Funny we both come from Washington, isn't it?" she said as they bumped onto the paved road that led to the park entrance, the staff housing and the Visitor Center. "Such a coincidence."

"Not really. This is federal land." He shrugged, eyes on the road. "We're federal employees."

"Did you like living in Washington?"

"I thought I did."

"So you really do prefer living here?"

"Uh-huh." He paused. "My daughter doesn't."

"You said she's fourteen?"

"Yes."

'I can imagine. This is a little…isolated for a teenager."

He said nothing, but she noticed the now-familiar tightening of his jaw, and the lines from his nose to his mouth deepened.

"If you don't mind my asking," Anne said, "where's her mother?" She knew, though. So why was she pushing the issue?

"Las Vegas," he said, offering nothing more, leaving the unspoken question—Why wasn't Brooke with her mother?—hanging in the air.

Anne wondered, was it a custody fight? Some sort of problem with the mother? Denise—that was her name.

He was silent again, and Anne felt a certain amount of discomfort. He didn't like her, either as a bureaucratic paper pusher or as a woman. That bothered her. Ridiculous. Why did she care what he thought of her? She reminded herself she was here to do a specific job. And this man knew something; she was sure of that. Perhaps it was unimportant, but she wanted to know what it was. How was she going to pry it out of him? Should she try to befriend him? Turn nice and accommodating all of a sudden?

Discreet, she'd been told. *Be* discreet.

Surely someone else in the park had an idea, a hint, a clue to who did it. No proof, maybe, but something more than she had. Maybe Martha knew something. Or that Chick Draco Mitch had mentioned, the archaeologist. She'd have to talk to them. Both of them. And soon.

Funny, she thought, watching the scenery move by her window, the sun gilding the jutting rocks, spreading long shadows across the flat areas, lighting up the western sky in bars of purple and mauve and orange. *Funny.* If she really were a budget analyst for the Park Service, she'd agree with Mitch that this huge mass of federal land was woefully underfunded.

What would he say then?

Mitch parked in front of Anne's staff apartment.

"Thank you for the tour," she said. "I know you're busy..."

He was staring straight ahead through the windshield, the sun hitting his mirrored sunglasses and glinting off the wire frames. "Will you need me tomorrow?" he asked.

"Well, yes, I will. I want to see more of the park. Is that a problem?"

"I'll...manage."

She gave a short laugh. "I only hope we won't be nearly killed. That boulder was too close for me. I'm a city girl."

"Yes, it was too close," he said in a strange voice, and she looked at him, trying to discern what was behind his tone.

"What time, then?" she asked.

"Let's say eight tomorrow. Same place."

"Okay, I'll walk over."

"Do you have everything you need? You can get things at the Outpost."

"I'm fine. Thanks."

"Well then, see you tomorrow." He seemed anxious to be gone.

"See you at eight," she said, and she watched him drive off to the Visitor Center, where no doubt a mountain of work awaited him. She felt a twinge of guilt.

In the cool apartment she slumped onto the couch. She was tired, hot and dusty. Heat always drained her. What a day. Dealing with a reluctant park ranger, nearly crushed by a rock, trying to delve into the mystery of Zachary Sterner's murder without giving herself away. She was weary, physically and mentally. She didn't have the mental energy for this sort of thing anymore. She should have stayed in Washington, made them send someone else.

She shed her clothes and took a long cool shower, letting the water sluice down her body. She held her face up to the spray, once more feeling a little guilty at the pleasure she was having. She'd thought for a long time she'd never feel pleasure again, not even in ordinary things like showers or good food or new scenery, but pleasure did sneak in, whether she was willing or not. Somehow life had its own mandates. God, she resented being dragged back into a normal world; nothing could ever be normal again, could it?

She turned the shower off and stepped out. Naked, leaning over the sink, she rested on both arms, hair dripping.

Yes, Mitch knew more than he was telling her.

She'd perhaps been too flippant with him, but he was a man who would not be comfortable confiding in anyone, especially a strange woman.

The boulder. Clearly, he considered it more than a random accident. Something was going on, and she didn't like being in the dark.

Mitch's daughter, Brooke. Did he have problems with her that distracted him? He'd alluded to some discord. Being out here alone with a teenaged daughter must be tough. He obviously loved his new life, but his daughter didn't.

She wrapped a towel around her wet hair and opened the bathroom door. The cool dry air sucked the moisture off her skin so rapidly she was abruptly covered with gooseflesh. So different from the soft damp eastern air. And the land, like the air, was desiccated and sharp edged and spare, its ancient secrets preserved for millennia because of that very dryness.

She pulled her nightgown over her head and went into the kitchen, where she opened the refrigerator to see what there was to eat. Not that it mattered. Nowadays she ate only to live, all food sawdust to her palate. It was the easiest diet she'd ever been on.

What was Mitch eating for dinner? Did his daughter cook for him? What did they talk about over their meal? Or perhaps he was still at his office in the Visitor Center, working late. Because of her.

She pulled a frozen dinner out and turned the oven on while eyeing the package.

Why was she thinking about him, anyway? But even to her inner ear the question was absurd. She was thinking about the ranger because he was a man, and a good-looking one at that.

She found a cookie sheet and put the frozen dinner on it, then shoved it in the oven.

Mitch. James Mitchell. Who would have thought a total stranger who lived worlds away from hers would be the one to ignite a spark in her dead soul? And yet he had. She wouldn't lie to herself. There was some curious sort of magic to that man, this place, and she couldn't help wonder what tomorrow had in store for her. More magic? And if that was true, would she embrace it or run for her life?

CHAPTER SEVEN

PAUL KASPER WAS A PARODY of a bodyguard. Six foot two, two hundred pounds, buzz-cut blond hair, eighteen-inch neck. But an intelligence lit in his blue eyes, and he was smart enough to keep his body honed in order to avoid trouble. He'd been a Navy SEAL, undergone rigorous training, worked at various jobs in security until he'd met David Draco.

Mr. Draco paid him well, but demanded absolute loyalty and service at any time of the day or night.

The job he'd been sent on was pretty basic: find this character Jerry Hawkins and instill the fear of God into him. Mr. Draco hadn't told Paul all the details, but he was well aware that this Hawkins dude had killed someone and that this act was endangering the arrangement between Hawkins and Mr. Draco.

Paul pulled up to the Rivers Saloon and parked. The neon sign was poison green, and one of the *O*s was dark, so the sign read "salon." *Right,* he thought.

He'd actually stopped by last night but had been told that Jerry Hawkins wasn't around. Tonight, however, Paul hit pay dirt, finding his quarry sidled up to the bar. He wore a tank top, dirty jeans that looked as if they could walk out of the bar by themselves, dusty, scuffed, low-heeled cowboy boots.

And there was the cousin, Harv, listing badly, his

cowboy hat pushed back crookedly, a beer in his hand. The dumb one.

Okay, so he'd found them, but by the appearance of things, this was not the time or place to discuss business. Disgusted, he made his way through the smoke and sweat smell, until he reached Jerry.

"Hey, Hawkins," he said.

Jerry turned, one elbow the bar, and eyed Paul. "Well, well," he said, "if it isn't Draco's gorilla."

"Yeah, sure. Listen, Hawkins…"

"Okay, I'm listening. What does Mr. Big-Shot Art Dealer want this time?"

"Not now, Hawkins."

"Okay, so when?"

"Tomorrow."

"I have to work tomorrow. You know, *work?*"

"Where can we meet?"

"I'm leaving for the dig real early, Gorilla. You city folk don't get up at the crack of dawn like us country bumpkins."

"I'll go anywhere anytime you like," Paul said without expression.

"Tell you what." Jerry turned all the way around to face Paul, a long-neck beer dangling between thumb and forefinger. "We're going to be up there a couple of days, and it's too far to go back and forth. You meet us in the park, come along, you'll see the operation, report back to Draco."

"All right. Tell me when and where to meet you."

"At 6:00 a.m. sharp," Jerry said, and he gave him directions. "You can leave your car and catch a ride with us."

"I got four-wheel-drive."

"Suit yourself."

"You wouldn't consider skipping out on me, Hawkins, would you?"

"Certainly not, my friend. Would we, Harv?"

"Huh? Would we what, Jerry?"

"Skip out on Gorilla here."

"Skip out? We sure wouldn't."

"See, I told you."

"Six tomorrow morning," Paul said. "And we'll get everything straightened out then."

"We sure will. Now, you bring enough gear along to stay up there. And water."

"Yeah, yeah."

"Wouldn't want anything to happen to Draco's right-hand man. It gets dangerous up in those canyons."

Paul gave him a contemptuous look. "See you tomorrow," he said, then he started making his way through the crowd to the door. He didn't like turning his back on Hawkins; he felt the man's malicious gaze between his shoulder blades like a dagger.

He wouldn't put anything past that slimeball. Certainly not murder.

Back in his motel room Paul checked his map and marked his route. He'd have to start early—it was miles down 191 to the road leading into the park. What a pain. But, hell, that was what he was paid to do.

Mr. Draco had warned Paul to be careful. *He's no pushover,* he'd said.

Well, neither am I, Paul thought, taking his gun from his overnight bag—the heavy nine-millimeter semiautomatic that he'd carry with him tomorrow.

He had a feeling he might need it.

BROOKE MITCHELL AWAKENED in a foul mood. She used to be happy when she woke up, look forward to each new day. But that had been when she was a kid, before her life had been ruined.

It wasn't fair. Mom and Dad had gotten divorced. It wasn't *her* fault, but she had to suffer anyway. It had been bad enough when her parents had both still lived in Washington, but now her mom had gotten married again and moved to Las Vegas and had a baby. *A baby. God.*

It embarrassed Brooke to think of how her mother had gotten that baby, her *brother,* no less. Charles. Charley. *Prince* Charles, Brooke had secretly dubbed him. He was a year old and spoiled rotten. How come they hadn't spoiled *her?*

She got up slowly, lethargically, knowing she had to face one more day in this awful, isolated park, stuck out in the middle of nowhere. And she couldn't drive yet, so she was really and truly stuck.

She pulled on a pair of shorts and a T-shirt and ambled out into the living room, yawning.

"Brooke—oh, good, you're up," her father said.

"What's good about it?" she mumbled.

"It's a beautiful day out and—"

"It's *always* a beautiful day out here. It's so boring."

"Come on, honey, isn't it time you got over this stuff?" It was the voice she hated, his long-suffering voice.

She took a bowl out of the cupboard, ignoring him. Cereal, milk from the fridge. The same thing every day. Boring.

"Did you hear from Mom?" she asked.

"No, not yet."

"Mmm."

"Look, honey, your mom's busy with the baby."

"Well, I'm her daughter, just as much as he's her son."

"Of course you are. And she loves you as much. She just needs some time to adjust, with the move and all."

"Yeah, *right*."

"I have to go soon, Brooke. That lady from Washington. She's a pain in the neck, but I have to be nice to her. You got your day planned?"

"I'm baby-sitting. As usual."

"Great. I'll see you when I get home. I don't know how long it'll take, showing her all over the damn place."

She didn't bother answering. What was the use? He was so dense.

"There's stuff for lunch in the refrigerator, unless you're going to eat where you're baby-sitting," he offered.

"Don't worry about me. I'll be fine," she said sarcastically.

Her dad sighed. "Gotta leave, honey. Be good."

When he was gone, Brooke wandered around the apartment, restless. She wanted so badly to call her mother. She'd been waiting all summer for her mom to answer the letter she'd sent, begging to be rescued from the park, pleading to be allowed to visit Las Vegas.

True, her mother was preoccupied with the baby and her new husband, Jeffrey, but their new house had a pool and Vegas was at least a city. There'd have to be kids her age around. It'd be better than *here*.

Brooke went to the Visitor Center every day to check the mail drop for letters, but so far there weren't any. It was as if she no longer existed now that Prince Charles was there.

She turned the radio on, trying to get the Moab station, but all she got was static. As usual. She did the breakfast dishes and drifted into her bedroom, listless, her narrow shoulders drooping.

The full-length mirror on the back of the door reflected a sad sight: a gawky teenager, tall and skinny and flat chested. Long, stringy dishwater-blond hair. Last week's zits drying up, this week's crop sprouting.

Tears gathered in her eyes. Frustrated, miserable, teenage tears. She cried for a long time, no one to tell her to stop, to be annoyed with her; no one to comfort her.

It wasn't fair.

Then she dried her eyes, because there wasn't anything else to do, took a shower and got ready to go off down the row of staff housing to her baby-sitting job. The kids were cute; the money was good. It was an easy job, but it was boring.

Before she went to take care of the kids, though, she walked over to the Visitor Center.

"Hi, Martha," she said, "any mail for us?"

"No, nothing today, button. How you doing?"

"Okay, I guess."

"You sitting for Renee Dickerson's kids today?"

"Uh-huh. Well, I better get going. See you."

No mail, nothing from her mother. She was going to have to call. She'd beg, she'd sob, she'd do anything to convince her mom to get her out of this place.

It just wasn't fair.

THIS TIME ANNE PUT ON the sunscreen and even a little zinc oxide with no prompting from Mitch as he drove out into the wilds of the park, obviously determined to make his rounds before she screwed up his day.

Which was exactly her plan.

She was about to ask him to drive her to Chick Draco's archaeological dig site, when the call came over his radio.

Mitch steered with one hand while lifting the handset to his mouth.

"Mitch, here. Over," he said, depressing a button.

Then the dispatcher's voice. "Got a rock climber in trouble. Leg injury. Over."

Mitch. "Location? Over."

"Firepit Canyon, Lil Cap Wall. You should be the nearest vehicle with a Stokes Litter. Over."

"Can the chopper make it in? Over."

"Not this canyon, Mitch. You'll need to litter the victim out to Tapioca Flats and radio for the chopper then. Got it? Over."

"Got it. Over and out." He turned to Anne, a look of apology in his eyes. "Sorry," he began.

"Mitch, hey," she said, "you have someone injured here. There's no apology necessary."

"This could take a while."

"I understand," she replied, but little did she know the rescue would take over half the day.

It started when they parked the Bronco at Tapioca Flats and had to hike a mile into the canyon toting along water, medical supplies and the Stokes Litter. To Mitch's credit, Anne saw, the slight halt in his gait did not slow him a bit. She wasn't aware of it, anyway, huffing as she was over the grossly uneven terrain in the narrow canyon.

"You sure can move along," she breathed.

"You mean considering my leg?"

"Well," she said, suddenly embarrassed, "yes."

"Hey, I had plenty of training while I was with the veep. You know, running beside his car during motorcades, that kind of stuff. I also run myself—*used to,* that is, in Rock Creek Park. I like moving. Being outside. How about you?"

"Right now," she said, "I think I better join a gym when I get home, if you know what I mean."

"Sure," he said, and she could have sworn she saw a corner of his lip curve into a smile before his eyes switched back to the uneven ground. Imagine that; she'd made the man smile.

They reached the site of the climbing accident by eleven and found two men and a woman, who'd clearly broken her leg, awaiting them at the base of Lil Cap Wall, named after its big, grown-up cousin El Capitán, in California's Yosemite National Park.

"Thank God you're here," one of the young men said, "Shelly's really hurting."

Lucky for Shelly, Mitch was trained as an EMT—emergency medical technician—and he was able to splint her leg. Still, the girl's face twisted in agony when the men loaded her into the specially designed Stokes Litter.

Anne became the frightened girl's best friend, holding her hand, reassuring her, as they began the long hike out to Tapioca Flats, where the chopper from Moab could make a safe landing. Mitch took turns with the two other men on the litter, and Anne made sure Shelly stayed hydrated in the brutal sun.

"You're so kind," Shelly said once as Anne held the water bottle to her lips.

"Well," Anne said, "I've had a little nursing practice. Not much, but..." She was aware of the glance Mitch threw in her direction, but she didn't say more. The last thing this group of young climbers wanted to hear was how she had cared for Lyle at home in his final months. Oh, yeah, *that* would cheer them up.

"So," Anne said, smiling at Shelly, "how did this happen, anyway?" *Safer subject.* "I don't know a thing about climbing."

"It wasn't the equipment," the girl said, looking away.

"It never is," one of the men muttered.

"I...I forgot to hook my safety rope into this one carabiner, and then I slipped, which happens sometimes, but instead of falling ten feet, it was more like fifteen. So stupid."

"Well," Anne said, "I bet it can happen to the most experienced climber."

The helicopter picked the trio up by one in the afternoon, and Anne gave Shelly a hug before backing away and shielding herself from the undulating currents of dust the rotors created when the chopper lifted off and headed north.

"Phew," Mitch said, watching as the big machine disappeared over the rim of spiral rock and crossed a distant mesa, "that was a job."

"Yes," Anne agreed, but just to say something. The crazy truth was that she'd enjoyed the experience. Not Shelly's pain, of course, but the challenge of the rescue, the satisfaction of having in some small way helped the girl get through a very scary time. Anne hadn't felt of any use to anyone—except Yoda,

that is—since Lyle… Then again, her cat was content
so long as someone was there to feed and cuddle him.
Yoda wasn't terribly particular who that someone
was.

"Well," Anne said, facing Mitch.

"Good Lord," he said, and he reached out and
touched her cheek with a finger. "You're fried."

She almost leaped back at the contact. "Oh," she
said, "I guess I do feel hot, huh?" But that didn't
explain her skittishness, not to him, obviously, and
not even to herself.

"Are you okay?" he was asking, his head pitched
to one side, the mirrors of his glasses reflecting her
embarrassment right back at her.

"I'm fine. Perfectly fine," she said quickly. But
she wasn't. Something was happening to her in this
primitive, windswept land of rock and color and
strange beauty. *Something.*

"Huh," was his answer.

They drove off Tapioca Flats and into an area of
the Needles District known as Muriel's Quilt. Here
the land opened up a bit as the dirt track Mitch followed wended its way across a wide, pockmarked expanse of sandy desert floor and huge boulders scattered haphazardly, some the size of houses. Boulders
that appeared to have had no origin, as the nearest
canyon walls were miles away now.

"Weird," Anne said. "Everything about Canyonlands is weird. It makes you stop and think."

"It sure does that," he agreed. "It's like being in
an ocean of rock."

"Yes," she said, "that's it. And the place is almost
fluid, isn't it? I mean, it changes before your eyes."

He nodded. "That's the light playing with all the shadows and colors. Takes getting used to."

"I think I could do that," she said, and then she sat up straight and had to shake herself. What was she doing? She wasn't here as a tourist, for Lord's sake; she was here to help get to the bottom of that poor boy's death.

Wake up, Anne.

"How far are we from the Red Canyon dig?" she asked abruptly.

"Ah, maybe sixteen, twenty miles. I don't know for sure. Why?"

"Well, the government is thinking about a hefty raise in permit fees to conduct a dig on federal lands. One of the things I need to review is the entire process. License to the actual land use, such as—"

"Hey," he cut in, "that *really* isn't my area. Like I told you—"

"But I do need to see one of the digs going on."

"You don't mean—now?"

"No time like the present."

"I still have to stop by two camping sites. No one has checked them in days. It's got to get done, and they're in the opposite direction from Red Canyon."

"I'm sorry."

"You're *sorry?*"

"Look, Mitch, I have a job to do, too."

"Then we'll stop at this dig on Sandoval's Mesa. The University of New Mexico's anthropology department is conducting it, and it's only a few miles from one of the campsites."

"I want to see Chick Draco's dig."

"Then, hell, Anne, see it on your own."

"No. I'd get lost."

"I'll draw you a goddamn map tonight, and you can make it in the rental car you've got. You won't get lost. Hell, I'll lend you a radio if you—"

"No," she said firmly, "it's Red Canyon today. That rescue has me a half day behind."

She could see a muscle in his jaw working furiously and a vein in his temple was swollen with his frustration. She didn't blame him. She knew there was no way he could comprehend her obstinacy or think her anything but incredibly selfish. And she *was* being selfish. She didn't really need Mitch in order to visit the dig or speak to this Chick Draco or his students. It was just that with Mitch along, she knew cooperation would be greater. And she sure could use all the cooperation she could find.

Mitch made a ninety-degree turn, his knuckles white on the steering wheel, that muscle still ticking away in the flat plane of his jaw.

He was furious.

Anne stared out the passenger window and tried to ignore the silence that enshrouded them. She reviewed in her mind what little she knew about the murder, what little she'd found in the files. A .22-caliber bullet had killed the boy. The hanging had been for show, as if the murderer had wanted to send a message. But what? A big "screw you" to the boy's family or the authorities? Why? Who'd want to kill a student?

Anne felt curiously certain of one thing: the killer's intimacy with the park itself. Having seen the isolated spot where Zachary had been strung up in that tree— and the uniqueness of the lone, dead tree on the floor of the canyon—she was positive the murderer knew the land very, very well.

A ranger? A frequent visitor? A Native American? One of the other archaeologists here? *Who?*

She pivoted toward Mitch, who was still driving along, with his broad shoulders set rigidly. *Fuming.* Someday he'd find out the truth about her. Someday he'd understand. She suddenly wished she could tell him the truth right now. Would it wipe that anger off his face if he knew? She'd like it if they could work together instead of at cross-purposes, if she could confide in him; talk to him; ask him about his wife, his daughter, his job.

He was so blatantly honest, his attempts at hiding things from her so transparent. Like now, when he was unable to hide his anger.

Someday he'd understand, but then it would be too late—she'd be gone.

"Mitch," she said, her voice carefully neutral, "what sort of people are intimate with the park? I mean, other than the rangers and archaeologists? Who comes out here all the time?"

He was slow in answering. For a long minute he stared straight ahead, then merely turned and shot her a look, before putting his eyes back on the track they were now negotiating. "A few campers, maybe. Couple local-yokel families."

"Families? You mean like from Moab?"

"Actually," he said, "I'm referring to the moki poachers."

"The...what?"

"Moki poachers. It's a Hopi Indian term that means those who steal from the dead. Grave robbers."

"I don't—"

"The concept's not that hard to grasp," he said

curtly. "Anasazi artifacts have a worldwide market. They can bring incredible prices on the black market. Even in Europe and Asia. Artifacts from the Southwest are very trendy."

"Really," she said, digesting this, mulling the new information over. "Tell me more about these moki poachers."

"What has this got to do with the NPS budget?" He threw her another look.

"A lot. Hey, you're the one complaining about lack of manpower to police the park. So tell me."

"There's a family in Moab, the Hawkins family. They settled this area right after the Civil War. They've looted the ruins in the park for three generations. The worst offender is Jerry Hawkins."

"Well, if you know who he is…"

"Oh, yeah, we know who he is. He's the best known moki poacher in the Southwest."

She tucked the name away for future reference. *Jerry Hawkins. This* was the kind of information she'd come here to find.

"Why isn't this Hawkins behind bars?" she asked.

Mitch made a disgruntled noise. "You have to catch him first, and that takes manpower. You know, budget money. The truth is," he went on, "no matter how many rangers are out in the park at a given time, you can believe Jerry Hawkins knows their schedules and patrol routes as well as they do. Better, probably, because he's far more knowledgeable about the park than anyone. Right now, I have three rangers who've been patrolling for over twenty years each, and that's nothing. Jerry and his clan have spent a lifetime in this area. They are just too damn hard to outwit."

"What about aerial surveillance?"

"It's been tried. You can hear a plane or a chopper coming for fifty miles, long before it can spot you, anyway. And Jerry must have a thousand places to stash his vehicles when he's looting."

"He has to drive the stuff out sometime. What about the roads?"

"See what we're on right now? Does this look like a road to you? Hell, Anne, out here you make your own roads. Hawkins can take hundreds of routes in and out of the park. And if he waits till dark?" Mitch shook his head in disgust. "There's little chance of catching him. Late last winter, right after I got here, we thought we had him. Stopped him leaving the park on a road up in Island in the Sky, but his truck was empty. He was either playing decoy, or he has a stashing spot right in the park and he only hauls stuff out once in a while. We'd like to follow him every second of every day, but that's impossible."

"Manpower," she said.

"You got it."

Moki poachers. Archaeologists, students. Priceless Anasazi treasures. This was big. Big money. And money and black markets and murder were certainly bedfellows in her book.

Anne was beginning to see a pattern. Hazy still, but becoming clearer by the minute. She wondered, too, if Mitch and his rangers didn't have similar thoughts. They had to, didn't they?

"Red Canyon," Mitch said, nodding to a gash between two distant plateaus.

Should she ask him if he saw a connection between the priceless artifacts and the student's murder? Or would that just make Mitch suspicious of her?

Discreet. She'd be discreet for a little while longer. There was always tomorrow.

ANNE'S FIRST LOOK at the Red Canyon dig left her awestruck. It was huge, much larger than she'd imagined, covering at least three acres of the canyon floor and climbing up the red-rock face of a southern-exposed cliff.

People worked everywhere, hunched over or on their knees in the fine, sandy soil, using tiny brushes to dust away earth or sifting handfuls of earth through screens; tagging potsherds and splinters of wood or fibers or bones at long, grimy worktables; crating the tagged items; shoveling near crumbled walls. The site was an anthill of activity under the baking, high-desert sun.

Anne got out of the Bronco, shielded her eyes from the slanted afternoon light and took it all in. She could almost see the Anasazi village as it must have been a thousand years earlier—the copper-skinned people who'd inhabited the clusters of stone rooms, their dark hair blunt-cut and shiny, their animal-skin clothes the color of the sand itself; children playing by firepits; women tending irrigated fields, giggling, gossiping as they labored, some tanning hides in the sun, others fetching water from the now dried-up stream that had meandered along the valley floor. In her mind's eye, she watched men climbing rough-hewn ladders, carrying timbers and stones; stonemasons chinking mud into new walls as the village grew; young men arriving home from the day's hunt with deer or rabbit; hawks soaring overhead; strange-looking dogs, barely domesticated, barking, fighting over bones. And in the center of all the activity the holy man, a mystical figure who had the power to call on the gods to bring rain or to heal the sick, and the kiva, smoke rising from the pit in the center of it, forming a question mark in the clear, dazzling blue sky.

Amazing.

"Anne? You coming?" Mitch's voice.

"Ah, yes, sure. I was just taking it all in," she said a little breathlessly.

"Chick Draco is over this way. You may as well meet him."

"I'd love to," she said.

Draco was the picture-perfect archaeologist in her estimation, with his dusty khaki shorts and sweat-stained khaki shirt, smudges on his ruddy cheeks and nose, grimy broken fingernails, matted thin blond hair, weathered skin, his wire-rimmed glasses literally held together with duct tape. She guessed his age to be close to Mitch's—a little under forty—but he was stooped even when he straightened from the table he'd been hunched over and took her hand, shaking it. *Old beyond his years,* she thought, or at least his back had given out a long time ago, making him appear closer to fifty.

"Funding, funding, funding," Chick said, giving her an apologetic smile. "Even the park must have its funding. I spend half my time trying to find new grant money. All us scientists do, you know. Being an archaeologist is not what it appears on TV—all the wonderful discoveries and years spent in exotic locales." He shook his head. "No, no, much of our time is spent looking for money so we can continue to unearth a few treasures."

Anne nodded and returned his genuine smile. "This is amazing, Doctor," she said.

"It's Chick, please. Doctor is too formal."

"Chick, then."

"And are you giving my friend Mitch a hard time, young lady?"

"Oh, over the budget? No, not yet. But I'm afraid he's getting sick of playing tour guide." Out of the corner of her eye she caught the wry twist to Mitch's mouth before he excused himself, saying he needed to speak to a couple of the students while he was there.

She watched him go. He'd been sitting in the car a long time, and obviously his leg was stiff, because his limp was quite pronounced. Her heart squeezed abruptly. *My fault,* she realized, and strangely, unaccountably, she had the urge to run after him and tell him that. Tell him everything. He'd take her by the arms and hold her still, his blue eyes boring into hers, and he'd be furious...at first. But then he'd understand and his hard grip would soften. "It's all right, Anne," he'd say in that slight gravelly voice, "I forgive you." And then... What? What did she want from Mitch?

Chick cleared his throat and she was wrenched back to the moment. "Ah, Mitch," she began, nodding after the ranger, "is he going to question some of your students about that poor boy's death?"

"I suppose so. It was a tragedy. I can still see Zach as clear as day, working right over there." He glanced toward a firepit in one of the rooms.

"Hard to imagine why anyone would do such a thing. You must have a theory, Chick."

"None, absolutely none. I've been racking my

brains. I can't even understand why he was so far from here.''

''Maybe he was taken from here. He *was* shot first, before he was...''

''Oh, God, don't remind me.''

''I'm sorry.''

''Not your fault. It's barely been a week.''

''I wonder,'' she said, ''well, if they'll ever find the person who did it. They don't seem to have a motive yet.''

''No, they don't seem to.''

''Maybe,'' Anne reflected out loud, ''Zach had an enemy among the students, got in an argument over one of the girls, something like that.'' She glanced around at the dozen or so student workers she could see. And there was Mitch, talking to a couple of girls right now.

His face was grave and very intent on what the girls were saying. He was a good listener, she could tell. She was curious what he'd asked them. Something about their friend Zachary, of course.

And she noticed it again—that aura of integrity that surrounded Mitch like a force field. One girl was speaking to him earnestly, looking very sad but sincere, and Anne had a fleeting moment of unaccountable jealousy. Mitch had established an instant rapport with these girls that he never had with her. Never wanted to have with her.

But Chick was saying something, and she hadn't really heard him.

''I'm sure you're wrong about that, Anne. Zach had no enemies here. Not a one.''

''Pardon me?''

''I said, Zach was incredibly well liked.''

She tore her gaze from Mitch and fixed it on the archaeologist. "Well," she said, "somebody killed the kid. And if it wasn't a crime of passion, then you tell me, Doctor, what was the young man really into?"

The minute she'd spoken, Anne realized by the horrified look on Chick's face that she'd been unfeeling, even cruel. Too late to take the words back, though, and the truth was that she was right, had to be right. Mr. Zachary Sterner had gotten himself involved in something dangerous. She eyed Chick. Did this innocent, absentminded professor know what his student had been involved in? And if he did, how was she going to pry that information from him?

You catch more flies with honey, she thought, and she gave the doctor a winning smile and started anew with her questions. Much more innocent ones.

CHAPTER EIGHT

JERRY HAWKINS WAS PLAYING cat and mouse with Paul Kasper. Draco's bodyguard bulged with muscle, but that wouldn't help him out here. What a person needed in this country was a whipcord-thin body that was efficient—didn't sweat too much, didn't use too much energy.

Paul was sweating like a pig, his thick neck running with precious liquid. They'd driven as far as they could, Paul behind them in his SUV, then they'd parked in the usual place in the brush beneath a rock outcropping where their vehicles were virtually invisible and started the uphill trek.

"I call it New Ruin," Jerry was saying. "Catchy, huh?"

Paul only breathed hard, following Jerry and Harv doggedly up the narrow trail between striated red-and-white rock walls. He was dressed like a city dude—pleated linen trousers, a salmon pink polo shirt, tassel loafers.

He must be getting blisters, Jerry thought, grinning inwardly.

"Now, this site we found," Jerry explained, moving along just quickly enough that the big gorilla couldn't catch his breath. "It's real special. I told Draco. We're still waiting for the tree-ring dating, but it's old. Older than old."

"Uh," Paul grunted.

"They left quite a legacy, these Indians. I'm not even sure you can call 'em Anasazi. They're different. Yeah, a little different. How you doing, pal? Some water?"

Paul shook his buzz-cut blond head. "How far?"

"Oh, not far. A mile more, maybe," Jerry lied, then continued his monologue. "You know about the Anasazi, pal? The name's Navajo, actually. Nobody knows what they called themselves back a thousand years ago. No written language. But a very advanced civilization, twice as many people living in this area then than there are now. You know that?"

"No."

"Yeah, but the climate got drier."

"Jerry," Harv whined, "can you slow down."

"Shut up, Harv. Hey, Paul, how you doing?"

The bodyguard stopped and glared at Jerry, sweating, puffing.

But Jerry didn't slow down. "The Navajos came in the 1400s, down from the north. They're related to the Inuit. So they got here and found all these ruins, towns of stone houses, found 'em empty. Scared the bejesus out of them. Navajos hate death, dead people. Won't touch 'em. So they called the lost race Anasazi—Ancient Enemy Ones."

"That's nice," Paul puffed.

"Those old Anasizi, they were real spiritual, like the Hopi nowadays. Very advanced. And this ruin—wait till you see it."

Paul stopped, hands on knees, sweat dripping off his nose, dark dots on the dust-dry ground. He looked up and asked, "What was the point of hanging the kid?"

"The Anasazi told me to."

"Right."

"Hey, they want their city protected, same as all of us. And that kid blundered onto the site. He was not wanted, pal."

"But to *hang* him?"

Jerry shrugged. "Call it a whim."

"God, a whim," Paul breathed. "Why couldn't you have made it look like an accident?"

Jerry eyed the big man. "Oh, sure, an accident. Like, accidentally shot through the head?"

Paul grimaced in disgust.

Jerry started walking again, picking up the pace. He didn't like Draco sending this guy to look over his shoulder. He didn't tell Draco what to do, did he? Goddamn, he resented this jerk.

They were nearing the plateau and the narrow valley that split it, the valley that held New Ruin. Despite his dislike of Paul, he wanted the man to be impressed by the find and to report back to Draco on his cell phone just how spectacular it was. The more leverage Jerry had the better.

"It's just around the corner," he said. "Tucked away in the valley, all up one side. You can't see it from the air or even from the plateau." He motioned Paul to precede him. "Take a look."

Paul went ahead first, his back rigid. *Distrustful bastard,* Jerry thought.

There it was. Jerry never got over the first view. Even though he'd been working here for months, it surprised him every time.

"Damn." Paul stopped and stared.

"It's something, isn't it?"

"I'll say." Paul craned his neck to look at the myriad rooms stepped up the valley's wall. Some even had intact roofs. And a stream still ran at the base of the ancient pueblo. Unheard of. All the other streams in Canyonlands were dry in the summer.

"It's big," Paul said.

"It's not just big. It's different," Jerry replied.

"So, where's all that stuff Mr. Draco's been promised?"

"Can't see it, can you? That's because we're being real careful, hiding our excavations. There's an art to looting," Jerry said proudly.

"But it's here?"

"Except for what we've already taken out to my place."

"And you're trying to tell me that the kid stumbled on this?" Paul asked.

"Yup."

"How?"

"Damned if I know. He was out hiking around probably, all inspired by Chick. Looking for shards like a good student. It was just dumb luck. *Bad* luck for him."

"You could have done it differently, Hawkins. I mean, talk about brutal. And now every television station and newspaper in the country has people here."

"Big deal," Jerry sneered.

Paul faced him, recovered from the hike. "You've put Mr. Draco in real jeopardy," he said, poking a finger in Jerry's chest. "It was stupid."

"David Draco can go screw himself." Hawkins eyed the finger poking him.

"You *need* Mr. Draco, you idiot," Paul said.

"No, Gorilla, Draco needs *me*."

"Ah, God, you're thick as mud," Paul muttered, turning away.

Jerry said nothing, but his temper smoldered. He'd love to tell this jerk about how he almost got rid of their biggest problem, Chief Ranger Mitchell, but he'd keep that little secret.

And he wasn't going to forget Paul poking that finger at him—or calling him an idiot. Hell, no.

"Should I set up the tent?" he heard Harv asking.

"Sure, go ahead."

"You mean, we're gonna sleep in *tents,* on the *ground?*" Paul asked.

Jerry grinned, enjoying the situation once again.

MITCH HAD SEEN Chick's horrified expression and wondered what Anne could have said to elicit such a response.

Interesting, he thought. There was a lot more to Anne Winslow than she let on. Something about her just didn't jibe. He still couldn't imagine her sitting in an office all day, crunching numbers. He couldn't have said why he thought that, but the feeling persisted.

And another thing, he mused. There was that way she wanted, *demanded,* to see everything, no matter his irritation. Did a budget lady *really* have to drive all over kingdom come and visit a murder site?

He narrowed his eyes behind his sunglasses and studied her. She was still talking to Chick, but the doctor had gotten over his reaction to whatever she'd said, and he was enthusiastically showing her a case of pottery shards. She appeared interested, but Mitch could have sworn she was holding back impatience.

"Have you gotten any new leads?" one of the students was asking him. Cute, petite, upturned nose covered with freckles from the sun. Sharon? Cheryl? Charlene, that was it.

"No, not yet. But these investigations take time."

"My mom is really nervous about me being here, you know?" the girl said. "She keeps saying a murderer's running around loose."

"Did you tell her you've got armed rangers guarding you?"

"Yes, but she's not convinced."

"I can understand her fear. I have a daughter, too."

"But I don't want to leave the dig. I'd feel like such a fink. Dr. Draco needs us all."

"Yeah, I know."

"Well, I better get back to work," she said, dispirited.

"Take it easy, Charlene. Tell your mom you're safe here."

"Sure, okay..." And she drifted away, back to sifting desert sand for bits of history.

Damn, he wished he could put these kids' minds to rest. He felt so darn helpless, rusty in the area of crime investigation. And he was basically an administrator here. That was all well and good when things went along normally, but a murder had been committed in his park, in his district, and he was getting absolutely nothing accomplished.

Except driving a budget lady around.

She'd sure asked a lot of questions. The moki-poacher information had interested her. Was that the realm of an accountant? Was she, as she'd said, trying to get a feel for the overall picture? Or was she here for some other reason?

Forget Anne Winslow, he told himself. He had

more important matters to think about. Murder, for instance. And that boulder yesterday. Had it really been an accident? He'd confronted Jerry Hawkins one night and a day later he almost had an accident that shouldn't have happened. Coincidence? Hell, he wouldn't put anything past Hawkins, not the kid's murder or the near miss or any other goddamn thing.

He checked with several other students to make sure one of his men had taken their statements, and then he made his way back to where Chick was showing Anne a map of the entire site.

"We think there's more under that hill." Chick gestured with his hand. "It's probably the midden, where they threw all the broken pottery and stuff."

"How big was this settlement?" Anne asked.

"Oh, I'd say about fifty families, a few hundred people." He pushed his glasses up on his nose, leaving a dust smudge. "None of these towns was very large because of the limitations of resources and climate. That's why Chaco Canyon is so unusual, a huge settlement…"

"Chaco Canyon?" she asked.

"A large set of ruins, over in New Mexico. Dozens of towns very close together in what used to be a river valley. But we've come to believe Chaco was a trading or religious center, only populated a few times a year. Sort of like Mecca."

"I had no idea there were so many ruins," she said.

"Thousands." Chick waved a hand. "Millions. And I have to beg for funding." He shook his head. "And now Zachary's murder. I hate to be selfish, but it will make it even harder to get funding and student workers. Awful, awful."

"No one's going to hold you responsible, Chick," Mitch said.

"I hope you're right," the man replied fervently.

Catching Anne's eye, Mitch said, "We better get going. I still have to finish my patrol route."

"Okay." She turned to Chick. "It was wonderful meeting you. Your work here is fascinating, and I hope I can come out and visit again."

"Anytime, Anne," Chick said.

"Ah, Anne, you want to go on up to the Bronco? I have a little technical problem to put to the doctor here."

She shot him a look, and for a minute he thought she was going to give him a hard time, but she made a gracious exit.

"What's up, Mitch?" Chick asked, his pale eyes enlarged by his glasses.

"The shard."

"Oh, God, I forgot all about it. I'm so sorry. I'll check on it today—really, I will. It's here somewhere." Chick looked around distractedly, as if he could locate it on the spot.

"I need it, Chick."

"I know, I know." He ran a hand through his hair, leaving spiked strands behind. "Look, I'll get it this afternoon and bring it to you tonight, okay?"

"That'll work."

Anne was waiting for him in the Bronco. He expected her to ask what he'd been talking about with Chick, but she didn't. Instead, she asked him to drive her to a site that had been looted.

"What?"

"I'd really like to see one. I think it's important.

It'll figure in my report. Mitch, they don't know about these things in Washington.''

"Can't you just take my word for it?''

"No,'' she said firmly.

"I don't have time for this.''

"You'll have to make time. It's part of your job.''

He clenched his jaw, twisted the key in the ignition and spun the vehicle around, spewing rooster tails of dust behind him.

"Okay,'' he said, "but it'll be a small one, not far from here, and you can't stay long.''

She said nothing, only clicked her seat belt shut.

He drove her to the nearest site he could think of; a set of round granaries in a gully. Not a very interesting site, but looters had removed many of the building stones, and some buried pots had been dug up and sold on the black market.

"That's it,'' he said. "Some storage silos for grain. You can find them all over the park, but this one is closer to the road, so it's been picked over.''

She got out and walked up to the jumble of fallen sandstone blocks and empty, gaping holes in the ground, then stood there eyeing the site, hands on her hips. Finally she turned to where he sat, drumming his fingers on the steering wheel.

"What kind of pots were here? The kind that sell for a lot of money?'' she called.

Impatient, trying to keep his temper in check, he got out and strode toward her. "I don't think so,'' he said. "There were probably only rough storage jars. Not worth much.''

"Was this place looted by those moki poachers?''

He shook his head. "Doubtful. Most likely they

were tourists looking for souvenirs. They don't realize they're breaking the law.''

''Ignorance of the law is no excuse.''

''Of course not, and we have signs all over warning people not to touch archaeological sites. A warning is printed on every map and guide and pamphlet. But they don't seem to notice.''

''Or they don't care.''

He shrugged.

''But there are other sites that have been scavenged by professionals,'' she said.

''Oh, yeah. The way the market works, only pots in good shape and with good artwork on them are worth much, so the professionals are knowledgeable. They wouldn't bother with a place like this.''

''Mmm. Can you show me a site they *would* bother with?''

''Not today.'' *Damn this woman.*

She cocked her head and studied him. ''Okay, but tomorrow or the next day?''

''I might have time on my day off,'' he said. ''They tend to be really out in the boonies.''

''Okay, well, I guess I've seen enough here.''

Thank God, Mitch thought. He still had to cover his route, get back to the center, check with the sheriff on the forensic tests…

He drove for a while, not saying much, wondering how long Anne was going to stay, when he could once again devote his full attention to the murder investigation, if Chick would find that shard and return it to him, what those odd, unidentified fibers on Zach Sterner's shorts were, when she spoke.

''You know a lot about this area.''

''I've been reading up on it.''

"I can tell. But it's more than that. You have a...well, a feeling for this park."

He cast her a sidelong glance. "Yeah, I guess so."

"It's so different from what you were used to, isn't it?"

"Oh, yeah. I came out willing to give the job a trial period, but I got hooked. I'd never heard of the Anasazi before, never knew one single thing about the most advanced civilization in North American before the Europeans arrived. I still haven't gotten over the surprise."

"Your enthusiasm is duly noted."

"Oh, that'll go in your report, too?"

"It might."

"Tell me, is all this driving around helping you?"

"It certainly is."

"Good," he muttered. "Good."

"So you love it here, but you mentioned that your daughter doesn't," she said with a certain amount of care.

He drove past the entrance to a campground, stopped the vehicle, got out and picked up a bag of trash someone had dropped by the side of the road.

"Slobs," he said, tossing the bag in the back of the Bronco. Then he got back in and they drove on, bouncing over the rough road. He didn't reply to her question.

She didn't give up, though; she tried a different tack. "Where will your daughter—Brooke, right?—attend school in the fall? Will she be going back to her mother?"

This woman was certainly nosy. Questions, questions. "No. Her mother lives in Vegas and she's remarried, has a year-old baby. I'd like Brooke to stay here.''

"Is there a school nearby?"

"No."

"I see. So where…?"

"There's a high school in Monticello and one in Moab. I'll move into Moab when the season's over, and Brooke will go to school there." He shot a look at her. "Will that be a part of your report?"

She crossed her legs. "You never know." She paused, then asked, "But your daughter isn't keen on living in the park?"

"No, she wants to be in a city. Other kids, malls to hang around it. I wish," he said regretfully, "I wish she'd appreciate this place."

"But you can't force her to appreciate it."

"No, I can't. I realize it was hard for her. Just when she was getting used to us being divorced we both moved away from Washington. I feel for her, but, boy, can she make it difficult."

"Being a teenager," Anne said. "It's a hard time."

"I really can't recall that it was so bad. I was busy, played football and ran track. I didn't think about it."

"*Men,*" she said, then she fell quiet, as if suddenly confronted with a somber notion.

He drove through his route quickly—there was no time to stop at every site, every overlook, every campground. Plus, he needed to get back to Brooke tonight. He'd been neglecting her—because of Anne. He was aggravated all over again; his time was just not his own. When was she going to leave him in peace?

Finally she spoke. "That Red Canyon dig is impressive."

"Mmm."

"Is there enough funding for Chick to continue his work there? I was afraid to ask him. He seemed so upset over it."

"I think he can last the summer, then he'll work alone until winter shuts him down. The kids have to go back to school, and they're unpaid volunteers. He can't really afford to hire anyone."

"Too bad," Anne mused.

"The only reason he's lasted this long is that he has a rich uncle who helps fund the dig."

"That's convenient."

"Well, the man has a vested interest. He's a collector and art-gallery owner."

"But he can't use anything from the dig."

"No, it's on federal land. But Chick excavates on private land in the off months, and that's when David Draco gets his rewards."

"*The* David Draco?" she said.

"That's right."

"The Arizona philanthropist? The one they talk about as possibly the next governor?"

"Uh-huh."

"I should have made the connection," she said to herself. "Draco the archaeologist and Draco the money man."

"So?"

"Oh, nothing, I'm just surprised I didn't recognize the name sooner," she said smoothly, and again Mitch was struck with the sense that Ms. Winslow was not quite leveling with him. She was a curious one, a real enigma. Ordinarily, he would try to find out just exactly what made her tick. It was in his nature. But the truth was he didn't have time for any of this right now. Anne Winslow might be bright and inquisitive and, he had to admit, a real good-looking woman but, man, he wished she'd just finish her crazy budget review and get the hell out of his hair.

CHAPTER NINE

"PHONE CALL, MR. DRACO," the sales associate said. "The caller says it's important."

"Excuse me, Mrs. Nielson. Debby here will take care of you. Thank you, Debby."

David took the call in his office. Sitting back in the black leather armchair, he pressed the button for line one. "Yes, Draco here."

"Mr. Draco, it's Paul."

"Where are you?"

"I'm up at the place, out in the park."

"Okay, good, fine. Jerry is there?"

"Yes, Jerry and his cousin Harv. We'll be spending the night, Mr. Draco, but I wanted to check in with you first."

"Has Jerry been a problem?"

"Not exactly, but he has a real bad attitude."

"Can he hear you?"

"No."

"Okay, so, do you feel that the man will listen to reason?"

"No, not at all."

"Damn!"

"He could be dangerous. He's very arrogant."

"I was afraid of that. Well, you do your best to convince him, Paul, but as I said, be careful."

"Don't worry."

"Now, to change the subject, what's it like up there?"

"It's quite fantastic, Mr. Draco. It's all Jerry said and more. Not that I'm any judge, of course."

"Oh, I trust your impression, Paul. So, it's good, huh?"

"Yes, it's good."

"And he gave no reason for killing that boy?"

"No. Only that the kid had accidentally discovered the place."

"All right, well, do your best."

"Yes, sir."

David hung up and sat there thoughtfully for a time, his forefinger pressed against his upper lip. He was going to have to fly up to Utah and meet with Jerry himself. There was no other choice, he was afraid. Damn, he'd wanted to avoid that, but he could see it was necessary. Someone had to talk sense into Hawkins and it would to have to be him. Face-to-face.

He'd use Chick as the excuse for his visit, of course. Easily done. But confronting Jerry Hawkins would be an ugly chore.

Goddamn the stupid redneck. Goddamn him and his arrogance.

Then David stood, straightened the already-perfect knot of his silk tie and went out into the front of his shop.

"Well, how's it going, Mrs. Nielson? Will it be the Santa Clara wedding vase or the Hopi polychrome?" he asked, smiling brilliantly.

CHICK DRACO felt a terrible hand of sadness grip him as he watched his family around the dinner table, Ellen scolding their precocious daughter, Kiva; their eldest, Miko, snickering. Normal family stuff. Typical. But Chick wondered if he would ever again feel anything but that awful sinking sense when he looked at his children, who were strong, happy, healthy. How could he feel otherwise with the death of someone's child weighing so heavily on him? If only he hadn't let Zach take the afternoon off to go on a hike. If only the young man had stayed close to Red Canyon. If only, if only, if only…

Chick pushed himself away from the table, the chair legs scraping the tile floor. Then he stood, rubbed his chin, and felt suddenly nauseated. His dinner plate was untouched.

"Honey," Ellen said, "you have to eat something. I know how hard this past week has been, but you won't be any good to anyone if you make yourself sick. Please."

But he shook his head vehemently. "You don't understand. No one does. Zach was *my* responsibility."

Ellen looked at her suddenly silent children, seeing the confused fear in their eyes. That the children should suffer wasn't fair. This wasn't their fault. *Damn it, get a grip.* But she held in her frustration. "Zach was a grown man," she said. "You aren't a camp counselor, Chick. These students will be holding down their own jobs next year. They'll be out in the big wide world looking for grant money, all that stuff. They *are* adults. All right, this has been a tragedy, and everyone is just as concerned as you whether or not the authorities will ever find that…that evil person who did this. But life goes on. You owe it to us, Chick, and you owe it to the other students. Now, please, sit down and try to eat something."

Chick met her gaze for a long moment, and then

he felt a sob well in his chest. Wordlessly, he walked out of the kitchen, through the tiny living room and out onto the patch of yard in front of the adobe apartment, a hand clamped over his mouth as though he were holding down his insides.

"Oh, God," he sighed against his fingers, and he stared out across the canyon toward the row of striated red spires that had given the name Needles to this section of the park. The sun had set, and the sky was splashed with oranges and purples, and he felt a hot burning behind his eyes. So beautiful, so beautiful. And Zach would never see it again.

MITCH WAS FRESH from a shower, clad only in clean blue jeans, no shirt or shoes yet, as he watched his daughter fussing at the stove. Not fifteen minutes ago, when he'd gone for the shower, Brooke had proudly announced she was making spaghetti and meatballs for dinner.

"I got the recipe from my friend Lisa in Moab. Her mom's teaching her to cook. Go take a shower, Dad, and we'll eat in like a half hour, okay?"

He'd showered and felt the best he had in weeks about Brooke, who'd looked so cute at the stove, her hair in a loose ponytail, an apron tied around her. She was trying, making a real effort to help out, and he was grateful to Lisa and her mother, who owned a little ma-and-pa restaurant in Moab. Cooking, at least, was constructive.

But something, obviously, had gone wrong in the fifteen minutes since he'd left the kitchen.

"It's not *working*," Brooke yelled when he reappeared. Then she threw a spatula in the sink, raising a hell of a racket in the process.

"What's wrong?" Mitch said. "Everything smells great."

Brooke whirled on him. "Oh, like the store-bought sauce smells great. Bid deal, *Dad*."

"Okay, whatever," he said. "So what's the problem?"

"The stupid meatballs. Like you'd really know. You can't even make toast."

He tried a smile. "That's true. But maybe we can figure this meatball thing out together."

"Forget it," she snapped, her eyes flashing, "I'm not hungry anyway."

And that was when the knock came at the open front door. "What now?" Mitch said under his breath.

Then he saw her, the budget lady, standing behind the screen door.

He pushed open the screen door and said hello. She, too, looked fresh from showering off the day's heat and dust. She was wearing loose-fitting tan slacks and a sleeveless white T-shirt with a scoop neck. He couldn't help noticing how nicely her skin glowed in the last light of evening, and that her hair seemed more blond, clean and bouncy, falling over one eye a little. He could smell shampoo and soap and some sort of flowery skin lotion. A heady scent.

"Hi," she said, and she peered past him. "I, ah, gosh...You're in the middle of something."

"No, no," he said.

"Really. It can wait till morning. I don't know why I..."

Mitch stood aside. "Come on in."

"No, I really shouldn't have..."

"Anne," he said, "will you please come in? I'd

like you to meet Brooke, anyway.'' He nodded toward the kitchen area behind the living room. ''How about a beer?''

She hesitated, then finally smiled, a little embarrassed, and stepped inside. ''A beer. Wow. I haven't had a beer in ages.''

''I could get you something else.''

''No, no, the beer will be fine. If you're sure, that is. I mean, you're about to sit down for dinner, aren't you?''

''Not at all,'' he said, and he noticed then that she avoided looking directly at him—his bare chest, anyhow. No beer in ages, squeamish about a man's chest. Where had she been—on a different planet? There were a lot of perplexing things about this woman. Deciphering her was like trying to peel an onion; the layers just kept coming and coming.

Mitch got them both a beer out of the fridge and introduced Brooke, who was now standing by the sink, checking Anne out, a guarded expression in her eyes.

Anne shook the girl's hand and smiled warmly. ''I'm the pain-in-the-neck budget lady,'' she said. ''But I bet you already figured that out.''

Brooke dropped her hand and shrugged. ''I guess.''

''Yum,'' Anne said then, ''something smells great.''

''Brooke's making—''

''*Dad.*''

''Well, it's not a state secret. She's making spaghetti, and—''

''*Dad,* don't.''

God, Mitch was thinking, when Anne managed to step in and save the moment.

"You cook at your age, Brooke? I am so impressed. Lord, I couldn't boil water till I was in college. Honest."

Brooke eyed her warily. "I screwed this up," she finally said, a defensive edge to her voice.

"You know," Mitch cut in, turning to Anne, "if you haven't eaten yet, maybe I could make a run over to the Outpost and..."

"Oh, no," Anne said quickly, "you already have dinner here. And I wouldn't dream of—"

"*Have* you eaten?" he inquired.

"Well..."

"Then we'll make do, won't we, Brooke?"

"But it's ruined, Dad," Brooke began, sudden tears in her eyes.

Again Anne came to the rescue. "Ruined? No such animal, not when it comes to spaghetti. What's the problem?" She peeked past Brooke's shoulder to the stove. "Uh-oh, the old crumbling-meatball situation. I know that one well."

Brooke seemed at a loss, awkwardly stepping aside, shy, embarrassed still. "I followed the recipe. My friend in Moab's mom make these really good meatballs..."

"They smell wonderful, but I wonder," Anne said, "did you remember to put an egg in to hold them together?"

Brooke bit her lower lip. "The egg."

Then Anne cocked her head. "Like maybe that poor little old egg over there by the sink?"

Brooke sighed. "*That* egg."

"Let's do it," Anne said, and Mitch, feeling like a third wheel, disappeared to put on shoes and a clean shirt. *Phew,* he thought, escaping.

Dinner was really good. Especially the meatballs, the very same meatballs that had been his daughter's undoing an hour ago. The three of them sat in the cramped alcove between the kitchen and living room, their knees practically touching beneath the square oak table, and chowed down.

"Anne showed me how to put a little Parmesan in them, too," Brooke said, "and they came out good, huh?"

"Excellent," Mitch agreed, mouth full.

"Well, I have to admit," Anne said, "I used to be a pretty good cook. I liked cooking."

But you don't anymore. Why? Mitch wondered.

"I'm just learning," Brooke was saying. "I have a cookbook. I want to learn how to make Chinese. Do you know how to cook Chinese?"

"Um, stir-fry used to be one of my favorites. A lot of vegetable chopping, though."

They talked about food and grocery stores and then about their hair, how the dry desert heat did something to it. The only thing Mitch had to offer was that keeping it short seemed simplest—which caused both women to eye his military-short haircut.

For the most part he just sat there, ate his spaghetti and sipped on the beer, happy to listen, grateful for Anne's obvious kindness and understanding with his difficult daughter.

"…my *baby* brother," Brooke was telling Anne now. "I don't know how my mom stands it. He like cries *all* the time and he's so spoiled it's sick. I call him Prince Charles." Brooke laughed at her own joke.

"I have a sister," Anne said, "and we just hated each other when we were kids. She could do no wrong, and I was in trouble every waking minute. I swear my parents liked her better.''

''But then you grew up, I guess,'' Brooke said, ''and you realized how dumb that was? Dad's always telling me that I'm making a mountain out of a molehill and it's just because Charley's a baby that he gets so much attention.''

''Well,'' Anne said, uncertain.

''Well what?'' Mitch said.

''Maybe I shouldn't say it.''

''You have to now,'' Brooke insisted.

''Oh, all right, I guess I do. And don't take this wrong, because my family is sort of different, but I still think my folks like my sister better.''

''Really?'' Mitch looked askance.

Anne nodded. ''Really. My sister's life is so… normal. Mine… Let's just say I've traveled a bumpier road.''

''Interesting,'' he said, and the cop in him wanted to dig into that statement, to peel away that layer. He wouldn't, however. Anne was a stranger. A guest in his house. Her life was none of his business.

''How long are you going to be here?'' Brooke was asking her.

''Oh, gosh, I'm not sure. These budget analyses are strange. Some go quickly, others…'' She shrugged.

It struck Mitch that aside from jotting a few notes in that notebook of hers, he hadn't actually seen Anne Winslow do a thing that resembled budget analysis.

Anne helped Brooke with the dishes, and then Brooke took off for a neighbor's apartment. ''They have a satellite TV.''

''Well, it was nice to finally meet you, Brooke,''

Anne said, and Brooke went banging out the screen door.

"Thanks," Mitch said, standing there in his living room, studying Anne. "If you hadn't stopped by I think World War III would have erupted. I'm having…a rough summer with her."

"Fourteen years old," Anne reflected. "Not a fun age, as I recall. I had braces and god-awful stringy hair and zits. Oh, yes, the trials of a teenaged girl." She rolled her hazel eyes.

"She'll probably live through it," he said, "but I don't know if I will."

He cocked his head at her. "Okay," he said, "at the risk of sounding rude, I'm wondering why you really stopped by. Not that I mind. But…"

She let out a breath and smiled. A little too broadly, he decided "Well, I was putting together my notes, the budget, you know, and I had a couple questions."

"Really."

"Yes, really. Can we, ah, sit for a minute or two? I mean, it isn't too late?"

"Sure. I'm all ears," he said dryly.

"Well." She sat opposite from him on the couch, Mitch in his favorite easy chair, one ankle resting over his other knee, arms folded across his chest. "My questions have to do with the excavations in the park. I realize I'll have to get my facts and figures as to license fees and that sort of thing from another department, but I am wondering about artifacts."

"Artifacts," he said, his gaze on her. Such a pretty woman, he noted again, and when she let her hair down and smiled every so often she was downright sexy, had a laugh that reached inside him and made his heart beat too damn quickly. But it seemed Anne kept that smile in reserve, as if it were a precious commodity, and he'd be darned if he could remember once in the past couple of days when she'd bestowed it on him. Not that he cared, but he was curious what it was about him she didn't like. Hell, he wasn't *that* hard to look at, and he'd been working for years on softening his stern façade. Was it something else? His mannerisms? The way he'd first greeted her? Okay, so he had been rude; but then, she had been, too. Still, he thought they'd gotten along okay these past few days. Maybe he was wrong.

"...polices the removal of the artifacts?" she was asking.

"I'm sorry." Mitch sat up a little straighter. "What was that?"

"Who polices the removal of artifacts from a dig?"

"Well, say at Red Canyon. Chick would catalog everything that left the park. That's part of his job."

"So he has to be trustworthy."

"Sure. As do all the permit holders. But I can't imagine—"

She held up a slim hand. "I understand," she said. "You can't imagine a man of Chick Draco's renown doing anything underhanded. I only asked because of his uncle."

"David Draco?"

"Sure. The man has galleries in Santa Fe, Aspen, Palm Springs and his main one in Scottsdale, and—"

"Just how did you suddenly become so knowledgeable about David Draco?" Mitch cut in.

"Well, there's no mystery. I made a couple calls early this evening."

"Oh?"

"I was intrigued. Here's Arizona's wealthiest entrepreneur, with shop after shop full of Native American artifacts commanding some pretty hefty prices. Where do they all come from?''

"Private land. Estate auctions." He shrugged.

"And all David Draco's merchandise is on the up-and-up?''

He kept his gaze on her. She didn't squirm, though, not Anne. Just met his eyes calmly, unruffled by his scrutiny. *An accountant?* he thought.

"What the hell does any of that have to do with the budget?" he finally asked.

"Like I said, Mitch, I was intrigued. I mean, I arrive here on the heels of a murder, and it doesn't seem to have a motive. I simply wondered if there was a connection between the boy's death and a lot of priceless artifacts. Anyone would wonder the same. My goodness."

"You know what, Anne? I suggest you leave the police work in the park to me. You really are out of your element."

"No need to get testy."

"I'm not testy."

"The hell you aren't."

Anne rose. "Anyway," she said, coolness in her voice, "I won't need you tomorrow. I have some errands to run in Moab. I'll be out of your hair. That should make you happy."

Mitch also came to his feet. "Hey," he said, frowning, "it's not like that."

"Oh?" She walked to the door, opened it, went out and let it shut before he could follow.

"Hey," he said again, but she was already moving quickly toward the road. Over her shoulder she called out a thank-you for the dinner, and she disappeared into the black night.

Mitch looked down the road after her for a long time and then he turned back to his empty house. "Well, that was good," he mumbled.

JERRY HAWKINS blew a stream of smoke out of his lungs and watched it turn blue-purple against the half moon that hung above the canyon across from where he sat on a crumbled wall, feet dangling.

It was late, almost midnight, and Harv and Paul had hit the sleeping bags over an hour ago. Jerry could even hear Harv snoring where he was sacked out some thirty yards away near an old firepit. Yeah, good ol' cousin Harv had never had a sleeping problem. Jerry figured it was because the guy never had anything on his mind to keep him awake.

Jerry, on the other hand, never slept well at a ruin. Too damn many ghosts, too much *power* electrifying the ancient stones and beams and pathways. A ruin might look dead to most people, but as far as Jerry was concerned the places crawled with an otherworldly life force. Especially New Ruin. He could sense a peculiar energy in the night shadows that moved along the crumbled walls. The air crackled with it. Yeah, the air. Despite the dryness, the air always seemed heavy to him, heavy with the burden of those who'd come before.

Jerry flicked the cigarette butt toward the firepit and watched the ember glow hot, then die out. On the far side of the pit the bodyguard slept restlessly under the canopy of desert stars.

The man was a pain in the ass. So was his boss, and it pissed Jerry off endlessly to realize Draco had sent the gorilla to snoop on him. Who the hell did Draco think he was?

Then there was another big pain in the butt—Chief Ranger James Mitchell, the friggin' *hero*. Well, Jerry had almost put the man's lights out for good. Almost. But somehow the boulder had missed. Next time the hero wasn't going to be so goddamn lucky, not if he kept sticking his nose into Hawkins family business.

Too damn many people involved in Jerry's life right now. Too many. And all because of that kid stumbling across New Ruin.

There were ways of *uninvolving* people, though, lots of ways out in this untamed land. And the first person Jerry was going to *uninvolve* was Gorilla over there.

Jerry lit another cigarette and tipped his head back, tilting it to get a better view of Orion's belt.

Yeah, the bodyguard had made a real mistake when he'd poked that finger in Jerry's chest. A real fatal error there.

He dragged on the cigarette, shifted his attention to the Big Dipper.

Harv snorted once, very loudly, then must have rolled over, because he quieted down.

"Bunch of morons," Jerry grumbled, then he stabbed out his cigarette, slid off the wall to retrieve the other butts he'd flicked into the firepit and pocketed them. He stared over at the bodyguard and thought—never leave anything behind. Never leave any evidence. Then he walked away from the sleeping men, alone with his thoughts, alone to make his plans. When push came to shove, he mused, it was always better to be alone.

ANNE WASN'T SLEEPING WELL. She sat on the embankment behind the staff housing, still clothed, and studied the awesome display of stars overhead.

This was unbelievable country. More than she could have imagined on the plane ride out here. Certainly more than she'd imagined when the attorney general had handed her this assignment.

She let out a sighing breath and found herself smiling, strangely at peace. It was this place, that curious magic she'd discovered, and she suspected that Mitch must have felt it, too, when he'd chosen to live here. Sure he had. And he'd started over, left his life in Washington behind, even brought his child here—though *that* decision was still up in the air.

Mitch had the guts to pull it off. Maybe it had been his brush with death and he'd said, *screw it,* life was too short to play by the rules.

I could live here, Anne thought, hugging her knees. *I could do this.* It just took intestinal fortitude.

She finally went back inside and put on her nightgown, but sleep was elusive. She couldn't stop thinking about that student and the ruin at Red Canyon and moki poachers. And, of course, there were the Dracos, both intricately involved in the procurement of artifacts—priceless treasures.

This was all connected. She knew it was.

And Mitch, she was positive, knew it, too.

That near miss with the boulder… Had it been an accident? She'd never forget the look on Mitch's face. As if he'd been more angry than surprised. He knew plenty, all right. And maybe she'd know more herself tomorrow when she did some snooping around Moab. She wanted to find out a lot more about that Hawkins clan Mitch had mentioned. A lot. She'd stop at the sheriff's for sure; she might have to let Warner in on her real assignment in order to get the info, but she'd tell him to keep it quiet.

Tomorrow, she mused, tossing in the bed. She'd learn a lot more tomorrow.

She was almost asleep, hanging on that fine edge of consciousness, when Mitch's face popped unwanted into her head.

Darn.

Mitch. There was something about him, something other than his tall good looks. A competence and self-assurance, the feeling he gave people that he was living the exact life he'd chosen. He pulled no punches and he made no compromises with himself. His integrity was magnetic. She couldn't remember the last time she'd been so impressed with a man. Lyle, her husband, had exuded the same brand of competence and honesty, but other than Lyle…

Go to sleep, her mind told her, but instead she thought about Brooke. Nice kid. Typical teenage problems. The girl needed a mom, or at least she needed friends her own age, close by. Anne could easily understand how isolation was making the teenager crazy. It was one thing to be an adult and opt for the wide-open spaces. But kids needed their peers.

She wondered then about Mitch's ex-wife and the new baby. Prince Charles. One of those broken-up family situations where the kids inevitably got hurt.

Yes, Brooke needed a woman and close friends. Did Mitch go out with anyone? Perhaps one of the lady rangers? Or maybe he'd met someone in Moab. That would be nice for Brooke, what the doctor ordered.

But none of this was Anne's business. She was here

to do a job. Period. Tomorrow she'd gather more information and hope the sheriff had some files on the Hawkinses. And maybe the lab results on the bullet would be ready. She'd sure ask.

Anne rolled over and punched her pillow, and there was Mitch again, invading her peace of mind. Silly, she chided herself, because as much as she admired his choice of life-style, she and he were for all practical purposes ships passing in the night. She had to remember that. So what if she finally, after all this time, felt a physical attraction to a man? It meant nothing.

Ships passing in the night....

CHAPTER TEN

THE LAST THING MITCH had time for was another trip out to Red Canyon dig, but Chick had not returned to the staff housing last night, which meant Mitch still didn't have the black potsherd.

He drove the isolated canyon road and consoled himself with the notion that at least he could kill two birds with one stone: get the blasted potsherd back and finish up the interviews with the student workers—not that the interviews were providing any help in the investigation so far.

He steered across a gully and thought about Anne. She had errands to run in Moab, she'd said. What errands? Getting her hair done?

She wasn't sitting in the Bronco next to him today, but her presence hovered, wraithlike, and the scent of her hair lingered on the air. He had to admit that he missed her a little. She'd been interesting company. Okay, she asked too many questions, made him take her all over the park, but she'd sure handled Brooke like a pro.

Pretty lady. Smart. Gutsy. Some accountant.

What errands? he thought again.

He found Chick labeling artifacts. "The potsherd?" Mitch asked, his irritation undisguised.

"Oh, my gosh," Chick Draco said, banging a hand against his sun-creased forehead, "I totally forgot."

"You mind looking for it now?"

"Of course, of course. I recall bringing it out here with me. It's got to be somewhere."

While Chick searched, Mitch spoke to the last three students and took notes. No one had a clue why someone would have murdered one of their peers. Evidently, Zachary Sterner was shy and quite immature with the opposite sex, capable of pulling pranks on girls but not much more. As far as Mitch could ascertain, no jealousy was involved in his death. As for the boy's relationship with his family, his fellow students believed it was normal stuff. If anything, Zachary was the pride of the family, soon to graduate and begin work on his doctorate.

"He was brilliant," one of the young men told Mitch.

"I see," Mitch said. "Do you happen to know where he'd gone the day he was killed?"

"On a hike." The young man shrugged. Same story they'd all told.

"How did he get there?"

"Caught a ride, I guess."

Another student who was close by piped up. "He hitchhiked. He said he could catch a ride there and back with tourists."

Mitch had heard this before, too. He also knew that no one had witnessed Zachary leaving the dig, much less catching a ride. A dead end there. All anyone could say was that he'd had a spot in mind to explore.

There were still so damn many unanswered questions, and Mitch was beginning to wonder if he'd ever get those answers.

The lab tests were crucial. The ballistics on the bullet and the nature of the fibers found on Zachary's clothing could tell Mitch a lot. But the tests still hasn't come back.

Frustration gnawed at him.

Chick had not found the shard when Mitch returned. "I just can't remember to save my life what I did with it." Chick gestured to the dozens of tables and crates, all containing artifacts. "If it got mixed up with any of these…" He frowned and shook his head.

"You *will* keep looking?" Mitch urged, his temper flaring.

"Of course, of course, and I'm so sorry."

"Me, too," Mitch said, and he left to check on Lonnie Whitehead, one of the rangers who was keeping an eye on the dig.

Lonnie, as expected, was bored out of his mind. "Man, I hope we solve this crime soon, Boss. This is dull, dull, dull. You know?"

Mitch knew. "Lab tests should be back within the week," was all he could offer. "Let's keep our fingers crossed they'll tell us something."

"Sure," Lonnie said, and he wandered off to help one of the women students lug a crate up to a pickup truck.

What a damn waste of precious manpower, Mitch fumed as he climbed into the Bronco and took off for the Visitor Center.

He was halfway back to his office, when he thought about Anne once more. Anne and her errands and all her questions. Curiously pointed questions for a budget review.

He drove the bumpy track and mulled that over, and then finally stopped the Bronco on a rise, his brow furrowed.

He picked up the handset and radioed his secretary. "Martha, can you do something for me? Over?"

"Anything, Boss. Over." Her voice faded in and out with some kind of interference.

"Phone the NPS in Washington and ask them if an Anne Winslow works in Budget. Over."

"Are you kidding? Over," came the crackling replay.

"Not in the least, Martha. Over and out."

"OH, GOD. Oh God," Harv sobbed. "Why'd you have to kill him?"

Jerry thumbed his sweat-stained cap back. "He pulled a gun on me. What'd you think I'd do?"

"But—"

"Look, no one threatens me, and no one tells me what to do. Don't you understand? If we let Draco think he can get away with that, we're goners."

Harv said nothing, but he didn't take his eyes off Paul's body, sprawled in the dust, a red spot spreading on his chest. He made a noise deep in his throat.

"Get over it, Cuz. Draco sent this gorilla here to punish us, don't you see?'

"He did?"

Jerry made a disgusted sound and pulled a cigarette out of the pack in his breast pocket. He lit it and took a drag. "Draco will get the picture now. *Me,* I'm the one in control, I'm the one sticking my neck out every damn day. I'm the one goes to jail if I get caught with the stuff he sells in his nice clean gallery."

"I know, Jerry, but—"

"It's done, okay? Just keep your friggin' mouth shut."

A raven landed on a rock nearby, a big black bird

glistening iridescently in the afternoon sun. It croaked, its heavy beak opening, closing.

Harv flapped his hands at the bird, which flew away, but Jerry knew it'd be back. With lots of pals. Maybe the bird was one of the Anasazi spirits, come to see what had been done in its ancient dwelling place, Jerry mused. One of those spirits returning in bird form. One of those spirits that led Jerry to the ruins, watched him every second, their lifeless eyes on his back while he dug among their bones. *Him,* not anyone else, not this dead bozo here and certainly not David Draco.

"What're we gonna do with him?" Harv cried.

Jerry sucked on his cigarette and studied the body for a moment. There was nothing to tell who had killed Paul Kasper, only a bullet hole in his chest. And Jerry had shot him miles from New Ruin. Even if someone happened upon the body, the crime couldn't be connected to Jerry unless the authorities got hold of his gun and matched the bullet. Not that *that* was going to happen.

And Draco—he would never squeal and end up incriminating himself. No problem.

"Look, we roll him over the edge and leave him for the Anasazi," Jerry said.

"The Anasazi? God, Jerry, you're turning crazier than a fruitcake."

"Shut up, Harv, and help me."

When it was done they walked to where the old red pickup truck was parked, got in and drove away. Already the ravens had come back, and were circling overhead, ready to begin.

"DAD, PLEASE HURRY, I'm going to be late," Brooke said.

"I'm going the speed limit, and you'll only be a couple minutes late."

"But they're probably all there already. I'm always the last one."

"We'll be at Suzy's house in ten minutes, Brooke. Just cool it."

His daughter subsided into silence. She couldn't wait to get to the slumber party in Moab; she was jumping with impatience. She'd spent a long time this afternoon preparing. Just for a bunch of girls? Mitch pondered the concept—dressing up and doing your hair so you can go to sleep with your friends? He didn't get it.

Or maybe boys were involved. Did the boys find out about the girls' party and saunter by?

"Are boys invited to this slumber thing?" he asked.

"Oh, God, Dad, no."

"But do they come by, you know, out of curiosity?"

She stared sullenly out of the passenger side window.

"Brooke..."

"Well, maybe."

"Aha."

"It's no big deal. I mean, they might come by, but it's not like we have *dates* or anything." She turned toward him. "Don't you want me to make any *friends?*"

"Of course I do. I was just wondering, that's all."

He dropped her off at Suzy Chandler's house, said hello to Suzy's mother and told Brooke to call him the next day. How eager his daughter was for him to leave bothered him just a bit. When she was tiny, she'd always wanted to sit in his lap, to hold his hand, to hug him, her little chubby hands usually sticky with something.

He drove away from Suzy's house telling himself to get over it. Brooke was growing up. It was a *good* thing she was independent.

Despite the late-afternoon hour, he stopped by the sheriff's on the off chance that Warner had heard back from the Salt Lake City forensic lab. Warner had gone home for the day, but the evening duty deputy had news for Mitch.

He handed him a fax. "Sheriff tried to reach you at the Visitor Center," the deputy said. "He knew you'd be interested."

Mitch read the fax and raised a brow. The tests on the fibers taken from Zachary Sterner's hiking shorts and T-shirt were turning out to be puzzling. They were yucca fibers, common enough, but they carbon-dated to 200 A.D., a time when primitive hunter-gatherers lived in the area.

The report went on to state that those early tribes used yucca for many things: the fibers for thread and sandals and baskets, the roots for soap, the fruit for food. But—and here the technician was obviously intrigued—the dye used in the fibers had never been seen before the fourteenth century. The lab technician was sending the fibers to a lab that had state-of-the-art testing abilities for further analysis.

"Strange," the deputy said when Mitch looked up.

'I'll say," Mitch put in, and he left the building, the report still in his hand, a frown etched on his forehead.

Where had those unusual yucca fibers come from? He had a feeling—a gut instinct—that if he knew the answer to that he could solve the crime.

He was still mulling over the fax, waiting at a traffic light on Main Street, when he heard a car horn and noticed someone behind him waving out the window. He looked in his rearview mirror—Anne Winslow.

They both pulled over to the curb, and he watched her get out and stride up to the Bronco. She probably had a question, or a dozen of them.

"Hi," she said, leaning against his open window. "Where were you going?"

"Back to the park. I just dropped Brooke off."

"Oh." She was regarding him curiously.

"Did you need something?"

"Oh, no."

"How did your day go? Get your errands done?"

"My errands? Oh, yes, sure, all done." She hesitated. "How about I buy you dinner? I owe you one."

"Oh, well, really, I was just heading back..."

"Come on. My treat."

"Anne, there's no need..."

"I figure you'll know the best place to go."

Not for one minute did he believe she was being sociable, and the last thing he was in the mood for was a bunch of her bullshit questions.

"Gosh," she said, "you're embarrassing me. I haven't asked a man to dinner in...well, maybe never, and you're going to make me beg?"

"It's not like that. I..."

"Where's the best place for western color? Someone today mentioned the Rivers Saloon. Said it had good food. Of course, I could go by myself."

He gave in. What else could he do? And, maybe, he thought as Anne followed him to the number-one local hangout, he could pour a few drinks down the lady and hear the truth about all her damn questions.

The minute he pulled into the parking lot at the Rivers Saloon he spotted Jerry Hawkins's pickup truck. *Figures,* he thought, shoving the gearshift into park. He considered Hawkins and the myriad Anasazi ruins in the park and moki poaching, and he felt as if he had an itch in his brain that he couldn't reach. Those old, old fibers with impossible dye—what was he missing?

He ushered Anne inside. It was early, so the weekend band wasn't set up yet, but men were lined up at the long bar, people were playing pool in the back room and several tables were filled with diners.

The old plank floor gave a little as Mitch led Anne to a table. The truth was he liked this place; partly because it was authentic, different from the trendy fern bars in Washington. He didn't look directly at the men bellied up to the bar, but he recognized Jerry Hawkins out of the corner of his eye.

He and Anne sat at a small round table overlooking the river. No linen, only paper place mats that displayed the menu. Bottles of ketchup and steak sauce, barbecue sauce, mustard and Tabasco crowded the center of the table like a bouquet of flowers.

"Full of atmosphere," Anne commented, glancing around.

"It's real, though. This place has been here for a long time and from what I hear it hasn't changed a bit."

"Interesting," she murmured, staring at the men at the bar.

The waitress was skinny and middle-aged, clad in threadbare jeans, a red-checkered cowboy shirt and pointy-toed boots. They gave her their orders—draft beers and ribs—and she nodded curtly, didn't write anything down and left without a word.

"So," Anne said, folding her arms on the tabletop, "anything exciting happen today?"

"Such as?" *Here we go,* he thought.

"Well, I guess I was thinking about that murder investigation. Anything new?"

"Not really," he replied.

"Oh," she said, then she shrugged and smiled. "So, where did you say your daughter was?"

He hadn't said. "At a slumber party at a friend's house."

"Funny term—slumber party. Girls never sleep a wink at them."

"Really." Mitch frowned. "What do they do, then?"

"They talk, gossip, giggle, you know."

"All night?"

"Oh, sure."

He shook his head, puzzled.

"It's a rite of passage for girls. And then the boys come over."

"How'd you know that?"

"A bunch of cute young girls? Of course the boys show up. Didn't Brooke tell you that?"

"Yeah."

"She's a darling girl."

"She seemed to get along all right with you. Oh, thanks," he said to the waitress, who had set their beers on the table. Then he turned back to Anne, "But she sure gives me a hard time."

"Um." Anne sipped her beer, licked the foam off her lip. "She's at a difficult age, trying so hard to be an adult but really not able to be one."

"Let's not talk about Brooke," he said.

"What do you want to talk about?"

"Where do you live in D.C., for example?"

"I have an apartment in Arlington."

He had a strong impression that she lived alone, but he couldn't help asking, "Do you live there by yourself?"

She gave him a closed look. "No, I have a cat, Yoda."

"A cat."

"Uh-huh, a cat."

He'd been fishing, but he hadn't caught much. He switched the subject. "What do you think of our Wild West?"

"I'm not sure how wild it is. So far I've noticed a lot of tourists. The scenery, of course…" She looked pensive. "Have you ever gone river rafting or mountain biking? I see signs all over."

"I've been rafting. I took Brooke in June. It's a lot of fun. Mountain biking? I haven't tried it yet." He glanced down. "My leg."

"Does it bother you a lot?"

He shrugged. "Some." He didn't like to talk about it, hated sympathy, despised pity; those reactions from people embarrassed the hell out of him.

The food came, huge plates piled with coleslaw and French fries and a rack of ribs slathered in barbecue sauce.

"Wow," Anne said.

He knew she was trying to be pleasant, but he still suspected an ulterior motive. Or was she just trying to gain his cooperation? And all the time he ate and talked to Anne, he was aware of Hawkins and his cousin at the bar. At one point Jerry had seen him, and even now the man was staring, his eyes roaming from Mitch to Anne, whom he studied without blinking. It aggravated Mitch to see how brazenly Hawkins leered.

"What are you watching?" Anne asked, twisting in her seat.

"Nothing."

"You keep staring over there. Is it someone you know?"

"Not really."

The band wandered in, began setting up on the raised bandstand. Drums, speakers, seedy-looking musicians in cowboy garb.

"Do you like country-western music?" Mitch asked.

She looked doubtful. Attempting to be polite. "I've never listened to it."

"It's loud." He found himself smiling. "People get up and dance. Old, bowlegged cowboys. They're really something to see."

"I used to love to dance," she said thoughtfully, and he tried to picture Anne Winslow dancing. What? Waltzes? Jitterbugs? With whom? In his mind an image coalesced: Anne in a flowing gown, spinning around a dance floor in a man's arms, but the man's face was a blur.

She was nibbling at a rib, her fingers sticky with sauce. There was a dot of the red stuff on her chin, and Mitch couldn't take his eyes off it. She put the rib down and wiped her fingers on a napkin.

"They're very good," she said.

"You've got sauce on your chin."

"Oh." She lifted her napkin and wiped at it, but it was still there.

"Did I get it?"

"No." He reached across the table and dabbed at the spot. She drew back a little and looked down.

"Sorry," he said.

"No, no, that's okay."

And he had to think again: *What does she want with me?*

When the damp washcloths were set down on the table, and Anne was reaching for one, he excused himself.

"Oh, sure, go on," she said brightly.

He went to the men's room, trying very hard not to let his limp show, because he knew Jerry Hawkins was tracking him with his eyes. When he emerged, he'd made up his mind. He walked right up to the Hawkins men.

"Well, if it ain't the hero again," Jerry said, turning from the bar very slowly, the way a snake readies itself to strike.

"You have a sore back, Jerry?"

"A sore back? No, why?"

"I thought you might have strained it pushing that boulder into the canyon the other day."

"Boulder? Canyon? What in hell you talking about?"

"I'm real glad you didn't hurt your back."

"Oh, hey, my back's fine." Jerry grinned wickedly. "Dangerous in the backcountry, Ranger Mitchell. You gotta watch your step."

"You know, Hawkins, you're going to get caught

one of these days.'' Mitch felt his temper begin to
heat up.

Jerry raised his eyebrows in mock innocence.
''Caught doing what? I don't know what you're talking about.''

''Your time's almost up. Remember that I said
that.'' Mitch took a step forward, into the smaller
man's space, almost chest to chest. He could smell
Hawkins's stale sweat.

Jerry narrowed his eyes. ''Back off, ranger-man.''

''When I feel like it.'' Mitch knew he was being
childish, indulging in such playground bravado, but
hell, he'd started this, and he wouldn't give in.

''Go back to your park and harass some tourists,''
Jerry hissed.

''I'd rather harass you.''

''I mean it, Mitchell.''

''Is there a problem here?'' came a cool, feminine
voice. Mitch and Jerry stood perfectly still, eyes
locked, not acknowledging Anne.

''Come on, fellas, lighten up,'' she said. ''You both
look like idiots.''

''Hey, Jerry,'' Harv said.

The bartender ambled over, a squat, dark-browed
man. ''Okay, guys, enough.''

Mitch let out a pent-up breath, felt his racing heartbeat, the adrenaline flowing. He stepped back, and
became aware of Anne's hand on his arm, drawing
him away.

''Later, Hawkins,'' he said.

''Anytime.''

Anne pulled him along, back to their table, pushed
him down in his chair. ''Goodness, I figured I'd get
to see a real Old West bar brawl.''

"Sorry," he said in a tight voice. But he wasn't.

"I think you did that deliberately. I think that's why you went to the men's room."

"Hey…"

"Don't bother, Mitch," she said dryly. Then, "I heard you call him Hawkins. Is that Jerry Hawkins?"

He nodded, noticing his hands were trembling. *Stupid,* he thought, *dumb thing to do—tip off your suspect.*

Anne looked across the room, as if studying Hawkins. "So that's him."

"That's him."

"And what exactly did you hope to accomplish by that confrontation?"

"Not a damn thing."

She stood up then and shook her head. "Well, Ranger," she said, "you certainly did accomplish your objective. *Men.*" And she walked out. When he tried to pay the bill, the waitress informed him the lady had already gotten it. He followed Anne out into the gathering dusk and felt like an A-number-one jerk.

CHAPTER ELEVEN

THE SUN HAD BARELY RISEN over the canyon walls when park ranger Joe Staghorn spotted the birds of prey circling low over a cut in the rock.

"Not good," the ranger said out loud as he turned the Bronco west, toward the hovering birds. Whenever a ranger spotted a large group of scavengers he assumed something was dead—a deer, a rabbit, or any one of the protected animals that lived in the park. Then again, a tourist—a hiker, a camper, a bicyclist—could be in trouble. Birds of prey circling warranted investigation.

Joe couldn't navigate the narrow rock crevice with the vehicle, so he got out, looked up to make certain this was the spot—yes, there were the birds, the shadows of their big wings flitting across the rough ground—and went the rest of the way on foot.

When he saw it, first he whispered a few Navajo words, then he said, "It can't be. Eyes are playing tricks on me."

Joe kept walking toward the object, his vision tunneling in on it, his breath coming quicker now.

"Can't be," he said again, and then he was standing over the body—the corpse of a man, face up into the morning sun, eyes wide-open, a bullet hole square in the middle of his chest.

Joe stood stock-still and stared, his brain rejecting

what his sight took in: the salmon-pink polo shirt, good trousers, tasseled loafers; a big, fit man... partially mutilated now. One side of his face...

The vomit just came. Fast and furious, a liquid projectile out of Joe's mouth.

Then he was running, stumbling over loose rock, desperate to get back to the radio in the Bronco, his brain screaming, *no no no*.

MITCH TOOK MARTHA'S phone call on the kitchen extension while he scrambled eggs and burned the toast. No way to start a day off, he mused, shoving the toast down the garbage disposal, starting again.

"Sorry to bother you at home," Martha said, "but I figured you'd want to know that I got an answer on your request about Anne Winslow."

"Go on," he said, keeping a close eye on the toast.

"Well, it was kind of weird. When I first contacted headquarters in Washington, they told me there was no Anne with the last name of Winslow working for the NPS. Not even a Winslow. So I asked them to check further and explained she was with Finance."

"So?"

"So I just got a call from the secretary of the head of the entire park service, no less, who apologized every which way and said that of course Anne Winslow was with the service and had been sent to do a budget review."

"Mmm," Mitch said, popping the toast up.

"Mmm is right. I know something fishy when I smell it," Martha said.

So do I, Mitch thought, and then he thanked Martha and hung up. What in hell was going on here?

He was pondering the whole question of who and

what Anne was when Martha called again. Not five minutes had passed.

"Oh, brother," Martha said over the line, "oh, man, you sitting down?"

"What in hell now?"

"We've got another one. Another body, Mitch. Joe found it while he was…"

"Another *dead* body?" Mitch cut in.

"That's the ticket, Boss. It's a man. Apparently, he was shot. That's all I know."

Mitch swore under his breath and tried to think. "Where?"

She gave him the coordinates.

"Call the sheriff and tell him what's happened," Mitch said. "Ask him to bring forensic men and the chopper. I'll get there as soon as I can, but he may beat me to the site. Tell him to get started—tape off the area, the whole nine yards."

"Got it," Martha said.

"And thank him, okay?"

"You bet. You know, this is getting awfully strange, Boss."

"'Strange' is not the word," Mitch said.

When he arrived at the site, well over an hour later, the place was teeming with activity. The county helicopter was sitting just off the four-wheel-drive road, and there were two Park Service Broncos and three San Juan County Sheriff's Department vehicles parked haphazardly near a narrow cut in a canyon wall.

Joe Staghorn strode up to Mitch before he'd even gotten out of his own Bronco. "Oh, wow," Joe said, pushing his straw ranger's hat back on his dark head, "this is a real mess, man. First that student kid and now this."

"Has an ID been made?"

"Don't know. I'm staying clear of the site. Bad medicine, Boss."

"I hear you." Mitch exited the Bronco and looked toward the rock cut into which two men were toting a stretcher.

"It's all taped off up there," Joe was saying. "They have photographers, a forensic guy, bunch of county cops. I just hope I didn't mess anything up."

"You touch the body?"

Joe shook his head. "No way, Boss. But I did leave my breakfast there. I'm real sorry about that. All our training… No way does it prepare you for this. You know?"

Mitch nodded. He knew.

He left Joe by the vehicles and made his way along a barely discernible path toward the taped-off area. He hadn't gone more than fifty yards when he saw the official group ahead, most of them outside the yellow tape, but he could make out the photographer and forensic specialist working inside, and there was Sheriff Warner. And with him…crouched, examining something in the dirt…was Anne.

Anne?

He stopped short about twenty yards away and stared dumbly.

Anne? Here? What the hell?

There was already enough manpower cluttering the scene, so for a time he stayed quietly off to the side and let the experts do their jobs. He needed to think, to let this new information sink in—a second murder in the space of little over a week, and Anne Winslow, working inside the crime-scene perimeter.

And she was actively participating in the investigation. As if intimately familiar with a crime scene. A couple of times he saw her direct the forensic man, and Mitch watched her collect dirt and rock samples, then carefully deposit them into plastic bags and mark the contents with a felt-tip pen.

She did not spot Mitch. Or if she did, she wasn't letting on. She was too absorbed in the work at hand to pay attention to Ranger Mitchell or anyone else.

He watched and considered, staying discreetly hidden in the sea of cops standing by. Anne, in her shorts and T-shirt, her nose free of zinc oxide this morning, her face already beginning to redden.

The *budget* lady.

He didn't know whether he was curious as hell or pissed as hell. A combination, he figured. One thing he did know—whatever was going on here, whoever she really was, Anne had lied to him.

The coroner arrived, spotted Mitch off to the side and strode over. "You sure are keeping me busy, Ranger."

"You could say that," Mitch acknowledged, then the man went to work.

They took the body away shortly before noon, carrying it out to the waiting chopper.

The sheriff walked over to Mitch. "I'm glad this is your turf, Mitch," he said.

"I bet." Mitch shook his head.

"You should have joined us inside the ropes."

"Hey, I would have, but I got here late and there was no point having an extra hand muddling up the works. I really appreciate your help on this, Ted, you know that. I don't have the resources.'' He looked down the trail where they'd just carried out the body. ''Any ID on the victim?''

''Driver's license, couple credit cards and a permit to carry.''

''Really?'' Mitch raised a brow.

''From Scottsdale, Arizona. Name's Paul Kasper. Had some sort of a private-security business, near as we can tell. Probably won't know for a day or so. I'm just hoping you can locate a next of kin and get a handle on what the heck is going on. You notice the way he was dressed?''

''Polo shirt and slacks. Loafers.''

''Go figure,'' Warner mumbled.

''He was shot?''

''Chest. Looks like it was pretty quick. Who the hell would do such a thing? Now you've got two murders and two bullets. I'd bet a year's salary the ballistics will be a match. What I can't even begin to guess at is a motive. How do that student and this man relate?'' Warner took off his big straw Stetson and scratched the side of his head.

''I'm not sure,'' Mitch said.

''But you have an idea?''

''I've got a few thoughts.''

''Care to share them?''

''If you don't mind, no. Not yet. But if anything pans out…''

''Yeah, yeah.''

Then Mitch had to ask. He gestured toward Anne. ''You know the lady?''

''Oh, Anne, sure. She came by yesterday and we had a long chat.''

''Really.''

"Nice lady. Tough job, though. I wouldn't want it."

"Huh," Mitch said, far too angry to ask for enlightenment.

"Well, I'm headed back to Moab."

"Sure."

"I'll keep you posted if I hear anything from the lab. You'll be around the Visitor Center?"

"I'm not sure," he said. "But Martha can find me."

"You mind giving the lady there a ride back?"

"No problem," Mitch said, twisting his head to shoot her a glance. "She came out with you?"

"Yeah. Actually, we had a breakfast meeting scheduled when the call came in. I grabbed Anne on the way out here."

"Huh," Mitch said again. "Yeah, sure, soon as she's done poking around I'll catch her."

"Thanks," Warner said. "And you'll let me know if you come up with a motive?"

"Soon as I figure anything out, I promise I'll call."

"Good, good. And I'll fax you the coroner's report on this one, and any ballistics as soon as word comes in."

"Thanks," Mitch said, and he watched Warner and four of his deputies head down the path toward their vehicles. When he turned back to the crime scene, she was staring at him. The first thing he noticed was that her already sunburned face turned even redder.

And damn well it should, he thought.

Anne didn't come over immediately after spotting Mitch. Instead, she instructed the forensic man to collect a few dirt and gravel samples from where the body had been lying. Finally, she turned in Mitch's direction, and he saw a pathetic attempt at a smile gather on her lips, as if she could somehow apologize at a distance.

Not a goddamn chance, he fumed, his jaw locked so tightly it hurt.

At last, she ducked under the yellow tape and made her way over to him, avoiding his eyes. ''Well,'' she said, ''what a morning.'' She dusted off her shorts and knees.

Mitch was stone cold silent.

''I, ah, guess Warner went on back into Moab.''

Silence.

''You, ah, wouldn't give me a ride to staff housing, would you?'' Then she turned beet red again. ''I said that wrong. *Would* you give me a lift?''

Mitch just stared at her, afraid to try his voice.

''I could explain about all this on the way,'' she offered.

''Sure,'' he finally got out through clenched teeth.

''Hey, come on, Mitch,'' she said, ''at least give me a chance to explain.''

''Why the hell should I?'' he fired back, and two of the sheriff's men who were still in the vicinity suddenly got real busy.

''Because, damn it, I'm just doing a job here, *Ranger.* This…farce wasn't my idea. I don't usually work this way.''

''And what work would that be?''

''I'm a special investigator with the Justice Department.''

''I see.''

''Meaning,'' she went on, ''that I get sent into crime scenes on federal property and try to coordinate the local and federal investigations.''

"Kind of like a spy for Justice?'

"No, not at all. My job is to observe and make recommendations. When a case goes to court, whether it's in federal court or not, I provide all the backup I can to the prosecution. Shall we walk down to your car? I'm hot and hungry and getting burned to a crisp."

"Sure, whatever."

Anne went ahead of him, and he made a supreme effort to keep his eyes off her legs and dusty round backside. *Damn.* The lying, sneaking...

"...personally sent in by the attorney general herself," Anne was saying over her shoulder. "That student's father is a huge campaign contributor, and I guess the White House wants to make sure this case gets solved and the investigation is sound, you know, so that the evidence will stand up in court. My being here instead of the FBI is a special favor, I suppose you'd say, to the White House."

"You don't have to impress me," he grumbled.

"I'm not trying to impress you—I'm merely explaining things."

"So you've explained them. Fine."

"The cover story of the budget thing wasn't my idea, Mitch. I would have played it straight. It's just that with the White House request...well, that's very unusual."

"I honestly don't care. You could have confided in me. I take it you confided in Warner, and he's not even in charge here."

"I confided in him just yesterday to get access to any files he had on the Hawkins family. But I was going to tell you this morning, and then this murder..."

Mitch grunted noncommittally then opened the passenger door to the Bronco for her. He did make a mental note, however, that Anne was smelling the same rat he was. Jerry Hawkins. But the missing element, the missing link, was motive. And now with this dead security man from Arizona… Hell, how did it all fit together?

After drinking a quart of water and pressing a damp cloth to her cheeks while Mitch drove, she said, "What do you want to bet that there's a connection between the man we found this morning and the Dracos?"

"I'm not the betting type."

"That dead man had a permit to carry and he's from Scottsdale. David Draco lives in Scottsdale."

"Uh-huh."

"Well, don't you think that's a little coincidental?"

"Could be." He wasn't going to admit she was right. He was still too pissed off that she'd lied to him.

"Mitch, we can work together, pool our resources…"

"Ah," he said, "that's why you were sent here— so we could pool our resources."

"Yes, damn it."

"So what do you do now?"

"I'm here for the duration, Mitch."

"I see."

"You're still mad."

"I never was mad."

"Liar," she said.

He gave her a sidelong glance and then shook his head. "It's none of my business what you do, and I don't engage in petty grudges. Like you said, you were given an assignment. It's just a job. But I can tell you one thing. This is *my* park, *my* territory, and I won't have you going off half-cocked and conducting your own investigation. It's too damn dangerous. I've already got two bodies on my hands.''

''And then there was the boulder,'' she said. ''I know you don't think it was an accident.''

''You don't know what I think, Anne. You really don't know me at all.''

''You *are* still mad.''

''I am not. I'm just telling you to keep out from underfoot and don't go getting in any trouble here.''

''I can take care of myself.''

''Yeah, right,'' Mitch said under his breath.

DAVID DRACO INSTRUCTED his pilot to change flight plans through the Salt Lake City tower and to land at the small Moab airfield before heading down to Phoenix and home.

He'd been in Jackson Hole, Wyoming, for the past two days, signing a lease for a new gallery in the heart of the old western town. The lease negotiations had gone well. What hadn't gone so smoothly were David's many attempts to contact Paul by cell phone. At first David had been sure Paul had either turned the phone off or his battery was shot. But after almost forty-eight hours now…

He phoned his nephew's place from the airport and got Ellen. Apparently, Chick was still at the Red Canyon dig.

''Ellen, it's David,'' he said, and she invited him over and promised one of her wonderful dinners. ''The girls will be so thrilled to see their uncle David.''

Then she dropped the bomb. "Oh, my, David, you can't imagine, but we've had another murder in the park."

His chest tightened.

"...There's so little news because they only found the poor soul this morning, but I understand he was from your neck of the woods. Scottsdale, I believe."

The tightening in his chest turned to a sharp pain.

"I heard one of the rangers' wives say he was a private detective or some such thing. Isn't this awful?"

"Dreadful," David choked out.

Ellen chatted on, but David barely heard. Somehow he managed to beg off from the dinner. "We were just refueling," he said, "and I have to get back home tonight. Tell Chick I'll be in touch."

And then he called Jerry Hawkins and reached him at home. It was one of the hardest calls he'd ever made.

"Is it true?" David asked.

"Is what true?"

"You know goddamn good and well what."

Silence.

"Listen. I need to see you. This has gotten way out of hand. Do you understand? God Almighty, Hawkins."

"I don't think we should meet in person," Jerry said.

"I agree. But we have to come to an understanding."

"Tell you what, Draco. I'll send Cousin Harv down to Scottsdale."

"Harvey?"

"Sure. You can tell him whatever you need to. In

the meantime, I'll have Harv bring along a couple nice pieces from New Ruin. How's that sound to you? They're real beauts, *Dave*. You like 'em, you can have 'em. But at a price, of course. You know?''

"Of course. And I...look forward to seeing the pieces. But this business...my bodyguard..."

"Hey," Hawkins said, "don't ever send another punk to check up on me. You got that?''

David said nothing. No words could pass the lump in his throat. The man was a maniac. A cold-blooded sociopath. This was insane.

He flew home right after talking to Hawkins. His brain was spinning, unable to comprehend how deeply he was involved in this horrible mess. Lord, just knowing about that student, and now Paul, made him an accomplice, for God's sake. An accomplice to murder.

Yet despite his terror, David remembered that Harvey Hawkins was coming to Scottsdale and bringing with him artifacts from New Ruin. Despite everything, David couldn't help being curious what they would look like, how much they would bring.

It was well past midnight when he pulled into his driveway and parked, then sat there wondering for an instant where Paul was, why he hadn't hustled out to put the car away for the night.

Dead. Paul was dead, David suddenly remembered, and the panic exploded in him again.

He found his wife still awake, reading in bed, waiting for him. She was wearing that pink silken lacy thing he loved and she looked absolutely beautiful. But for the first time in his entire life David could not become aroused. Too much death, too much. And now the icing on the cake. He was goddamn impotent.

CHAPTER TWELVE

BROOKE ANSWERED THE PHONE on Sunday morning with alacrity; she thought it might be her mother.

"Hello?"

"Hey, button, it's Martha. Is your dad there?"

"Um, he's in the shower."

"Okay, well, will you tell him to stop by his office before he goes out on patrol?"

"Sure."

"Now, don't forget. Somebody important wants to see him ASAP."

"I won't forget."

When her father came out of his room, freshly showered and shaved, dressed in that Smokey-the-Bear uniform, Brooke gave him the message.

"Who's the important person?" he asked.

"How should I know?"

"Okay, I'll leave in a few minutes. But before I do I thought you and I could sit down and talk. I'd like to hear your side of things. I'm prepared to listen, Brooke. I know you haven't been happy lately and..."

"*That's* an understatement. If you really wanted to listen to me, like you say, you'd already know how I feel. I hate it here."

He poured himself a mug of coffee and walked

over to the kitchen table. "Come on, honey, sit down, and tell me why."

She wouldn't sit. She stayed where she was, her skin feeling hot and crawly, her arms dangling awkwardly, tears near the surface. "You know why."

"It's more than just this place—I'm sure it is. Can we talk about it, like two adults?"

"You don't treat me like an adult and you don't listen."

"Please," he pleaded.

"I've said it all. For the whole summer. I don't have anything else to say. I hate it here. *I hate it.*"

"But why?"

"You know why."

He sighed then and ran his hand through his short hair. Brooke felt a kind of thrill getting to him like that. She knew she was making him miserable, and she reveled in her power.

"All right," he said, "maybe some other time. When you're ready."

"I'll never be ready."

"I have got to go, Brooke. You all set for the day?"

"Sure, I'm fine. Don't worry about me. I'm just bored out of my mind. No one to talk to..."

"All right," her father said, an edge to his voice. "See you this evening." He moved toward her, as if about to pat her hand or kiss her goodbye or something, but she shied away.

When he left she sat on the couch and cried. She felt so miserable, so ugly. Inside and out, she felt ugly and sad and she hated everything and everybody.

Deep down, she knew she didn't hate her father, but he was an easy target. She didn't know why she was so mad, so touchy, so awful to everyone but the kids her age. She just was. She only knew she felt a terrible, unfocused misery, and she wanted to lash out.

She sniffed and blew her nose; then, nervous and scared, she telephoned her mother in Las Vegas.

"Hello, Mom?"

"Yes, oh, Brooke baby, is that you?"

"Mom."

"Just a sec, honey. Jeffrey, will you take Charles?"

Brooke heard the stupid baby fretting in the background. She waited impatiently for her mother to pay attention to her. Only her.

"How are you, Brooke?"

"I'm okay."

"Only okay?"

"I hate it here, Mom."

"Just a few more weeks and then you'll be in that town—what's it called?"

"Moab. But that's what I wanted to talk to you about. I can't stand it here anymore. Please, can I stay with you for the rest of the summer?"

There was a frozen moment of silence. Prince Charles made mewling noises in the background. "But, Brooke, I mean, does your father know about this?"

"Yes," she lied, "and he thinks it's a great idea."

"Well, I guess so. How would you get here?"

"Bus," Brooke said promptly.

"Well, I guess if it's okay with Mitch…"

"God, Denise, do you think…?" came Jeffrey's muted comment, and Brooke's gut clenched.

"Okay, honey, just let us know when you'll arrive, okay? Charles will love to see you again. His big sister."

Oh, sure, Brooke thought. Spoiled little Charles wouldn't even remember her. But what did she care?

"I can't wait, Mom. See you soon. Tomorrow or the next day."

"You call and let us know what bus."

She hung up, feeling as if she'd won a battle, fought and outsmarted the enemy. Las Vegas, a big new house with a pool, kids, malls, movies, television. The world.

So what if Jeffrey didn't particularly want her there? It didn't matter. She was going to see her mother.

It occurred to her that she should ask her dad's permission, but what if he said no? He'd been against her going all summer, and he wouldn't change his mind now.

No, she'd do this on her own, and once it was done and she was in Las Vegas, there wouldn't be a thing he could do about it.

THE IMPORTANT PERSON awaiting Mitch in his office at the Visitor Center was Anne.

"Good morning," she said, brisk and businesslike, as if she hadn't lied to him, misled him, made him chase all around the damn park on false pretenses.

"Good morning," he said curtly, sitting behind his desk.

"Look, Mitch, I know you're irritated with me, but we really do need to cooperate on this case."

"Your point?"

She stood and folded her arms defensively, and he felt a small stab of pleasure that he made her uncomfortable. "Something's come up. I had a call from Justice."

"Did they want your budget projections?"

"All right, that's over. Believe me, it wasn't my decision to come here with a cover story. The powers that be wanted Washington involvement kept secret. They were hoping for a quick arrest. I was just going to make sure everything went all right. I told you. But with this second murder and no suspect in sight, everything's changed."

"The call?"

"Oh, yes…" She moved restlessly around the small office, touching things lightly, the morning sun turning her hair to copper and gilt. Finally, she stopped. "Paul Kasper's address has been traced to David Draco's house in Scottsdale. Just as I thought."

"I had that in the works yesterday," he said angrily.

"I know, but I had the use of a national database. Sorry if I jumped the gun."

He tried to control his irritation, but he knew it showed.

"I should have told you first. No, *asked* you first," she said.

"Yeah, you should have."

"We need to pursue this lead."

"*We?*"

"Yes, this is a cooperative investigation, I told you. I'm only here to…"

"Spare me your excuses." He cut off whatever she was going to say. "Has anyone contacted Draco?"

"No." She felt the bridge of her nose with a forefinger. It was probably burned and peeling. "Not yet."

"I'll call the federal attorney in Phoenix, have someone go to Draco's house and interview him."

"He'll surround himself with high-priced lawyers, remain absolutely silent, cover his tracks. And that would be that. End of investigation."

"I suppose you have a better plan."

"Actually, I do."

"Go on," he said warily.

"I'm going to Scottsdale to visit Draco's gallery under the pretext of being an art collector. See what he has."

"Ah, for God's sake, Anne, that's crazy. Do you think he's going to show you his illegal pieces just on your say-so?"

"Why not? I'll flash money around—*cash*. He has to sell the illegal pieces to somebody. Why not me?"

"*If* he's involved at all. If he even has stolen artifacts."

"Hey, Mitch, I don't believe in coincidences." She ticked the points off on her fingers. "Two murders in the park. *You* think Hawkins had something to do with one or both. One of the dead men works for Draco. Draco sells Anasazi art. Hawkins loots Anasazi art. Come on."

He studied her. "Okay," he said slowly, "so maybe I agree. I'll tell you what, though. I resent your being sent here to take over an investigation I'm in charge of."

"I know." She sat down on the edge of a chair. "And I'm sorry about that. But I have more leeway than you do. More resources." She paused. "And frankly, Mitch, I outrank you."

He wondered if she'd done that deliberately. Stuck it to him. Assert her authority. He didn't like it, and she knew he didn't like it. He realized he was frowning; she could read him like a book, and that pissed him off even more.

Then she relented, playing a double role—good cop—bad cop, all in one nicely shaped package. "Look, Mitch, I want those murders solved as much as you do. And I want to get Hawkins if he's guilty. Let's work together on this."

She made sense, but damn, it rankled. "What's the plan? Tell me how you see it going down."

She let out a breath, as if relieved. "Okay, well, I go to Scottsdale, stay in a ritzy hotel, visit his gallery. Feel him out. Keep asking, doesn't he have anything better, rarer, more spectacular?"

He thought for a minute. "Have you considered that it could be dangerous? If your theory is correct, and Draco finds out who you are… Hell, Anne, two people are already dead."

"The exposure is minimal."

"Yeah, sure, that's what they all say."

"I'll be careful. I've done this kind of thing before."

"Tell them to send someone else. A man."

She smiled. "A woman is less suspicious. Women buy art for their homes."

"Men are collectors," he said stubbornly.

"Yes, you're right. That's why I need your cooperation."

"You don't need it. Remember? You outrank me."

She leaned forward a little. "A couple is even less suspicious. If we pretend to be a couple, you know, you're my wealthy friend looking for a gift for me. Something very special. It would be a sound cover."

He was stunned. Is this what she'd been leading up to?

"It'd work, Mitch. It's a solid plan."

He stood and faced the window, staring out at the familiar scenery, the tourists' cars and the hot bright light. Then he pivoted to face her. "I'm no undercover agent."

"You can pull it off. I know you can."

"Who'll do my job when I'm gone? How long will it take? What in hell will I do with Brooke?"

"Moab will send someone. It's already been cleared. A few days. The last…Well, that may be a problem." She shrugged. "If you can't do it, I'll go alone."

"The hell you will." He knew he couldn't let her do the job by herself.

"So, you'll do it? Good."

"Give me till this afternoon," he said. "I have to talk to Brooke."

"Sure."

"I'll let you know." He thought for a minute. "Cash? Hotel, car?"

She waved her hand. "I'll take care of them. Money's on its way."

He cocked his head. "Efficient, aren't you?"

She smoothed her slacks over her thighs, her eyes down. "Yes." Then she said, "Thanks, Mitch, I appreciate it."

"I haven't agreed to do it yet."

She smiled again, and it transformed her face. "Sure you have."

When she left he sat there thinking. The plan was workable, except for one thing; although he hated to admit it, he felt very uncomfortable at the idea of spending so much time with Anne. Days. Pretending to be her friend, her lover. Despite her businesslike manner, her careful distance, despite their edgy relationship, something about that woman intrigued him more than he wanted to admit.

They'd be in a hotel together. They'd eat meals together. They'd go to Draco's gallery together, and Mitch would have to act as if he…loved her. He'd have to touch her, stand close, smile at her. He'd have to play the infatuated lover buying his mistress an expensive present.

Yet he couldn't let her go alone. She'd seen through his reluctance and understood that he'd accept the job. Goddamn, but women who wore badges could be infuriating. The smart ones, like Anne, knew exactly how to play on a guy's sense of honor and chivalry, and the strategy worked every time. He'd never let Anne go this alone. Anne with her pretty hazel eyes and those long beautiful legs.

And she knew it.

Later, as Mitch was catching up on paperwork, routine stuff that let his mind wander, he was going over the permutations of Anne's plan when he remembered something that made him sit straight up.

The shard. The black, shiny shard with the outline of a head on it. What had Chick done with it? Was it lost or deliberately hidden? Could Chick be covering up for his uncle?

He sat with one foot propped up on his desk, his index fingers steepled under his chin, and tried to envision the larger picture.

First, a student archaeologist is murdered. Kid's out hiking, maybe comes across someone—Jerry Hawkins?—looting a ruin. Mitch recalled the shard and then the unusual fibers on the kid's clothes. Fibers from something at a ruin? A basket? Sandals?

Anyway, the moki poacher panics and puts a bullet in the kid's head. The hanging? Just plain vicious. Again, Hawkins fit the profile.

The second murder: David Draco's bodyguard. Draco, the wealthiest art dealer in Arizona, whose very own nephew is working at a dig right in Canyonlands.

Did Draco send a man to set Hawkins straight because he was worried about the student's murder, and something went wrong?

Mitch considered the hypothesis, the same hypothesis Anne had come up with. Still, it was almost impossible to see Chick Draco involved in moki poaching and murder. The only thing troubling Mitch was the shard. Why hadn't Chick given it back?

There was, of course, the obvious answer: Chick was in on the whole damn mess.

HARVEY HAWKINS was a fish out of water in trendy Scottsdale. He walked down the sidewalk from where he'd parked his truck, and he could feel the heat burn up through the soles of his cowboy boots. The shop windows of Fifth Avenue astonished him, and he stopped to gawk. Elegant clothes so filmy and colorful they looked like costumes to him. Jewelry, diamonds, silver-and-turquoise creations, Navajo carpets, paintings, baskets, new artistic pottery.

Where'd people buy food? Or hammers and nails?

He'd been given explicit directions to the Draco Gallery. He was to go to the alley that ran behind it and ring at the locked delivery door.

He felt out of place and hot. Sticky in his long-sleeved cowboy shirt and jeans when everyone else on the street wore cropped tops and shorts. By God, it was hot.

He was nervous, too, carrying a big box that Jerry had packed real carefully, wrapping each piece in newspaper. Jerry had instructed him to deliver the box to Draco, not take an ounce of guff and return with not less than two hundred thousand dollars. Cash.

He figured he could do what Jerry wanted, but he was very nervous about what Draco's response to his dead bodyguard would be. Oh, boy, he sure was sweating that confrontation. He'd thought all the way down to Scottsdale about what he'd say and could come up with nothing better than to deny knowing anything about it.

"What?" he'd practiced uttering in his pickup. "What bodyguard? Who? Hey, man, Mr. Draco, I wasn't there. I don't know nothing about your guy."

He lowered his head and wiped the sweat off his forehead onto his arm. Couldn't use his hand because he was carrying the big box. If he dropped it and broke anything, Jerry'd kill him.

Oh, God, there it was again: talk about killing.

The Draco Gallery at last. Pretty damn fancy, gilt etching on the huge windows. Pots on display. Beautiful pots. Mostly new ones from the pueblos. Even Harv recognized a good pot. Large double glass doors with copper handles.

He hitched the box up, felt sweat trickling down his neck, and followed Jerry's directions to the alley behind the building. He had to set the box down to ring the bell, but someone answered right away. A pretty young woman, blond and slim. She was looking at him questioningly.

"I'm, uh, Harvey Hawkins. Here to see Mr. Draco. He's expecting me."

"Okay, right, just a minute. Come in, put the box there. I'll go get Mr. Draco…Mr. Hawkins."

David Draco bustled in, with his white hair and slate-gray Armani suit and gold chain and year-round perfect tan. But he wasn't smiling.

He gave a brusque nod. "Harvey."

"Hi, Mr. Draco."

"You brought some things, I see."

"Just like Jerry said."

Draco closed the office door. Harv was scared to death the art dealer would start talking about Paul, blaming and questioning, but he didn't. He reached for the box, undid the top flaps, extracted one well-protected bundle with his smooth hands. Harv stood back while Draco carefully unwrapped the piece, layer after layer, until the floor was littered with newspaper.

Finally, the pot was unveiled. Draco held it with both hands, not saying a word. Harv watched, knowing Jerry would ask how the man had reacted. The pot sure was pretty, more like a bowl. With the raised outline of antelope chasing themselves around the outside. One of the best pots they'd found.

Draco put it down on his desk, then reverently traced an antelope with his finger, still saying nothing. Harv was beginning to get nervous.

Draco spoke then, whispering hoarsely: "Magnificent."

Phew, Harv thought, then he said, "Yeah, it's pretty, isn't it?"

"Pretty?" Draco looked up at him.

"Yeah, Jerry found that one. It was in a room under—"

"*Pretty?*" Draco repeated. "My God, man, don't sully the perfection of this pot with a trite word like *pretty.*"

Huh? Harv stood there, puzzled.

"What else have you brought me?" Draco said, but more to himself than to Harv.

The art dealer unwrapped another piece, a more ordinary black-on-white jug, but in exquisite condition, without a chip or a crack. Then another bowl, tapered at the top, and a small pitcher in the distinctive polished black with a raised figure on each side. Then an intricately patterned black-on-red plate. Harv noticed that Draco's forehead shone with sweat. He uttered only a few words each time a pot came to light: "Fabulous, astounding, remarkable. Oh, dear God." His voice sounded strange, as if something were hurting him, but he liked the pots—Harv could tell he did.

Eventually, he had them lined up on his desk. He looked at them without speaking for so long Harv was getting fidgety, but he was afraid to say anything. He just stood there, awkward and out of place, masses of crumpled newspaper around his feet.

Mr. Draco finally spoke to him. "You have more like this?"

Harv nodded. "Oh, sure."

"Okay, all right. I have the money we agreed upon. These pots are worth it—you realize that, I suppose— but when New Ruin is discovered, when my nephew Chick stumbles across it, shall we say, they'll be worth even more. Priceless."

"Uh-huh."

"It's nearly time. Tell Jerry that. How many pots have you gotten out of the ruin?"

"Couple dozen or so."

Draco seemed to be figuring in his head. "Yes, that'll do. We can't be too greedy. We'll all be rich beyond imagination as it stands now." He paused, thinking. "This has got to be handled delicately, with perfect timing. Make certain Jerry understands. Once New Ruin is discovered, the place will be crawling with archaeologists and anthropologists from around the world. Those men will be quick to notice if anything has been disturbed."

"We're being real careful, Mr. Draco. Jerry is an expert when it comes to covering our tracks."

"Yes," David said dryly, "I imagine he is. So let's take the best pieces out and the rest will find their way to museums, of course. Private collectors will be in a frenzy to get their hands on one of these." He touched the black bowl with a finger. Lightly. With veneration. "You understand, Harvey?" He peered at Harv from under his brows.

"Sure, you think I'm some kinda dummy? I get it."

"Beautiful, glorious." Draco had turned again to the pots on his desk, crooning over them, his back to Harv.

"Uh, excuse me, Mr. Draco, but I need the money."

"Oh, yes." He straightened. "The money." He pulled a large bag from a cabinet built into the wall. The bag was constructed of heavy paper with handles, and it said Fendi on the side in elegant script. Whatever that meant.

"It's all there," Draco said. "Two hundred thousand."

Harv peeked in the bag. All he could see was white tissue paper. He looked up at Draco.

"I wrapped it up. Do you want to count it?"

"No, no." The thought of counting so much money made Harv's head spin. Jerry hadn't said anything about counting it, had he?

Harv reached out a hand to take the bag, but Draco didn't relinquish it immediately. His gaze met Harv's.

"No more *unpleasantness,* right?" he said, a hard glint in his eyes. "You tell Jerry that for me."

"Okay, I will." Then Harv had the bag, and Draco was opening the door and showing him out to the alley.

Back in the heat, Harv broke into a sweat again. But he was relieved. He'd done everything Jerry had told him to do, and hardly anything had been mentioned about Paul's murder.

He walked up the curving street to where his truck was parked. Boy, it sure looked out of place lined up next to all the shining clean Cadillacs and Lexuses and big old Range Rovers. He swung the bag onto the cracked vinyl seat and got in. The steering wheel was so hot he could hardly touch it. He drove out of downtown Scottsdale toward the interstate, and he felt good. He'd done everything right. Cool.

On the outskirts of town he stopped at a strip mall, went into a liquor store and bought a six-pack of beer to keep him company on the long hot ride home. Kind of a celebration.

At the interstate he headed north toward Flagstaff, beginning to climb right away, up into the mountains, where it'd be cooler. He was happy—Jerry would be proud of him. And he could buy a new truck, maybe, one that even had air-conditioning. And a new rifle— that Winchester Model 70, 7 mm magnum he'd been wanting. And a new cowboy hat—the real expensive felt kind. Yeah.

He patted the Fendi bag next to him and raised a can of beer to his lips. The brew was still cold; it tasted good. Dusk was falling. Hell, it'd be awful late when he got home. He turned on his lights and stepped on the gas, trying to get the best out of the laboring pickup, unaware that the taillight on his truck was blinking out for the last time.

CHAPTER THIRTEEN

ANNE INSPECTED the bedroom and the Jacuzzi tub in the bath, while Mitch tipped the bellman. *Nice, very nice,* she thought. But then, the Phoenician resort hotel in Scottsdale had a reputation as one of the best.

It wasn't cheap. Even in the hot summer months—off-season in Arizona—the ritzy resorts still commanded hefty room rates, and the one-bedroom suite, which sat at ground level, nestled among Egyptian palms near a spa, was half again as much as a regular room.

But they needed the living-room area and the pull-out couch.

"I'll take the couch," Mitch said when the bellman had adjusted the air-conditioning for them and closed the door behind him.

"You don't have to. I can just as easily—"

"Let's not argue over it, okay?" he said, and she gave in graciously.

The suite was soothing, done in desert pastels. The artwork on the walls of desert vistas was original, and two cactus plants flanked the front window, both in fine Pima Indian pots.

Anne checked out the closet and hung up the few clothes she'd brought from Washington, none of which would cut it for her assignment in elegant Scottsdale. That would require something new, something just right for the occasion. And that meant a shopping trip.

"I need a few things," she called from the bedroom, "something to wear to the gallery tomorrow."

"You mean...you're going shopping?"

Anne walked to the door. "When I left D.C., I had no idea I'd have to turn into a wealthy art collector."

"Fine. I'm sure there are plenty of stores around."

And then, for a moment, she studied his attire. He looked...good. Really good, she decided, in off-white cotton slacks, a teal polo shirt, loafers—no socks— and his perpetual tan, which somehow made the silver that tipped his light-brown hair seem to glow. He looked, well, she thought, like money.

"So when do you want to do this, ah, shopping thing?" he asked.

"The sooner the better."

At least he was making an effort to cooperate. She knew how reluctant he was to be here, but he was doing his best. And for that she was thankful. The situation was awkward enough as it was.

"Why not enjoy the pool," she suggested. "I have no idea how long this'll take."

"I didn't come here to sit around a pool, Anne. Let's just get your chores done."

"Okay, whatever you say."

She was trying to be pleasant. Tomorrow, when they visited Draco's Fifth Avenue gallery, she'd have to be a lot more than pleasant. She'd have to act the role of adoring lover. And so would he. That was unimaginable right now. She and Mitch, *lovers.* They'd have to discuss it, wouldn't they? Formulate a plan, talk about their roles? She dreaded it. She didn't know how to be a lover anymore—didn't know where to begin. Did he?

The shopping trip went far more smoothly than Anne could have imagined. Mitch, surprisingly, was patient while Anne fussed and complained and declared the whole thing hopeless.

They started at a mall close to the resort on Scottsdale Road, but she could find nothing more than a pair of sandals. Then they drove into the heart of Scottsdale and parked in front of a trading post in the old section of town, and she came across several dress shops where the clothes were decidedly *Arizona*. Lots of colors and gauzy, drapy linen things. Mitch was the one who suggested a long, sky-blue peasant skirt and a frilly, white cotton blouse. The blouse wasn't her, but she spotted a less frilly one that would work. She also spotted a short, beige linen skirt and a matching loose-fitting, double-breasted summer blazer, which she thought would be perfect for the visit to Draco's gallery.

She tried it on with a rich, green silk shell underneath, while Mitch waited out front in the hot sun, reading a local newspaper, and she even asked his opinion, standing in the door, modeling it.

"What do you think? Too much? Should I go with the peasant look? I can't make up my mind."

He shook the paper and folded it, eyeing her from behind sunglasses. "Wear the suit tomorrow and the long skirt tonight."

"Tonight?"

"We have to eat somewhere."

"Oh, sure, okay," she said, and for some inexplicable reason her skin suddenly prickled. She hadn't thought about things like meals. He was right, of course; they had to eat somewhere.

The jewelry was Mitch's idea, too. There were dozens of jewelry and trinket shops in the heart of old-town Scottsdale with lots of silver-and-turquoise bracelets and necklaces and earrings—very Indian, very desert Southwest, very Scottsdale. She bought three silver bracelets, a turquoise-and-silver choker, a simple pair of plain round silver earrings and a small silver clasp to hold up her hair.

"I wonder if I'll ever wear this stuff again," she said, her purchases stuffed into a big straw bag that Mitch purchased for her from a street market.

"You must have some sort of a social life in Washington," he offered.

"Not much," she said, and then she wisely dropped the subject. This was business. "Let's get an ice cream. I saw this soda fountain..."

They sat at a booth in Scottsdale's famous ice-cream parlor and cooled off with root-beer floats. "It must be over a hundred out." Anne sighed and lifted her hair off her neck.

"Yeah, but it's a dry heat," he quipped.

"I'll be a sagging mess tomorrow."

"I'm sure you'll do fine."

"I'm certainly going to try."

"You don't have to do this, you know," he said. "We could pack up in the morning and—"

"It's my job, Mitch." She held her long spoon in midair and cocked her head. "You're not backing out?"

"No. But I think our odds of getting Draco to sell us something illegal are slim to none. If he's into the black market, he has regular clients. He'd at least check out a new customer before showing his hand.''

"So? Let him check us out. I have it covered through the Washington office.''

"Things go wrong," he pointed out.

"Oh, Murphy's Law? If they can go wrong, they will?''

"Something along those lines. I know we've had this discussion before. But two people are dead already, Anne.''

She finished her soda, then looked pensively across the street at the row of art galleries. Scottsdale was famous for its galleries, and there were blocks and blocks of them, but the most elegant and most renowned were right there on Scottsdale Drive and along Fifth Avenue. She glanced at her watch. "Do you think we should case out a few galleries? Not the Draco Gallery, but some of the others? Get a feel for them?''

He finished his soda, peeled a ten off a wad of cash and left it on the table. "Why not," he said.

She never would have factored into the equation her response to Mitch that afternoon. There was something about him in this setting, something she hadn't counted on. Maybe it was his striking good looks, or the casualness of his dress, or the ease in his deportment as they window-shopped. Or maybe that undefinable quality about him had to do with his knowledge of Indian art, his likes and dislikes, the strength of his convictions.

"Oh, I really love this," she said in the spectacular May Gallery.

But Mitch shook his head. "Hardly very original. It's a knockoff on a Gorman.''

"Really," she said.

He knew his Indian pottery and the western artists who excelled in bronze, and he knew a few of the wood-carvers. She was quite impressed, and again she thought about how he'd come to the Southwest as an eastern dude and he'd made it a point to educate himself. He was interested in the area, its history and fine arts. He was interested in *life,* and for a short time, strolling by his side in the pounding August sun, she felt curiously vibrant despite the heat, even attractive. How had he done that? And why this particular man at this most inappropriate time?

She found it terribly hard to stay focused, to remind herself over and over that in less than twenty-four hours she had to be a hundred percent on her toes and not mooning over the park ranger.

They drove her rental car back to the Phoenician at five and she showered, then lay in the Jacuzzi for an indecent period. So much time had gone by since she'd felt this relaxed, her muscles liquid. Yet her skin was supersensitive and her senses seemed keenly alert. She finally got out and put lotion on, her nakedness hazy, dreamlike in the big steamy mirror, and she closed her eyes and dared to imagine that it was Mitch who was rubbing the lotion onto her thighs and belly; Mitch, with his strong, capable hands...

It was hard to shake off her crazy mood. Forcing her thoughts to practical matters, she dressed in her new skirt and blouse and put the silver clip in her hair. The air conditioner was at its coolest setting, but still her skin felt on fire. *God,* she thought, she sure had picked a bad time to come back to life. Wrong time and the wrong man. This was a job.

A job, idiot, she told herself, *and he doesn't even like you.*

Her mood, her private dreamtime, persisted with a will of its own no matter how hard she tried to get a grip on reality. It occurred to her to tell Mitch to get some dinner by himself—to claim she wasn't hungry—but when she emerged from the hotel and found him standing outside under the palms in the shadow of Camelback Mountain, the golden evening light catching in his eyes, something inside her melted, a hot liquid in her veins, and she couldn't, *wouldn't,* deny herself these few hours of girlish fantasy. Why should she? She was human; she felt alive again. Tomorrow, she thought, clinging to the notion; tomorrow she'd be sharp as a tack. But not now. Damn it. It had been too long. It didn't even matter that Mitch was oblivious to her emotional state. It simply felt too wonderful to let go.

They ate at a restaurant south of Scottsdale in Tempe. It was a Mexican place recommended by the hotel, a charming, old-fashioned restaurant cluttered floor-to-ceiling with every imaginable decor from south of the border: decorated gourd rattles, pressed-tin lanterns, sombreros, colorful blankets hanging on the richly painted walls, castanets, guitars, earthen jars, baskets, piñatas, huge dripping candles, strings of chili peppers, bouquets of garlic, a donkey cart on wooden wheels loaded with huge paper flowers next to a splashing blue-tile fountain in the center of the crowded dining room.

Of course there was a mariachi band.

And of course they insisted on serenading Anne over her glass of wine.

She flushed stupidly. Mitch looked on as the hand-

some mariachis sang and strummed their guitars,
looked on as if he were holding back a smile at her
obvious discomfort and pleasure. She felt the music
seep into her, dark and warm and velvety, and
Mitch's eyes pinioning her, eyes that were windows
to his soul. She listened, drifted in sensation, her
breath coming far too quickly. It was so silly, so immature of her, to get caught up like this, and yet since
that afternoon, for hours now, she'd been trapped in
this unreal void. Must be the hot desert sun, a handsome man, the thrill of the chase and the many
months, years now, that she'd put aside her own
needs. She'd wanted to put aside her own needs for
Lyle. She wouldn't have changed a moment of their
brief life together, but that life was gone, and it was
time for her to live again.

She suddenly wanted to come to her feet and say:
Look at me. I'm alive.

The band wandered off to the next table, and Anne
stared down at her wine, at her finger tracing the rim
of the glass. She could still feel Mitch's gaze on her,
the questions, and she so badly wanted to tell him
everything now, about her marriage and Lyle and the
cancer, how she'd shut the world out, how even her
co-workers sighed in relief when she was away on
assignment. Not to mention her family. God. They'd
washed their hands of her. But now something was
happening. She felt as though someone had blown on
the dying ember of her life and a spark was still there.

But how could she tell him all that? What would
he think? He had his own life, his own troubles. He
didn't want to hear about hers, and she'd only make
an utter fool of herself with a man who really didn't
give a hoot.

Get a grip, Winslow.

Anne had the burrito platter and Mitch had the que-sadillas. The food was excellent, as was the wine, and somehow she managed to collect herself, and they discussed the plan for tomorrow.

"I know I've got to be a total bimbo," she said over decaf coffee. "I just hope I don't say some-thing... But I'm counting on you to do the talking. You don't have a problem with that, do you?"

"No problem."

"You won't get bent out of shape if I fawn over you?"

"Fawn on me, Anne?"

He was playing with her. "You know what I mean. Don't make this harder than it already is."

"Okay, okay, I think I know the drill. Let's just hope Draco doesn't spot a bad act when he sees one."

"*Mitch.*"

"I'm kidding."

"I know. I guess I'm nervous."

He raised a brow.

"I usually work alone."

"Anne Winslow, loner."

"That's me." She looked up and smiled too brightly. *God.* Surely he could see right through her, surely he knew how...confused she was right now. But tomorrow. She'd do fine tomorrow. She always did.

The problem was, she still had tonight to get through. She hadn't counted on these crazy feelings she'd been having all day. *Great timing.*

They walked the grounds at the hotel when they got back, and sat for a while by the tiered swimming pools.

"I wish I'd brought my swimsuit," she said. It was still over ninety out.

"You could go skinny-dipping. No one around."

"It's probably against the law," she shot back. "I'd get arrested."

"Well, if you have the nerve, lady, I sure won't squeal."

"Imagine that," she said. "Why don't *you* go in?"

"You think I won't?" Then suddenly he stood, and showing a playful side she'd never imagined, he undid his belt buckle.

"Oh, stop," she said, uncertain.

"You think I'm kidding?"

"Yes. But don't prove me wrong, please." She couldn't believe it—Mitch, a lighthearted Mitch.

They even had a nightcap at the bar, where a pianist played forties swing music. It was hard to imagine at that moment they were anything but lovers, biding their time till they strolled, hand in hand, back to their room. Anne had a thought. Maybe he was as lonely as she was. Maybe his divorce had left him bitter and afraid to love. Maybe, just maybe, they were kindred spirits, and the magic of the desert, of the night and the beautiful setting, could somehow set them both free. Was it possible? Had she misread Mitch? *Did* he care?

She wasn't to have her answers. The bubble burst back in their room when he phoned his neighbors to check on Brooke.

Anne was in the bedroom, changing into her nightgown, when she overheard his end of the conversation. "She went where, Vicky? Moab? But..." Then there was a pause. "I see. Well, I suppose it's okay if she stays with Suzy in town... No, it's not your fault. I really didn't tell Brooke she had to stay in the park... Yeah, okay, I'll touch base. And don't worry. It's okay. I'm sure she's fine.''

With the hotel's plush white robe around her shoulders, Anne padded into the living room. "Everything okay with Brooke?" she asked.

But he was frowning. "I'm not... Oh, well, sure, she's fine. She just went into Moab to stay with her friend.''

"And you didn't tell her she could do that." It wasn't a question.

"I'm sure she's fine," Mitch repeated, avoiding an answer, then he stood and went to the door. "Look," he said, "I'm not all that tired. I think I'll just go for a walk around the golf course or something. You'll be okay?''

"Of course. And Mitch," she said, "try not to worry. Brooke will be perfectly all right.''

"Yeah," he said, "in about ten years.''

He left then, and she stared at the door. She wasn't sure if she was upset and disappointed or if she was relieved. She did know one thing. Mitch was right. This whole trip might have been a bad idea. But not for the reasons he thought.

HARV SAT ON THE SIDE of the hard bunk in the Flagstaff, Arizona, jail.

DUI, he thought. What a helluva mess. If only he had known about that broken taillight. That was why the cop had stopped him. It was the open beer that had prompted his arrest.

Goddamn cops.

He stared up through the iron bars and felt his gut roll over. The money. The bag stuffed with cash. The arresting officer had asked him about that. You bet he had. And Harv couldn't even remember what he'd said. *Shit.*

The cop had taken the bag, held it up and said at the desk, ''We'll just hang on to this. Write Mr. Hawkins here a receipt,'' he'd told the night-duty sergeant, and then they'd booked him.

Two hours ago, Harv thought, rubbing his fists against his temples, two hours ago and he still hadn't made that one phone call he was allowed.

Damn. He couldn't rot in here forever. Eventually, he'd have to get bailed out. He could call his wife… No. She'd never forgive him. It would be bad enough as it was when she found out.

He knew who he had to call. And he knew Jerry would drive straight down to Flagstaff and work everything out. The money, though. What had he told the cops? Goddamn it, Jerry was going to murder him.

Harv put his face in his hands and began to sob. He sobbed his heart out like a little kid.

CHAPTER FOURTEEN

"YOU FRIGGIN' IDIOT," Jerry snarled, his head close to Harv's.

"I'm sorry, Jerry. How was I supposed to know the taillight was out?"

"The beer, the money, for God's sake, two hundred thou in cash, confiscated by the cops. How're we supposed to get *that* back?"

Harv looked so miserable Jerry almost pitied him. Almost. The cops had let them use one of the interrogation rooms, but Jerry was sure they were watching and listening. He'd already warned his cousin to be careful what he said.

"Okay, let me think," he said. "The DUI won't stick. You didn't drink enough. Having an open container of alcohol in a vehicle is a first-offense misdemeanor. But the money. Shit."

"I don't remember what I said, Jerry. I was so shocked. I couldn't believe it. I was just driving along, minding my own business. Honest, Jerry."

"Shut up. Let me think." He got up and paced the featureless room. Deliberately, he stopped, faced the mirror and said loudly, "You sure did win big in Vegas, didn't you, Harv? All that money from gambling. Wow."

"Vegas?" Harv asked dully.

"Well, that's where you were, wasn't it?"

"Oh, sure, yeah. Vegas." Harv looked at the mirror and said equally loudly, "I guess I was just lucky."

Gambling, Jerry thought. It was the only reason he could think of to explain so much cash. Unless the cops asked exactly where, in what casinos, Harv had played. Then they'd check and... Or they might inform the IRS...but screw the IRS.

"We'll get you out of here, Harv. Don't worry. But, goddamn it, I'll never forgive you for this stunt. We'll get the money back, but it might take some time," he said quietly. "I'm going to pay your bail and get your truck out of the impound lot, and then I'm hiring a lawyer. By God, Harv, the money for all this is coming out of your share."

"Okay, Jerry, okay."

"All right. God—" he rolled his eyes "—you're my cross to bear, you dumb idiot. But you're family. Goddamn it."

One of the detectives in the Flagstaff office was hanging up the phone just as Jerry knocked on the interrogation room door to be let out. The detective had phoned Harvey Hawkins's hometown police and the San Juan County Sheriff's Department, checking on him, and he'd found out that Harvey had a record, dating from his high-school days. But there it was: he and his cousin Jerry were suspects in myriad moki-poaching schemes.

Moki poaching. A bag of cash. Not hard to figure out what was going on here. At least, that's what Sheriff Ted Warner of Moab, Utah, had said.

THE PHOENICIAN HOTEL was an oasis in the desert, Mitch thought, just as the ancient city-state had been.

The place was well named. Stately Egyptian palms bathed the breakfast table in stripes of muted light, while outside the tiered pool gave the impression of a cool, tumbling waterfall. An impossibly blue waterfall. Beyond the pool, the brilliantly green golf course stretched forever, and he could see a foursome teeing off, their pastel golf clothes bright in the morning sun.

"Nice, isn't it?" Anne said.

"Very nice. But I'm glad I'm not staying."

She was toying with her breakfast, and seemed a bit on edge. She was probably nervous about their visit to the Draco Gallery. Interesting—she was nervous, even though she'd assured him she'd done undercover work before. Yet she'd been cool and collected back at Canyonlands when she'd planned the operation out. Of course, operatives had to get up for their jobs, or so Mitch had always heard.

"Did you sleep well?" he asked, making conversation.

Her eyes switched away. "Sure, good. Was the pullout couch okay?"

"It was fine."

"Did you have a nice walk last night?"

"Very nice."

"I heard you come in."

"Did you? Sorry, I tried to be quiet."

"You were quiet. I was just lying there thinking."

He raised his coffee cup to his lips and sipped. *Thinking*. Was he now supposed to ask her what she was thinking about? He couldn't help the image that sprang into his mind: Anne lying in the king-size bed, tangled in the covers; lying there alone in the dark, hearing him let himself in the door, tiptoe around.

Had she heard the rustle of his clothes as he'd undressed? Or the water running, the toilet flush, the squeak of the springs as he'd gotten into bed? The situation was too personal, he thought. Two strangers thrown together. Too close, too intimate, when neither of them wanted intimacy. Why in hell had he agreed to this farce?

She wore the new linen skirt and blazer she'd bought yesterday and a green silk tank top that made her eyes look greener than ever. She'd taken the jacket off, and her slim arms were tanned from the days out in the park.

She bit off a corner of toast and chewed. She'd put on lipstick, and he noticed that her mouth was nicely shaped, with a deep bow on the upper lip. Her tongue flicked out to capture some crumbs.

"What time do you want to go to Draco's?" he asked.

"Not too early. He opens at ten, but I don't want to appear anxious."

She fiddled with the silver hair clip. She was definitely edgy, a different woman from the absolutely confident one he'd known in the park. Or maybe she was worried about how *he'd* play his part. "You're clear on our story?" she asked. "Don't forget our new last names."

"I've got it, don't worry."

"I've seen people blow their cover doing something dumb like getting their names wrong, the most obvious thing in the world."

"Uh-huh."

"Sorry, I don't mean to preach."

"That's okay. I told you, I'm no undercover agent."

She finished her orange juice, signed the check and turned to him. "I'm going to the room and make some calls."

"I'll wander around." He glanced at this watch. "Meet you in the lobby in an hour?"

"All right." She stood, and he contemplated her as she wended her way among the tables. Damn, this had been a bad idea.

They parked the rental car a block from the gallery. The heat was already starting to press on him, like a hot hard hand.

"I'm not sure whether Washington, or this place is worse in summer," he said.

"It's hot, that's for sure."

Meaningless chatter, he thought, or were they both getting into their roles, taut with nerves?

A pretty young lady greeted them at the Draco Gallery. "I'm Debby," she said. "Please let me know if I can help you. We have a new collection of Hopi polychromes done by a protégé of Nampeyo. Absolutely beautiful. Or are you looking for rugs or perhaps kachinas?"

The place was impressive. Large and airy, skylights and spotlights placed for optimum flattery. The walls hung with paintings, some Indian, some western. A corner alcove was softly lit, illuminating a collection of the best art the Southwest could offer.

"Actually," Mitch said, "we're in the market for something very special. We've come all the way from Salt Lake City because I've heard about Mr. Draco's reputation." He paused for a heartbeat. "Is Mr. Draco here, by any chance?"

"Yes, sir, he's in back. Can I give him your name?"

"James Melrose—Jim," he said, smiling broadly.

It wasn't long before David Draco emerged from the rear of the gallery. A handsome man, ageless, with a silvery-gray suit that shimmered like heavy silk, a crisp white shirt and a red-and-black tie. His smile displayed perfect teeth, and he wore a diamond ring on his pinky finger next to a heavy gold wedding band.

"Mr. Melrose," he said, holding his hand out, "how good to meet you."

"'Jim,' please, and this is Anne Walker."

Draco took Anne's hand and bowed over it like a European count.

"It's wonderful to meet you, Mr. Draco," she gushed. "We've heard so much about you."

The amenities over, they got down to business.

"I'm a collector, Mr. Draco…"

"'David.' Please, Jim, it's David."

"Of course. David. As I said, I'm a collector. I have an extensive collection of Anasazi and Kayenta pots. I recently learned of your expertise in this area, so we drove down."

"I couldn't wait another day," Anne put in, blinking big hazel eyes.

"I promised Anne a gift, something very special. Unique."

"Please, let's go into my office. We'll talk."

Mitch exchanged glances with Anne as they followed Draco into his office. *We got this far,* he thought.

They settled into chairs across from Draco's desk, which was an enormously thick slab of glass on an intricately forged, wrought-iron base. Anne crossed her legs, reached out a hand and laid it on Mitch's arm. Casually, as if she were used to doing it. As if they were lovers. His skin crawled with pleasure.

"What exactly were you thinking of?" Draco asked. "You aren't interested in contemporary pottery, I take it."

"No." Mitch leaned forward earnestly. "I want something old. Very old. And I'd like it in perfect condition. No cracks, no chips, no fireclouds."

"A firecloud," Anne said, batting thick lashes. "Jim, honey, what's that?"

"She's learning," Mitch said, "picking up stuff every day."

"A firecloud," Draco explained, "is a dark spot, often found on antique pottery due to incomplete burning of the wood they fired their pottery with. A smudge."

"Oh," she said, "and it doesn't come off?"

"No, unfortunately not. And it does reduce the value of the piece."

"Well then," Anne said, "we certainly don't want one of those."

"Old and in perfect condition," Draco mused. "Are you prepared for the cost? Something like that will be very expensive."

"Yes, I know," Mitch said, "but I promised. Anything for Anne." And he felt the warm pressure of her touch, felt it move along her arm to his hand, and he couldn't stop himself—it seemed so natural—from turning his hand over and folding his fingers around hers. He and Anne had to be convincing, he kept telling himself. A rich man with a beautiful woman for a mistress. Lovers.

"Thank you, darling," she murmured, and he caught the scent of her perfume. He swallowed.

"I do have a couple of things available," Draco was saying, "that might interest you."

He showed them a red-on-brown Mogollon pitcher decorated with a textile design—woven strips of color—from around 900 A.D., and an exquisite Mimbres platter with a feather design.

"This has been dated to 1150," Draco said. "Lovely, isn't it?"

"There's a crack in it," Mitch pointed out.

"The pitcher is perfect."

"Yes, but I have one almost exactly like it at home. I'm really looking for something entirely different."

"I see."

Anne moved in her chair, leaned toward him, her shoulder touching his. "Darling," she said, leaning even closer, "we could leave our names with David, and he could phone us at home if he finds something."

"I suppose, but I really wanted to see it. You know, touch it. *Collectors.*" Mitch shook his head in mock consternation.

Draco studied him for a moment. "I may be able to get hold of something you'd be interested in, Jim."

"Really?"

"Something very special."

"What exactly?"

"I'd prefer not to say yet. Can you come back tomorrow?"

"Well…" Mitch hesitated. "We were going to leave this afternoon."

"Oh, that's too bad."

"We could stay, couldn't we?" Anne said. "Just another day. Please, Jim?"

He placed his arm around her. "I'm putty in her hands," he said, smiling, smiling.

"Excellent. Come back tomorrow, and I'm sure you'll be happy with the piece. But I must warn you, it won't come cheap. And I do, ah, prefer cash."

"I'm willing to pay for quality, David."

"Then we may have a deal, Jim."

Outside, the heat bludgeoned him. They walked to their car, opened the doors to let the suffocatingly hot air inside escape, slid in. Mitch started the engine quickly and turned on the air-conditioning. All without a word. He pulled out into the heavy midday traffic and felt the first cool breaths of air on his face.

"Thank God," Anne finally said.

"That it's over? Or that the air-conditioning came on?"

"Both."

He glanced over at her; she was pale, sweat beading her upper lip. She wiped it away and let her head fall back onto the seat.

"You did well," he said.

"We both did."

"Think he bought it?"

"Yes. Yes, he did."

"So he wants us to come back, take a look at this special pot—theoretically, one that the Hawkins clan looted—and we nail him."

"When he said he preferred cash I knew we had him," she commented.

"That means it's an illegal piece."

"Right."

"Sounds easy." He was talking because silence seemed somehow too intimate.

She didn't answer. He looked over again and saw that she'd closed her eyes.

"You okay?"

"Yes," she whispered. "The tension and this heat…they take a lot out of me."

Back at the hotel, he steered her to their suite, a hand under her arm, then ordered lunch and cold drinks from room service. He was worried at Anne's listlessness, at her paleness. You could easily get heatstroke in Arizona in the summer, for God's sake.

There was a knock on the door: room service. A tray of sandwiches and a large pitcher of iced tea. Mitch handed the waiter a tip and shut the door after him.

"Here," he said, holding out a glass. "Drink."

"Yes, sir." She accepted it, tried to smile, sipped the tea.

He sat down beside her. "Goddamn heat," he said.

She put a hand on his arm, and the gesture took him back to the gallery, her smiles, her closeness, her scent. All pretend. A dangerous game.

"Thanks for worrying about me. No one's done that for a long time," she said.

He felt embarrassed, supersensitive all over. He wasn't used to being close to a woman, a beautiful woman. There was danger in this, too.

Yet he was powerfully, almost hypnotically, drawn to the moment. He leaned toward her and put a hand on her forehead. "You feel hot."

And then, as if someone had written the script, she pressed forward against his hand and closed her eyes, and he couldn't stop his hand, his fingers, from trailing to her temple, her cheek, her lips. Her eyes were closed still, her lashes dark fans on her cheeks. Her chest rose and fell under green silk.

He drew his hand away.

"No," she said softly, stopping him.

"Anne..."

She turned her face toward him and opened her eyes. There were tears welling in her beautiful hazel eyes. "Please," she said, and he brought his mouth to hers, touching her lips gently, not knowing what to do with his hands at first, then finding her mouth, her tongue, the sweetness of her, and then his hands knew what to do, one on her shoulder, the other tangled in her hair.

He pulled back at the same time she did, and she turned her head away.

"I'm sorry," she said, "that was stupid." She had one hand on his chest, between them, a barrier. He could feel it press into him.

He let her go as if scalded. "No, it's my fault. You were..."

She stood and moved toward the bedroom, ran a hand through her hair. "For God's sake, don't make excuses. I'm humiliated enough as it is."

"Okay, forget it. It didn't happen. We'll start over," he said, still shaken but angry. Yes, angry. What the hell did she want from him?

She disappeared into the bedroom and he was left standing there, a big idiot. But their game wasn't over yet. They'd just finished act one.

Shit.

BROOKE STARED OUT THE WINDOWS at the endless brown desert and small towns the bus passed along the route to Las Vegas and felt her body thrum with nervous excitement.

At last she was in control of her life, *Doing* something. And that made her feel so very grown-up. Okay, she thought, her dad would go ballistic—and that did frighten her—but she couldn't let his anger stop her. Never again was anyone going to tell her what to do or where to live. She was fourteen years old, for Pete's sake; no one had a right to order her around, much less ruin her life.

So, he was going to be pissed. *Tough,* she thought, and she stared out the window again, and her body tensed with a shot of pure adrenaline. *Free at last.* It was going to be heaven.

CHAPTER FIFTEEN

ANNE SAT ON THE SIDE of the bed, her face in her hands. *Stupid, stupid,* she kept repeating silently. Weak and foolish and stupid. It had only happened because he'd been so concerned about her. The way Lyle had been when she was sick or when the sweltering Washington summers got to her.

For the first time in more months than she wanted to recall she felt taken care of. It made her weak and stupid, and it made her want to cry.

Now she had to go back out there and face him. She couldn't give up on this job; they had David Draco on the hook. Her work was important, damn it.

She stood up abruptly and went to the mirror over the dresser. After dropping the silver hair clip on the top of the dresser, she combed her hair, and wiped the mascara smudges from under her eyes. She'd just shut her mind to him, deny that kiss ever happened. Start over with a clean slate. She could do it.

She took a deep breath and opened the door to the suite's living room. Mitch was eating a sandwich, seemingly unconcerned. Good, he'd really decided to forget it, too. For a split second Anne remembered the feel of his lips, his clean scent, the strength of his hands, and then she put the memories aside.

"Hungry?" he asked.

"Yes."

"There's plenty."

They sat on either side of the table, mannequins, eating the hotel's delicious sandwiches, pretending, trying impossibly to turn back the clock.

"Will we be able to drive home tomorrow?" Mitch asked. "I want to let Brooke know."

Home. "I don't see why not."

"Do you have any idea why Draco's making us wait?"

She shrugged. "He's probably got the stuff stored somewhere."

"Or he's checking on us."

"He has no reason to be suspicious. We're covered. The name and address you registered with at the hotel will stand up under scrutiny, don't worry."

Mitch was silent for a time, staring unfocused across the room. She wondered if he was chickening out.

"It'll be okay," she said. "He's greedy. He'll go for it."

"Mmm," he said. Then he turned the full force of his gaze on her. He was frowning, dark brows drawn together. "I haven't been entirely honest with you."

"I thought that was my line," she said dryly.

"No, I'm serious. I should have told you."

"Told me what?"

"I found the first body, you know that. But I found something with the body, and I should have... Damn, I really screwed up."

"Are you going to make me guess?"

"No. When I cut the body down, something fell out of the boy's pocket. A potsherd."

"And?"

"It could be important. I don't know, maybe a clue to exactly where Sterner was when he was killed."

"A potsherd." She waited.

"I asked Chick Draco about it, just in case it was something distinctive that he could place, but he said it was nothing...*unremarkable,* I believe was the word he used."

"And where is this potsherd?"

"That's the trouble. I don't know. I should have kept it, put it in the sheriff's evidence locker." He looked at her, troubled. "Either Chick Draco still has it or has lost it or..."

"He's deliberately keeping it from you," she said calmly.

"That crossed my mind, but I know Chick. He's as honest as they come. A gentle-hearted scholar. No way could he do anything like that. He's absent-minded, that's all."

"And yet..." Anne said, "he has an uncle whom we suspect of buying illegal artifacts. Couldn't Chick be funneling things to his uncle? Couldn't he be involved?"

Mitch shook his head. "Not murder, though. Not Chick. If you *knew* him you'd realize the idea is ludicrous."

"We haven't established that David Draco is involved in murder."

"No, we haven't."

"It's highly unlikely David Draco was in the park when the murders occurred. But we know Chick was."

"I told you... Look, didn't you see how undone Chick was by his student's murder?"

"He may not have liked it. He may not have com-

mitted the actual murder himself. But he may be involved. His emotional response could be a big dose
of remorse and guilt.''

"No, not Chick."

"Then you think the Hawkins men are the only
ones tied to the actual murders?''

"Yeah, that's how it appears to add up."

"Chick Draco may know more than he realizes.
David certainly does, I'd guess.''

"Maybe."

"Okay." She stood up, uneasy sitting so close to
him. "Tell me about the potsherd."

"It was black, about this big." He made a diamond
with his forefingers and thumbs. "Shiny black with a
raised design on it that looked like part of a man's
head."

"Why did it seem important to you? Maybe the
boy was hiking and found the piece and stuck it in
his pocket."

"Now *you're* playing devil's advocate. I know it's
important. The piece was unusual. Chick said it was
probably new, because none of the Anasazi potters
made black-on-black pottery. But why would Zachary
Sterner have a broken piece of *new* pottery in his
pocket?''

"Did you ask Chick that question?" She walked
to a window and leaned an elbow against the edge,
looking out at the dust-brown humps of Camelback
Mountain.

"No, I didn't."

"Do you believe Chick was trying deliberately to
mislead you about the shard?''

"No. I...damn, I don't know. I don't think so."

"But it's possible he recognized instantly that it was a significant find?"

"It's possible," he said doubtfully.

"And you asked him how many times to return it to you?"

"Twice. And I was going to go out to Red Canyon to look for it. Some night when the student kids were gone. But I'm here, instead."

"I see."

"And there's something else odd about this case. Forensics found fibers on the Sterner boy that were very old, too old, something about a dye that wasn't used until centuries later. It just doesn't add up."

"Very old fibers and a mysterious potsherd. Interesting. Maybe Chick, David and the Hawkinses have discovered something they don't want anyone to know about."

"Look, I'd believe ulterior motives of the Hawkins boys and certainly David Draco now that I've met him, but Chick is...naïve. He's a good person."

"Good people do bad things for reasons we can never comprehend."

"You mean money. Chick doesn't care about money."

"Except for his digs. He needs money for that. He told me so. I'd barely met him when he told me how hard it was to get funding. A motive?"

"You've got a suspicious mind."

"I'm paid to have a suspicious mind."

He put his head in his hands, scrubbed his fingers through his short hair, then lifted his eyes to hers. "So what's David Draco's motive?"

"Money. He may be overextended or just plain greedy."

"You think the worst of people, don't you?"

"In my experience that's usually wise."

He said nothing, but his eyes never wavered from her face. Dark-blue eyes, honesty and integrity so clear in them. She sounded like an embittered old shrew, yet *he'd* been the one shot, nearly killed. Why wasn't *he* bitter?

"I think this changes our plans a bit," she said.

He waited.

"I'd like to go around to every gallery we can find, check each out for anything resembling the missing shard."

"It looks something like a very popular type of modern pottery. I'm not sure I can tell the difference. There's Santa Clara black-on-black and San Ildelfonso black-on-black. We'll find them all over."

"With the design you described, a raised outline of a head?"

"Probably not."

"Then we better get going, don't you think?"

They visited dozens of galleries that afternoon. Pottery shops, curio shops, tourist souvenir shops. And saw many shiny black pots. But none like the missing shard.

At one place Mitch thought he'd found a similar pot, but then he realized the design was engraved. Some designs were carved, some incised; some were smooth; but none had the fine raised lines of the missing piece.

"We could drive to Phoenix," he said. "It's only a few miles away. Start over there."

"Oh, my God." She was fanning herself with a road map, even with air-conditioning on in the car. Her hair lay wet on her neck; her green top was rumpled. She kicked off her new sandals. "Would you find different sorts of pottery there?"

"Not really. We've seen about all that're commonly sold. Of course, I'm no expert."

"We don't have time to dig up an expert here."

"I know. But I could be missing something."

"Look, we can safely assume the Sterner boy had that shard in his pocket because it interested him. And he was an archaeology student. He would recognize its value."

"Maybe."

"Oh, this heat. I'm wilted. I can't think straight."

"You're thinking okay."

"What if the shard came from a stash of pottery so unique that Zachary was literally killed for finding it?"

"Whoever killed him missed the piece, remember?"

"But he only had that small piece because he could carry it back and show it to Chick. He was killed for finding the stash."

"That sounds like the legend of the Seven Cities of Cibola, streets paved in gold. Nobody ever came across even one city."

She waved a hand. "Ruins. Hawkins. We've got a motive now. Hawkins kills to protect a valuable site he's discovered. He's selling the stuff to Draco, who sends his bodyguard up to the park, and Hawkins kills him, too."

"Why?"

"Some altercation or other. You're the one who said Jerry Hawkins was capable of murder."

"Yeah, I did."

"We have to be on our toes tomorrow," she said.

"If he shows us a piece you suspect...Mitch, I'm not the expert here. I have to depend on you to judge what he's got."

"I already told you, I'm no expert, either."

"You know a lot more than I do."

He drove for a time without saying a word, past shops and hotels, past incongruous green rolling golf courses and tennis courts, empty now in the heat of the late afternoon.

"You must realize," Anne finally said, "Chick knows you found that shard. He even knows you want it back as evidence."

"Yes, so what?"

She looked down at her hands. "If he's involved..."

"He's not involved."

"*If* he's involved, then you're a threat. You know he's got the shard."

"I told you, Chick's innocent."

"I remember what you told me, Mitch, but you really do have to consider the possibility that you're in danger."

She gave him a sidelong glance and saw his jaw muscles clench. He stared straight ahead through the windshield. She ventured a thought: "The boulder that darn near killed us."

"An accident."

"You didn't look like you thought it was an accident."

"How do you know what I looked like?"

"It was pretty obvious."

"Spare me your crackpot theories."

"Stop being so damn stubborn," she said with a

touch of anger. "You could be in danger. It's worth it to consider all possibilities."

"If anyone caused that boulder to fall, Jerry Hawkins did. But I'd say that's a pretty remote possibility."

"Fine, call it remote. It's still a possibility. Mitch, you have a daughter. You *can't* just go around threatening people without thinking about Brooke and—"

"Leave Brooke out of this."

She subsided into silence, feeling the sun burn through the tinted window and sap her energy. She tried to keep focused on the problem at hand, but her mind kept slipping back to the feel of Mitch against her, his lips, the roughness of his cheek, his hand in her hair, the sweet taste of him. She shuddered inadvertently and forced herself back to the present, to the neutral zone they'd both chosen to inhabit.

He was turning into the Phoenician Hotel. The stately Egyptian palms laid a deceptive shadow on the roadway. My God, it was hot, she thought. An inferno. It truly did affect her judgment.

When Mitch stopped the car they both sat there for a moment, delaying their plunge into the heat. Anne looked squarely at him. "We have to get our hands on that shard," she said doggedly.

"You never give up, do you, Agent Winslow?"

She simply shook her head.

BROOKE'S MOTHER PICKED HER UP at the bus station in downtown Las Vegas, and she was a very welcome sight, because the station was full of scary characters and weirdos and bums. They had made Brooke nervous as she waited impatiently for her mother.

She'd told Brooke to look for a new white Cadillac.

"And I won't be able to park and go in for you, because Charles will be in the car, honey, so please keep an eye out, okay?"

A new white Cadillac. Brooke sat in the car, feeling the air-conditioning wash over her, thinking of her father's dusty old Bronco.

"So, how was your trip?" her mother asked.

"Long," she replied.

"Bus trips are always long, aren't they?" Denise smiled and patted Brooke's leg. "Wait till you see our new house. So much nicer than Washington. We have lots of space here."

"Is there a room for me, Mom?"

"Of course there is. Well, right now it's still full of boxes and things from the move. But I'm going to fix it up for you as soon as I get a chance. It'll always be there for you, honey."

Brooke wondered if Prince Charles's room was still full of unpacked boxes.

Charles was in a baby seat in the back of the car. He'd fallen asleep, his head flopping to one side, his mouth open, a pacifier hanging out of it.

"He's such a good baby," her mother said, glancing in the rearview mirror.

"Was I a good baby?"

"Pretty good."

I must have been awful, Brooke thought.

"He's almost walking," her mother went on. "Any day now."

Denise drove away from the downtown area, past all the famous signs of the gambling casinos and hotels. Brooke gazed out the tinted window, curious. She'd never been in Las Vegas before; her mother and Jeffrey had moved there only a couple of months ago. Last time she'd seen her mother it had been in Washington.

"Do you like it here?" Brooke asked, staring at the massive edifice of a pyramid—a *casino*.

"It's okay. Too hot for me, but it's quite a move up for Jeffrey. We'll probably be here for a year or two. Then hopefully back to the East Coast again."

"I miss Washington, Mom."

"Oh, honey, I know you do. I wish Mitch had stayed there. Dragging you out to Utah..."

But you moved, too, Brooke wanted to say, knowing she couldn't.

The brown desert stretched away on all sides now, punctuated by emerald-green golf courses. The sun was low in the sky, deceiving you into thinking the temperature was cooling down, but it was still blazing hot out.

"Here we are," Denise said, turning into an entranceway flanked by adobe walls, flowers and steel gates. "Our country club."

There was a guardhouse and a guard who came out to check on the car.

"Oh, Mrs. Arndt, hello."

"Hi, Lloyd. This is my daughter, Brooke."

Brooke leaned forward to smile and say hi.

"Nice to meet you, Brooke. You'll love it here," Lloyd said.

The gates parted; they drove through. The roads in the subdivision curved artfully. Each home sat amid exquisite Xeriscaping—palms and cacti and stones, no irrigation. On man-made hills.

The new house was another sprawling, single-storied mansion. It was stepped up a slight incline, constructed of natural wood and adobe, with lots of glass to catch the view.

"Isn't it nice?" Denise asked proudly.

"Beautiful. Where's the pool?"

"Around back. You can go in for a swim right now while I get dinner ready."

"Wow, cool," Brooke said.

Jeffrey was home from work. He was tall and thin, very blond and tan. He played golf, Brooke remembered. He was an executive for some company—she never could remember the name of it—and he did something with computer systems.

"Hello, Brooke," he said, smiling, "welcome to our new house." He obviously wasn't sure whether to hug her or shake her hand or do nothing.

Brooke avoided the awkward moment by holding out her hand. "Good to see you again, Jeffrey." She would *not* call him *Dad*. No way.

"Brooke's going for a swim before dinner," Denise said.

"Oh, sure. Use that pool," Jeffrey said enthusiastically.

Her mother showed her to a bedroom that contained only a bed and a dresser. Boxes were piled in the closet and in a corner. The walls were bare. But she did have her own bathroom.

"Here it is. I thought I'd do it in wallpaper, something pastel. And a new bedspread with shams to match. Would you like that, honey?"

"Sure, just please don't do it in pink, Mom. I can't stand pink."

"Okay, no pink. Maybe peach or pale green." She was carrying Charles on one hip, and he started squirming and making impatient sounds: *uh, uh, uh.*

"I better feed him. He's getting hungry," Denise said. "Go on out to the pool, Brooke. It's wonderful."

The water was lukewarm, but it felt good. Brooke paddled around, then lay on one of the inflated rubber lounges, relaxing, staring up at the bright blue sky. It occurred to her that her father might know she was gone by now. Maybe not, though. Maybe he was too busy down in Scottsdale and hadn't even checked on her.

She felt sort of sorry for Vicky, whom she'd lied to. Vicky would be in a panic, having an absolute hissy fit. Brooke cringed inwardly, thinking of Vicky telling her father she was gone. But it served him right. A person could only take so much of being stuck out in the wilderness.

Dinner was a hurried affair. Charles had eaten, but he sat in his high chair, chewing on a cracker, gumming it to mush, and her mother was harried, trying to keep the baby occupied while she served hamburgers cooked outside by Jeffrey.

"Sorry I couldn't do anything fancier for your first night here," her mother said, "but I didn't have time."

"It's fine, Denise," Jeffrey said. "You don't have to try to impress Brooke. We're all family."

Family. Not really, Brooke thought. This man was a virtual stranger, and Prince Charles was just as much a stranger, even though he was her half brother. And her mom was different, as if being remarried and having another kid had changed her.

A hard sad knot settled in Brooke's stomach. This wasn't home. This would never be home. But at least it wasn't isolated, out in the boonies.

"Any kids my age around here?" she asked.

"Well, gosh, I don't really know. I only know the people who have kids Charley's age."

"Of course there are, Denise," Jeffrey said. "We'll find them for you, don't worry, Brooke."

She smiled brightly, but the knot in her belly stayed.

"Hadn't you better call your father and let him know you got here safely?" Jeffrey asked.

"Yes, Brooke, you better do that."

"Oh, sure."

She lifted the cordless phone from its base and punched in the familiar number. No one was home, and her father didn't even have an answering machine. No problem.

"Hi, Dad," she said blithely as the phone rang in her ear. "Yes, I'm here. It was a long ride." She paused. "Yes, Mom picked me up. The house is beautiful. And I already swam in the pool." She paused. "Okay, I'll call you."

"Let me talk to him, please," her mother yelled.

"Oops," Brooke said, "sorry, Mom, he already hung up."

CHAPTER SIXTEEN

DAVID DRACO HAD NOT reached his powerful position by being a fool. Something, some instinct, had told him to put off showing that couple from Salt Lake City the New Ruin pots.

Had they been too eager? Too good to be true? Too…ingratiating? He couldn't put his finger on it, but something about them didn't ring true. He thought hard, went over every moment of the meeting yesterday.

He believed in their attraction for each other, and their clothes certainly looked expensive enough, but… He frowned as he got dressed to go to the gallery. Was he just being paranoid these days?

Goddamn Jerry Hawkins. If only he didn't need the man.

David considered his alternatives: chance it and sell a pot to the couple, Jim and Anne, or give them some excuse and lose out on a cool hundred thousand. Better to be safe than sorry or to take a risk and make a killing? He shuddered at the phrase.

Where had that couple said they were staying? The Phoenician, right.

Claire was off at her morning tennis game, so he had the house to himself. He picked up the phone on the night table and called information, had them connect him to the hotel.

"Do you have a Jim, uh, Melrose registered?" he asked, sitting on the side of the unmade bed.

"Why, yes, sir, Mr. Melrose and Ms. Anne Walker."

"Thank you."

Well, they hadn't lied about that. He could try Salt Lake City information, but Jim might have an unlisted number. David sat there, pondering the possibilities, tapping his teeth with a fingernail.

"Okay," he said aloud, "what if they were, say, undercover agents?" It was possible someone had connected the murders to Jerry Hawkins and then to him. Unlikely but possible. There was no proof, but if he sold the couple a pot, an *illegal* pot, he could be linked. Damn.

The maid would be up to change the bed soon, but David didn't want to make this call from the gallery. His sales associate, Debby, knew too much already.

He dialed the number quickly, from memory. *Be there,* he said silently, *be there.*

"Yeah," came the familiar voice.

"Listen, I don't have much time. Just answer this."

"Oh, it's you."

"Yes, it's me. Tell me, do these people sound familiar?" He described the couple. "The man is tall. Short hair, gray. Military bearing. Limps a little."

"Limps?"

"Why, do you know him?"

"Go on. Does he have a name?"

"Calls himself Jim Melrose."

"Okay, and the woman?"

"Medium height, light-brown hair, hazel eyes. Pretty. Anne Walker."

A chuckle traveled over the line.

''What?''

''Sure sounds like some people I know.''

''Who?''

''The guy is Chief Park Ranger Jim Mitchell and the woman is some chick who's been around for a week or so, nosy. I figure she's from Washington. FBI maybe.''

''Oh, dear God.''

''Why? What did you do?''

''Nothing yet. I told them to come back to the gallery today. They want to buy a pot, a very old pot.''

''They are definitely fishing.''

''I knew it. I knew there was something about them.''

''So the two of them are down there? Interesting.''

''It means they're smarter than we figured. Cool it, will you? Lie low for a while.''

''Yeah, yeah, anything you say.''

''Listen to me, you idiot,'' David began, but the man had hung up, leaving nothing but a dial tone in his ear.

Sweating, David finished dressing. His hands shook a little. God, that man could upset him. But at least he hadn't sold those two a pot. The closeness of his escape made him weak. Well, they'd be coming back to the gallery today, and he'd be ready for them.

Thank heavens he'd made that phone call.

THINGS WERE GOING along all right, Anne thought as they drove to the Draco Gallery. She was keeping the situation under control and so was Mitch. They were being civilized with each other. Mature. Two federal employees after the same end: the apprehension and conviction of criminals who'd broken federal law.

She pressed down any feelings she felt seep into her consciousness, buried them. She was adept at that, had lots of practice. Now Mitch looked at her with a kind of detached distaste. Good.

"Okay," she said briskly as they pulled up across the street from the gallery, "you have the money, all set with everything?"

"I don't like carrying this amount of cash," he grumbled.

"You've said that six times since it was delivered this morning."

He parked and got out, then opened the passenger door for her—in case Draco was looking out the window—and took the cash-filled briefcase from the backseat. Anne drew in a deep breath and put on her smile. They might nail Draco today. Hell, they *would* nail him.

Debby greeted them at the door as if they were long-lost friends. "Oh, yes, Mr. Draco is here. Please follow me."

Today Draco wore a beige linen suit and a white linen shirt, suitably and elegantly wrinkled—a British peer in a tropical, foreign colony. He stood and shook their hands, one at a time, the perfect host.

"Would you like some coffee? Debby could run out and get you some. A cappuccino, perhaps?"

"No. No, thank you, really, David," Mitch said. "We're terribly eager to see the pot you talked about."

"Ah." Draco took a very long time sitting down behind his glass slab of a desk. He steepled his fingers and drew his brows together. "Ah," he repeated.

"Is there a problem?" Mitch asked.

"Well, you know, I had in mind one particular

piece in my Santa Fe gallery, but when I phoned last night, it had already been sold. I'm terribly sorry."

"Oh, no," Anne said.

"I apologize, but that was the only one I could think of that would have pleased you. Very old, a black-on-white bowl with birds on the outside. A real collector's piece."

"And it's gone?" Mitch asked.

"Yes, to a well-known collector, someone like you. I *am* sorry."

"So, you have nothing to offer us?" Anne asked.

"Well, there are the pieces I showed you yesterday. Both are lovely. And since I've disappointed you so cruelly, I'll sell either one for a discount of ten percent."

"Thank you," Mitch said, "but neither of them will do."

"I understand. Of course I do. But from time to time I get very nice pieces in. I can keep in touch with you, send you photos."

"No." Mitch shook his head. "I have to see a pot in person. It's a thing of mine."

"Yes, of course. I feel the same way." David shook his head sadly. "I apologize once again." He spread his hands. "But it happens."

"Thanks anyway, David. Anne?"

"Yes, Jim, I guess we'll have to leave empty-handed," she said, not having to feign disappointment.

"Goodbye, and be sure to stop by next time you're down this way. You never know what I might have in." David ushered them out, looking regretful and sober, and shut the heavy glass doors behind them.

"He made us," Mitch muttered angrily as they walked away.

"How?" Anne asked. She, too, was angry, hot and frustrated and disappointed.

"I don't know, but he made us. God, I could have punched him right in the middle of all those expensively capped teeth."

She strode to the car and waited impatiently for Mitch to unlock the doors, not caring anymore what Draco saw.

"Son of a bitch," Mitch said, tossing the briefcase in the car, then sliding behind the wheel. "I could have sworn he bought us yesterday."

"He did."

"Well, what happened?"

"I don't know," she snapped.

He drove back toward the hotel. "No sense sticking around here."

"No, it's pointless. We may as well check out and drive back today. What tipped him off?"

Mitch didn't answer. "Okay, so we go back to the park and try it from that angle. Run Jerry Hawkins to the ground, catch him with evidence. Find a witness. I don't know, something." She turned to Mitch. "Has anyone ever tried tracking Hawkins in the park?"

"I told you before, it's been tried for years. The trouble is, he's smart and he knows the backcountry even better than the rangers. Every road, every canyon, every rock in the park. No one can catch him in the act."

"I have a hard time believing he's good enough to elude the federal government."

"You mean a dozen rangers? *That* federal government? Damn it, Anne, trying to keep tabs on Jerry Hawkins is like trying to find a needle in a haystack.''

"Okay. I've heard that line before.'' She was quiet, thinking, pushing her anger into the background, not letting it cloud her judgment. "There may be a way,'' she said.

"Yeah, how?''

"Satellite tracking technology.''

"Star Wars?'' he scoffed.

"No,'' she said, "but something pretty high-tech. I could get hold of it.''

"Describe this thing to me.''

"You put a tracking device on Jerry's truck, a satellite tracks it, we follow the coordinates right to him.''

"Hey, sounds easy as pie,'' he said sarcastically.

"Got a better idea?''

"Not at the moment.''

"I'll make a call when we get back to the hotel.''

"Look, Anne, if you're considering doing something crazy—crawling under Jerry's truck, following him into the park—forget it. I'm the law-enforcement officer in the Needles District. It's my turf, my jurisdiction. You're here as a consultant. And don't pull that crap about outranking me. It won't fly.''

He spoke in a hard voice, not angry but matter-of-fact, and he was very, very sure of himself. The male chauvinism made her mad, but at the same time she had to respect his stand. Oh, yes, James Mitchell demanded respect.

"I'll clear everything with you.''

"Damn right you will.''

"And we have to find that shard,'' she reminded him.

"Yes, I know," he said tightly. "If you hadn't dragged me down here on this wild-goose chase I might have found it by now."

They were snipping at each other—typical behavior, she thought, for operatives on a failed mission. It wasn't really anyone's fault. Just bad luck.

"Okay," she said, "but it was worth a try."

"Huh."

How far apart they were in reality, so different. It had been ludicrous of her ever to imagine they could be… What? *Friends?* No, never friends. Lovers, perhaps, but it was too late for that. They'd drive to Canyonlands and soon she'd fly back to Washington and her empty, sterile life. How hard it would be, she mused, to return to being not quite alive.

Mitch had stopped at a red light, and she stole a glance at his profile. A handsome profile. It was hard to believe that those lips had pressed hers. And that his hands, on the steering wheel now, had held her. She realized, without a bridging thought, that she'd stopped him because of her own sudden wild abandon. Mitch was utterly trustworthy; the person she hadn't trusted was herself.

They packed quickly, Anne stuffing her new clothes into her bag. She'd probably never wear them again. Her new lease on life, her attempt at illicit passion—they were over. How pathetic.

Mitch was phoning Vicky to check on Brooke. He wanted to be sure she knew he'd be home tonight. Idly, Anne listened to the conversation with one ear as she packed the last few toiletries in the bathroom.

"Vicky? It's me. We're—" He stopped abruptly and listened. "What?" he shouted. "Slow down. What? Since Monday? My God, why didn't you…?

All right. She went to Moab and then when you called she wasn't there? You mean she never came home?''

He was pacing, a hand on the top of his head. ''And you called the police? No, no, Vicky, it's not your fault. I think, I think Brooke did it on purpose. Yes, I'm leaving right now.''

He hung up and stood there for a minute, looking down.

''What is it?'' Anne asked.

''Brooke hasn't been home since that night I phoned Vicky. She isn't at Suzy's in Moab. She's gone,'' he said dully.

''Oh, no.''

''I should have known. She ran away. She planned it out and left.''

''Oh, Mitch, I'm so sorry. But she's all right—I'm sure she is. Maybe she's at her mother's.''

Mitch shook his head. ''I seriously doubt that. Brooke... Let's just say that when Denise got remarried and had the new baby, well, it broke Brooke's heart.''

''Still,'' Anne said, ''you might want to try calling Denise.''

''And what if Brooke isn't there?'' he snapped.

''Oh...I see. Well, you could... Better yet, I'll call and ask for a Brooke Mitchell. That way...''

''Would you?''

''Of course.''

But in the end Anne only got an answering machine. ''We'll try later, okay?''

''Sure, sure,'' Mitch said, troubled.

''She's fine. And don't blame yourself. Teenagers are difficult.'' She could see his anguish. If she had children, maybe she could comprehend what he was going through. But she didn't. She had put it off too long, and then Lyle was sick and then it was too late. Mitch didn't want her pity, and she could offer him little else.

"Let's go," he said harshly.

"Do you want me to drive?"

"Hell, no."

He stopped short at the door and passed a hand across his face. "Brooke needs more than I can give her. She needs a real home. She needs a woman around."

They fell studiously silent, Anne closing her bag, Mitch pulling the car keys out of his pocket with far too much concentration. The moment was terribly awkward, his words so plainly truthful. Even worse, he obviously realized the implications of his statement.

"Well, I guess that's it," she said.

"Let's get out of this place," he replied angrily.

And Anne wondered if he was angry at her or himself. Or Brooke. Or all of them.

BROOKE LAY IN THE POOL, her head on the edge, her eyes closed to the burning sun, her legs floating out in front of her, pale and wavering in the turquoise water. She'd spent quite some time in the pool in the past day because she was left alone there. No one else in the house used it, it seemed.

She was almost as bored here as she was in the park. Jeffrey was at work, thank God. When he was home he tended to be cloyingly nice to Brooke, and she could tell it was false. She figured he resented her being around.

Her mother tried; she'd give her that. She'd taken

Brooke to a mall that morning and bought her some shorts and a cute new bikini. But then Prince Charles had fussed and needed his nap, so they'd had to go home.

Brooke had eaten lunch and then realized she had nothing to do, so she'd gotten into the pool.

It'd be better once she met some kids her age, she thought, but when was she going to do that? She so desperately wanted this to work—the nice house, the car, the pool, the city. She so desperately wanted her mother to say, "Let's plan on you staying here for school, honey. What do you think?" But she hadn't, even though Brooke had complained about Moab and the park and Utah and her whole life there. She could tell her complaints had upset her mother, that Denise didn't want to hear about it, but she wasn't willing to take her daughter back.

Nobody wanted her.

Brooke rolled over and rested her chin on her folded arms. Her father must know by now that she was gone, but he probably didn't care, either.

Oh, yes, he did. She knew he did, and for a moment she experienced a flash of homesickness so powerful it made her heart contract. Her father and the small apartment and the neighbors' kids and Chick Draco with his wonderful stories of ancient Indians. And the view of the Needles across the valley, the spires blood-red against the blue sky. And Suzy and her other new friends in Moab.

No. Those things weren't enough. She wanted to be here with her mother, in a city, a real civilized place.

"Brooke," she heard her mother call from the patio door.

"Yes, Mom?"

"Could you watch Charles for a second? I have to get the laundry and he's being fussy."

"Sure, Mom."

Brooke got out of the pool, toweled herself off and padded inside. The air-conditioning hit her wet skin like a blast of winter, and gooseflesh rose all over her.

"He's in the playpen. Just hand him toys. It's great of you to take care of him, honey. Gives me a real break," her mother said. "Behave, Charles, that's a good boy."

Brooke picked the baby up and set him on her lap. He was clutching a red plastic car, and his face screwed up as if he were going to cry.

"Now, come on, Charley, no crying. I'm your big sister."

"Ma-ma-ma," Charles said.

"She'll be back in a minute. Here, Charley." Brooke pulled him up by his hands so that he stood on her thighs, his fat baby toes gripping her bare skin. She bounced him up and down, his dimpled knees bending and straightening. Then he laughed, his nearly toothless gums showing. "Guh, guh," he said.

"Yeah, Charley, that's right. Guh, guh. Hey, kiddo, do you have any advice for me?" She sat him back down in her lap and bent her face to his fragrant baby scent. "How do I tell him, huh? How do I tell my dad I'm not going back to that park? Ever."

"Guh, guh, ooah," Charles replied.

"Well, you're no help." And she thought, suddenly, that maybe no one, not even the smartest grown-up, had an answer.

CHAPTER SEVENTEEN

MITCH FINALLY REACHED his ex-wife that evening when he arrived home. The conversation was far worse than he'd anticipated.

"Hi, Denise. Say, did Brooke get in touch with you?" he asked.

"Get in touch with me? You mean since she left without saying a word?"

"She left?" He pondered the words.

"Yes, she left. Sometime this afternoon. I'm really upset with her, Mitch."

"She was there, then?"

"Why are you asking *me*? She phoned you when she got here."

"She phoned me? When?"

"Right after she got here. What's going on? What do you mean?"

"She never called me, Denise. I wasn't even here."

"What?"

"She was there, you say, but she left?"

"Yes. Mitch, what's going on?" She sounded frightened.

"I'm not sure, but I'll find out, don't worry."

"Where is Brooke? Where's my daughter, Mitch?"

"I don't know. She's obviously trying to show us something. Acting out. Teenage rebellion. I'll find her."

"You better, goddamn it!"

"I'll call the local police right now. Just in case. You call the Vegas police. What was she wearing?"

"Oh, my God." He heard her voice break. "Slacks—oh, I don't know, baggy khaki pants and a red sleeveless top. Oh, Mitch…"

"She's fine."

"I thought you knew. She called you. I stood right here and heard her. And I thought you knew she was on her way back to Canyonlands, but she just left and I was so mad. Oh my God, my little girl."

"Did she have any money?"

"I don't know. I…"

"All right, do what I said. I'll be in touch."

"Mitch, do you think…?"

"She's fine, Denise," he said firmly.

He hung up, feeling his insides turn to jelly. Brooke, his daughter, out there somewhere.

Lost and alone.

ANNE COULD SEE Mitch's apartment from her window. His lights were on, but the curtains were drawn. She wondered whether he'd managed to reach his ex-wife and what she'd had to say. Maybe Brooke was with her mother, safe and sound, and Mitch wasn't even worried anymore.

She really wanted to know.

She wished she had the kind of relationship with him that would allow her to just drop by, ask him what he'd found out, talk to him, comfort him if necessary.

There was something she needed to tell him, but it might have to wait; he was too distracted by Brooke's disappearance right now. She'd phoned Ted Warner's office when they had gotten back, and she'd been informed that while she and Mitch were gone, Harvey Hawkins had been arrested in Flagstaff, Arizona, with two hundred thousand dollars in cash on him.

She'd set the phone down with a satisfied thump and felt vindicated. Her theory had been absolutely right—David Draco and Jerry Hawkins were running a moki poaching operation. The murders were cover-ups for the looting. And Harvey... He must have been coming back from unloading illegal artifacts in Scottsdale. Damn, David Draco had had the illegal pots right in his gallery when she and Mitch had been there!

She paced, frustrated. They'd been so close. But Draco had suspected them. Why? Had she lost her touch?

The only thing she wasn't positive about was Chick Draco's involvement. Mitch believed wholeheartedly that the man was innocent, but he kept forgetting he'd given Chick the shard, which was conveniently missing. Too conveniently. It was a potentially vital piece of evidence from the crime scene, and Chick had *lost* it.

Damn. She paced some more and peered out her front window. The light was still on in his apartment. It wasn't that late. She wanted very badly to present him with her news about Harvey's arrest. She needed Mitch's expertise and his knowledge of the park.

And yes, she admitted to herself, she needed— wanted—his respect and his regard.

The trouble was, he was distracted by his daughter's situation. As he should be. Of course. Anne opened her door and took a deep breath.

Maybe Mitch didn't really want to be alone any more than she did.

MITCH WAS IN A BLACK MOOD. He sat on his couch, tense as a coiled spring. He'd called the Utah State Patrol; he called the Nevada State Patrol. He'd called the Las Vegas police, too, in case, but they already had the report. A Mrs. Jeffrey Arndt had just phoned it in.

He felt as if someone had cut off his arms and legs but left him with his brain so that he could suffer in full measure.

Where was his child?

There was a tap on his door. He jumped up, thinking for a split second it was Brooke. But she wouldn't knock. Of course not. Still, he stepped across the room swiftly—it could be news, someone come to deliver information.

"Hi," Anne said. "Is this a bad time?"

He ran a hand across his face. "No, come on in."

"Did you call Denise?"

"Yes."

"Well?"

He felt the fear hit him again, a hammer blow. "Brooke was there."

"She was there." Anne stood in the center of the room. "Well, that's good, isn't it?"

"But she left this afternoon without even telling them and no one knows where she's gone. She could be anywhere. God, Anne, the things I'm imagining."

"I bet. And I can't say anything that will make you feel any better."

"Nobody can."

"Mitch." She took his arm and led him to the

couch, then sat beside him. He went, an automaton, empty of all emotion but anxiety. Her face was serious, her hazel eyes worried, the perfect wings of her brows drawn together. "Mitch, maybe this won't help, but when I was Brooke's age... I told you about my sister, didn't I? How jealous I was? I wanted to run away so many times. I did once, but only to my aunt's in New Jersey.

"And you know what? Mostly I did it to imagine how much my parents would suffer. I enjoyed that a lot."

"Well, if that's what Brooke was after, she got it."

"I know. But I'm sure she's okay. She's out there, hoping you're worried. She wants proof you love her."

"Oh, boy, great." He squeezed his temples between his fingers.

"Have you notified anyone?"

He listed everyone.

"Good, you've done the best you can for now."

"The worst part is, I can't do anything else," he said. "I just have to sit here, waiting." He got up restlessly. "And we still have two murders on our hands."

"There's some news," she said. "Harvey Hawkins was arrested in Flagstaff with a bag containing two hundred thousand dollars in cash."

He stopped short and stared at her.

"Yes, and you know where he got the money."

"Draco." He shook his head. "I can't believe even Harvey could be so dumb...."

"He was stopped for a broken taillight, but he had an open beer and the money bag on the seat next to him."

"The idiot."

"Okay, I've been thinking. That tracking device I told you about. I'm going to call about it in the morning. It'll take a couple days to ship it out here and to retask a satellite for the job."

"You've lost me."

"To track the specific device they send us, they need to reposition the satellite. It's no easy thing, and it isn't cheap, either."

"All right. But we have to attach the device on our end. Where? Jerry's truck?"

She nodded. "That's what I thought."

"Fine, hell, let's try it. But who's going to bell the cat?"

"Let's worry about that later. You have enough on your mind right now."

"Don't goddamn patronize me," he said with a flash of anger. He liked that—anger felt good.

"I'm sorry, I didn't mean to," she said stiffly.

"No, no, I'm just…"

"I understand. Mitch, I really do. I may not have children, but I know what it's like to suffer a loss, not to be able to do anything. I've been there."

He was too full of his own fears to pursue her meaning. He would later, once he found out Brooke was safe. He'd remember, and he'd ask Anne what she meant.

She gave him a sorrowful smile. "You just concentrate on Brooke while we wait. And, you know, I have connections all over the country, in every federal office. If you think it would help…"

"Thanks. Let's give it a day or so. There's an APB out on her." He shut his eyes. "God."

She stepped close to him and held his gaze. He

could smell her fragrance and feel the heat of her skin. He wanted so very much to reach a hand out and touch her hair, to pull her to him. For comfort, only for comfort.

But she touched him first, a hand on his cheek, holding his face so that he couldn't turn away. "She's all right, Mitch. She's all right."

He put his arms around her, drew her to him. Yes, this is what he'd wanted since the moment she'd walked in tonight. Her scent, her warmth, her softness, her hands on his back. He needed this woman.

They stayed that way for a long time, clasping each other without words, just two people standing together against the storm of life that buffeted them and made them reach to each other for solace.

MITCH COULDN'T SLEEP After Anne had left him. She'd gone regretfully, with a soft smile. "It's better," she'd said. "You have to think about Brooke."

He'd wondered whether she'd left to protect herself or him. "If you want me," she'd said, "you know where I am. Get some sleep, Mitch."

"Sure," he'd said, holding her hand. "I'll sleep like a baby."

"Try."

He decided to take a shower, to wash off the sweat and dust of the long day, the drive from Scottsdale. There was nothing else to do; sleep was out of the question. He left the phone on the bathroom vanity so he could hear it. Just in case.

Where was Brooke? Maybe she *was* doing this as a prank to stick it to him and Denise... But what if she'd been kidnapped, dragged off? Worse. No, he wouldn't think of that. Yet the stories kept coming to him. Headlines. Lost children taken from their homes, raped, murdered. *No.* He stopped himself. Madness lay in that direction.

Anne had said Brooke would be all right. He hung on her words. Then reason asserted itself. How in hell did *she* know? Did Anne have a crystal ball? And anger drew his face into harsh lines.

He let the water splash on his head, rubbed absently at the scar on his thigh. The ache that reminded him of his mortality. *His,* not his child's.

The job. He'd focus on the job. Stupid Harvey Hawkins. Could the money in the bag be traced? He'd call the Flagstaff police about that. The satellite tracking device—well, Anne could play with her new toy. If it worked, good.

Those fibers… The forensic report on the bullets—yes, he had to check if the one from Paul Kasper matched.

The shard. Chick. He pictured the man's tortured face when he'd spoken of his dead student. Could that pain have been an act?

The shard. It came to him like an electric shock. He saw the scene in his mind's eye as if it had happened a moment ago. Chick absentmindedly looking at the piece of pottery, saying he'd take it out to Red Canyon and show it to his kids, see if anyone knew anything about it. Then Chick had opened the door of his truck, placed the piece on the cluttered seat and closed the door.

Maybe the shard had never been removed from the truck. Maybe Chick—all the junk in his truck, his preoccupation with the dead student—maybe he'd just left it there and forgotten.

Mitch turned off the shower, only half-toweled

himself dry and threw on some clothes. After picking up the phone to take with him in case Brooke called, he took his flashlight but didn't put it on when he went outside.

Yes, there was Chick's truck, parked in its usual spot. Dark-green, dented, rusty. Chick never locked it. Hell, no one locked his house or his vehicle out here.

He put the flashlight on inside the truck. Nobody would see him. It was late. The junk on the seat was truly remarkable: candy wrappers, dusty shirts, empty pop bottles, maps, photographs and drawings, sheets of paper with notes on them. A sandwich, moldy and green. Pieces of pottery. Mitch checked each piece out carefully. No black potsherd. Damn. He dug among the debris, inspected the floor and behind the seat.

Nothing.

He'd been wrong, then. Chick must have removed it from the truck. Mitch tried once more, swept the stuff aside and stuck his hand down between the seat and the upright seat back, inching his fingers along the tight crack.

His hand hit something sharp. He shone the light onto the spot, felt around, grasped an edge, pulled. His fingers slipped off. He tried again, tugging, and it moved. It slid and came out of the crack, dark, the flashlight beam glinting off its shiny surface.

The black potsherd with the raised lines on it. *Oh, yes*.

AS MUCH AS IT PAINED HIM, David Draco knew his business arrangement with Jerry Hawkins had to end. Between the looting and the two murders and now that park ranger showing up at his gallery, it was finished. The only problem was New Ruin and the priceless artifacts Hawkins still had stashed in Moab. David wanted them. The question was, would it be too dangerous to make one last deal with Jerry?

He pondered the dilemma, examining every angle. So far there was nothing to connect him to either New Ruin or the murders—short of the artifacts Harvey Hawkins had sold him, which would only go to David's most discreet buyers. He felt relatively certain he'd escaped by the hair on his chin. This time.

So the arrangment had to end.

But Harvey had mentioned a couple dozen pieces, a fortune in treasures from the distant past, and David wanted them. If he could get his hands on them without having to deal with that murdering maniac...

There was no way.

But nothing was to stop David from paying his nephew a long overdue visit up in Canyonlands. And once there, if he could meet with Jerry one last time, bringing along plenty of cash...perhaps he could return to Scottsdale with the bulk of the New Ruin artifacts and no one would be the wiser. Then he was going to wash his hands of Hawkins for good.

He brushed his teeth and looked at himself in his bathroom mirror. Was he pushing this? Should he walk away now, before something else went wrong?

No, he thought, and combed his hair despite the fact he was ready for bed. He would use a visit to Chick as cover. Contact Hawkins. Maybe he could even get a look at New Ruin. By the time he flew back to Scottsdale—hopefully with the artifacts—he would be home free. And very, very wealthy. More so than he could have dreamed possible only a few short months ago, before the discovery of New Ruin.

He'd do it. He flipped off the light switch and padded across the plush carpet to the bed where Claire sat propped up, reading.

Yes. This one last time.

The decision made, he pulled down the coverlet and climbed into bed. Claire took off her reading glasses and smiled at him, and he returned her smile. God, how he loved her, how he wanted her.

He reached over and drew a finger along her collarbone and shoulder.

"Mmm," she murmured said, and snapped off her light.

"I have to fly up to Utah," he said into the darkness.

"Oh? When?"

"Soon." He slid the strap of her pink nightie off her shoulder and found the firm roundness of her breast. "I'll only be gone a day, two at the most."

"Any time you're away is an eternity," she whispered, and she shrugged off the other strap and eased down next to her husband. He lowered his head to her. Claire moaned and held him, and David knew that all was right with his world.

CHAPTER EIGHTEEN

SOMEHOW MITCH MANAGED to doze off, but he was
jarred awake when the phone rang at midnight. It was
the Las Vegas police. And they had Brooke. Safe and
sound.

He couldn't believe the enormity of his relief when
they put her on the line.

"Oh, Daddy," his daughter sobbed. *Daddy*. She
hadn't called him that in years. "They're going to
make me stay in juvenile hall. What am I going to
do? I'm so sorry. Oh, Daddy..." Then she really
sobbed.

It took him fifteen minutes to get the full story, how
she'd run away from her mother's, how she'd been
hitchhiking on the interstate—trying to get back to
Utah, she claimed—and how that was against the law
and she was a minor...

"Honey," he said, "calm down, please. This isn't
the end of the world. I can be there by late tomorrow
and—"

"No! Daddy!"

"It'll take me that long to drive down, Brooke. Be
realistic."

"But I'll...die in here!"

"No, you won't. You'll get a good night's sleep,
in a safe place, and have a couple of meals and I'll
be there."

"They..." Sob. "They said you have to talk to a judge, Daddy. What if he won't let me come home?"

"I'll work everything out. You know that. I promise."

"I'm so sorry...I'm so sorry..."

"You calm down and get some sleep and I'll leave at daybreak, okay?"

"Can't you come now?"

"Let me catch a few hours' shut-eye myself. You don't want me falling asleep at the wheel. Now, go get some rest."

"Okay," she said, sniffing, "okay."

He spoke to the juvenile officer once more, then hung up and let out a long breath of relief.

God Almighty, he thought, heading into the bedroom, *kids.*

Amazingly, despite the long, crazy evening, Mitch dozed off again. The next thing he knew he was wide-awake, staring, at the blinking digital clock. 3:02 a.m. And in the next instant he realized something was very wrong. Something had awakened him. Someone was in his house.

He sat up quickly, sudden rage exploding in him. *How dare they?* he thought, and without turning on the light, he reached down next to the bed and felt around for his holster and gun. Where the hell had he dropped them?

Got 'em.

He was swallowing hard against a dry throat, drawing the gun silently from the holster, sliding off the safety, when he saw a shadow detach itself from the darkness beyond the bedroom door.

As he swung his legs to the floor, lifting the gun, half rising in the same instant, something—a fist?—

caught him hard on the jaw and propelled him backward.

Later, he wasn't sure if he'd been stunned or if he'd witnessed the shadow fleeing the room. All he knew was that he was hunched over, dazed, clinging to the back screen door, not even remembering how he got there, when he heard a voice at the front.

"Mitch?" It was Anne. "Mitch? Are you okay? Mitch, answer me!"

"Back…" He licked his lips. God, was *that* sore. "Back here."

Somehow the lights were all on and he was on the couch. He was aware of a dizzying headache and a sharp pain in his jaw and Anne…she was leaning over him, a rag in her hand, trying to press it against his mouth.

"Goddamn," he sputtered, pushing her hand away.

"Oh, stop it. Here, there's blood on your lower lip."

He let her touch his lip with the cool rag, but damn, it really did hurt. More than when he'd taken the bullet in his leg, for God's sake. He didn't tell her that, though.

"Got a glass jaw, huh?" she was saying, and she eased down next to him, still dabbing—more like stabbing, he thought—at his lip.

"Yeah," he managed to say, "I always did. It's in my DNA."

"Swell," she said. "Do you remember what happened?"

"Not much. I know one thing—my gun's around here someplace, and I think maybe the safety is off."

"I'll find it. Hold this to your lip. No, Mitch, the cut is in the corner."

His gun was on the kitchen counter, where he must have set it down before opening the back door and trying to give chase.

Some chase.

"I put it back in your holster by the bed," she said, and she sat down next to him. "Did you see anything at all?"

He thought for a moment. "No. Something woke me up. The next thing I knew I saw a shadow in the bedroom, and then it was pretty much lights out." He touched his jaw and tried to work it a little from side to side. *Wow.*

"Hurts?"

"You might say that."

"Don't you lock your doors?"

"No one here does."

"Hmm. I suggest that from now on—"

"Hey," he cut in, "what're *you* doing here?"

"I heard a noise out back, like loose gravel coming down off the embankment. I got up, but by the time I looked out my kitchen door, I couldn't really make anything out. I *thought* I saw something moving away from the back of your place, but I couldn't tell." She shrugged, then took the cloth, went to the fridge and wrapped ice in it. "Hold this on there for a while." She sat back down. "You may have a concussion, you know. I could drive you…"

"Will you stop it?" he growled. "I'm fine. I tried boxing once at college and this is the result I got then. It's no big deal."

"I'm embarrassing you," she said in a soft voice.

"Yeah, you are," he had to agree. Then, turning away from her, from the gaping vee in her robe, he saw the shard on the coffee table. God. He'd forgotten. "Here." He leaned forward and picked it up.

"What? What is it?"

"The potsherd."

"*The* potsherd."

"Yes."

Anne held it gingerly and turned it over several times in her hand. "Where…?"

"Right in Chick's truck. I got to thinking… Anyway, there it is."

"And it is…as unusual as you first thought?"

"Maybe. I don't really know."

"But shouldn't Chick Draco have recognized if it was?"

"Chick barely looked at it. And obviously he forgot, tossing it into his truck. I wouldn't try to second-guess the incident."

"You need fresh ice," she said, and she put the shard down. "Let me—"

"Will you stop?" he told her again. "Please. This is fine."

And then he saw her expression change, and the gap in her robe widened as she moved the slightest bit closer. He could detect the scent of her soap and night cream, and he broke out in a sweat.

"You might have been killed," she was saying, a catch in her voice. She reached out and placed her hand on his, and his skin seemed to burst into flames. "I should have been quicker to check on that noise when I first heard it."

"It's not your fault, for God's sake. Don't blame yourself. I think we both know who to blame."

"Yes. Our friends, the Hawkinses."

"You bet…" he began, and then suddenly he remembered. "My God. I forgot to tell you. Brooke's at juvenile hall in Vegas." He told her the whole story.

"Poor baby," Anne said, her hand still scorching his. "She must be awfully scared. Oh, gosh."

"She is. But I think she's even more worried about facing the juvenile court judge when I get there. I suppose it could be a problem."

Anne abruptly sat up straight. "I'll go with you."

"Hey, you don't…"

"Oh, yes, I do. I'm Justice Department. I've got the pull, and you never know about some of these juvenile judges. If the judge even *thinks* there're problems at home…"

"All right," he said.

"All right?"

"You can ride along. Wait, I didn't say that very well. I'd really appreciate it if you'd be there. Frankly," he said, meeting her eyes, "I had the same thoughts."

"It's a deal, then. What time do we go?"

"Six-thirty okay?"

"It's fine. I'll check on the tracking device from the road."

"You're sure?"

"Absolutely. But don't you think you should call your ex-wife? Does she knew about Brooke?"

"I better wait till morning. She'd have a heart attack if the phone rang at this hour."

Anne got up and went to the front door.

"What are you doing?" he asked.

"Locking your door." Then she went to the back door, and he could hear her latching that, too.

"There," she said, "I feel better."

"You lock your own doors," Mitch said. "I don't want to have to worry about you."

"I'm staying here," she announced. "It's ridiculous for me to be running back and forth, when you're leaving in only a few hours till, anyway."

"Anne..."

She shook her head. "I'll take the couch. I wouldn't sleep a wink in my place. I'd worry."

He didn't have the energy to argue. "God, Anne, you're treating me like a child."

"No," she said solemnly, "I'm treating you like a friend."

A friend, Mitch mused as he lay in his bed, trying to sleep. No, Anne wasn't a friend. She was much more. And if she thought her being on his couch, just outside his bedroom door, would allow him to get the rest he needed, she was crazy.

IT WAS 5:20 a.m. when Jerry Hawkins switched on the coffeemaker in the kitchen of the old family house, then leaned against the counter, arms folded stiffly across his chest.

He was wide-awake. He rarely slept more than five hours a night, but this night—or early morning—he'd never even gone to bed. Too busy down in the Needles District.

He lit a cigarette, blew out a stream of smoke and cussed, mad at himself for not finishing the job. Trouble was, he hadn't been sure just how dazed Mitchell had been or if he'd had his gun handy. And in the dark...

"Ah, hell," he said, dragging on the cigarette, he'd get the man another day. And maybe even that broad who was hanging around with him, the bitch from the government. Jerry didn't know which government agency, but he sure knew a cop, male or female, when he saw one.

"Yeah, maybe her, too," he said, and he poured a cup of coffee, tossing his cigarette butt into the sink.

Both of them, he thought again; he'd get two for the price of one. Maybe he'd use another boulder or, this time, a goddamn avalanche on them.

But they both had to go and Jerry didn't much care how.

CHAPTER NINETEEN

ANNE RINSED THE COFFEE CUPS while Mitch phoned his ex-wife to tell her Brooke was safe.

"No, Denise, I'll take care of it. She was my responsibility. Sure, call her if you want. And reassure her that I'll be there this evening." He listened. "Yes, I know, and maybe this will teach her something. Maybe..." He waited while Denise spoke. "Yes, I promise, I'll keep in touch."

He hung up and stood there for a minute, and Anne wondered what Denise had said to him.

"Divorce is the pits," he finally declared.

"There are worse things," she said, almost to herself, but Mitch evidently registered her words.

"You want to explain what you were talking about when you said there were things worse than divorce?" he asked when they were on the road, driving past Green River.

"Not really." She looked out the passenger window of the car, seeing but not seeing the endless dry expanse of the Southwest.

"Stop playing games. You've been hiding something. It's pretty damn obvious."

"It has nothing to do with you."

"The hell it doesn't." Then, "You want me to play guessing games?" He steered around a tractor trailer.

"Drop it, will you?"

"Anne, look—" he shot her a glance then put his eyes back on the road "—you said you were my friend. Okay, fine, friends tell each other their problems."

"Why do you think I have a problem?"

"Maybe I recognize someone who's hurting."

She hated how vulnerable he made her feel. As if he knew her inside and out. She didn't want him to see her weakness. She guessed it scared her, that loss of control.

"Come on," he said gruffly, and she felt his hand on hers.

She was quiet for a minute, watching the empty land slide by. Mitch said nothing more, and perhaps his very silence gave her the impetus to start.

"I was married," she said, "for seven years. To a man named Lyle. He was a civil engineer. We had a wonderful life. Then he was diagnosed with cancer, a particularly nasty kind, and he fought it for three years. And then he died."

Quietly, Mitch asked, "When did he die?"

"A little over a year ago." She spread her fingers in her lap and studied her nails.

"I'm very sorry."

"So am I. So was his family, so was everybody."

"That *is* worse than divorce. It explains a lot."

"What exactly does it explain?"

"Oh, I don't know. A certain, um, distance you have." He hesitated, then asked, "Has there been anyone since? Have you dated at all?"

"God, no," she said vehemently. "I don't want to have a relationship with anyone. Never again. I can't go through it."

"You usually don't have to go through it at all at your age," he said gently.

"I can't take that chance. It nearly destroyed me." But she was lying—she knew it. She *had* been taking a chance lately. Really living, feeling. And she'd put herself in jeopardy once more by accompanying Mitch to Las Vegas. She didn't have to; she'd wanted to.

"Maybe you need some more time."

"Maybe."

He drove on, and they sat there together, encased in the steel shell, hurtling along the interstate. She wanted to blurt out her pain and her fury. She wanted to tell him about the false hope, the agony Lyle had been through, the days and weeks and months of hoping and praying. The final, utter despair. The tears she'd shed. But she couldn't.

"I'm ashamed to have burdened you with my problems," he said at last. "They sure seem unimportant now."

"No, not at all. Mitch, your daughter, was missing."

"You never had children?"

"No."

"Why not?"

"We were going to."

"Oh."

The words came out of her as if they had a will of their own: "He told me...before he died...he said I should get married again and have children."

"He was right, I guess."

"How could I think of that when he lay there dying?"

"But now you could."

She closed her eyes.

"You're a young woman. You're smart, you're attractive. You have a long life ahead of you."

"Thanks, Mitch."

"Thanks for what?"

"For the compliment."

Soberly, he said, "My pleasure."

After lunch Anne took over the wheel, and Mitch fell asleep for a while. She studied his face in snatches while she drove. The stern lines from nose to mouth, the crinkles at the corners of his eyes, the cut on his lip, which was swollen. She liked his face; it was a strong face, filled with integrity. She couldn't believe she'd told him about Lyle—she never told anyone. Why had she chosen Mitch as confessor?

Las Vegas rose out of the desert like a mirage, a brightly colored make-believe land in the middle of a plain of desolation.

They drove straight to the juvenile detention center and parked in the visitors' lot.

"Okay," Mitch said, "here we are."

"Nervous?"

"A little. I hope there aren't any snafus."

"I can call my friend Matt Zwerling. I told you about him. He's a lawyer with the Justice Department office here."

"He probably deals with Mafia guys," Mitch muttered.

"Probably. But he'll help us out if we need him."

Brooke looked young and helpless and frightened. A woman accompanied her to the visitors' room, and left her there.

"Oh, Daddy," she said, bursting into tears as Mitch folded her in his arms.

"Did your mother call you?" he inquired finally, holding her at arm's length.

"Y...yes, and I asked her if she would come and get me, but sh-sh-she couldn't."

"I know. I got here as fast as I could."

"Daddy, can I go with you now? It's awful here. It's horrible!"

Mitch gazed at Anne over Brooke's head. His eyes were dark with helplessness. "I don't think so, baby. It might be tomorrow."

"Daddy..."

"You can handle it. One more night, Brooke."

She sniffed and wiped at her eyes. Anne handed her a tissue.

"Why can't I go now?"

"Because, honey, you're a minor and you broke the law, and a juvenile court judge has to release you into my custody, and judges are home watching TV by now."

Brooke peered at her father through her tears. "Are you angry?"

"Not yet, but I probably will be."

"Is Mom angry?"

"She will be, too. Once we get over being worried."

"I'm...I'm sorry," Brooke sobbed.

"Good," Mitch said. "Now, Anne and I are going to get rooms somewhere and I'll see you in the morning."

"Do you have to go?"

"Yes, Brooke. But you'll be out of here in the morning, I promise."

"Oh, Daddy, I can't stand it. I can't..."

"Yes, you can. You have to. You'll be fine. See you soon."

"Daddy..."

He sat in the car in the parking lot, his face gray, and Anne could do nothing. Her heart broke for both of them.

"It'll be all right," she reassured him.

"Yeah, yeah, that's what I told her."

She drove, and found them a hotel near the detention center. Two adjoining rooms. There was a casino next door, its lights gyrating over the surrounding buildings, the muffled sound of laughter and the clanking of slot machines emerging from it.

"You'll be okay?" she said, handing him his room key.

"Sure, I'll be fine."

"Look, I'll call Matt. He'll help. Just so there are no obstacles, okay?"

He finally focused on her. "That'd be good, Anne. I'd appreciate it."

She went into her room and closed the door behind her. Here she was in Las Vegas, the sun beginning to set, the neon blaring out the city's wares: gambling, music, girls, dancing, food and more food. With a handsome guy next door, one who knew her deepest darkest secrets.

A man who was making her feel alive again.

SOMETHING ABOUT THE frantic atmosphere of Las Vegas must have unsettled her, Anne thought later. Her mind whirled without letup: Mitch, Brooke, the attempt on Mitch's life, David Draco, the murders, the satellite tracking device. Jerry Hawkins. Mitch.

She paced her room, thinking, thinking. So strange

that fate had thrown her together with James Mitchell, the one man out of a world full of men, who could reach inside her and touch her.

She had the urge to go next door and hold his hand and ask him what it had felt like to be shot. And then she'd ask him about Denise and why they'd divorced and where he'd gone to school and… So many questions, so many things about him that she didn't know, that she wanted to know.

She looked out of the window. The city was coming to life, the long Strip outlined in garish illumination, everything sparkling, barely cooling off in the dusk. An unreal concoction of mankind's worst desires. But beautiful with the lure of the exotic, the titillating, all of it as false as a prostitute's smile.

She lay down on the bed, closed her eyes and tried to relax. She was exhausted, but sleep wouldn't come.

The potsherd. The shiny black piece that Mitch had retrieved from Chick Draco's truck. It was hard evidence, she knew, but they had to track Hawkins to his lair, and then the pieces of the puzzle would fall in place.

Had it been Hawkins in Mitch's apartment last night? *Had it?*

The knock on the door startled her.

"Yes?" she called out.

"It's me."

She got up and padded in bare feet to the door.

"I got us some Chinese takeout," he said. "Figured it was easy, and there was a place right next door."

"Chinese takeout."

"Sure, why not?"

"I love Chinese," she said. "How'd you know?"

"You told Brooke at dinner that night." He held a fragrant bag that made her mouth water. "Your place or mine?" he asked.

"Oh, mine, come in." Smoothing down her hair, slipping into her sandals, she was as nervous as a schoolgirl. "I phoned Matt, by the way. He's going to find out which judge is in court tomorrow and call him at home."

"Great. Wonderful. Hey, Anne, I appreciate it," he told her once more.

They sat at the small table and ate the spicy food. She was hungry for the first time in so long; she really tasted the flavors, felt the textures. She'd never forget this meal.

They made idle conversation, but tension hung in the air. Something between them.

"Do you like to gamble?" she asked.

"Don't know. Never tried. I'd go next door and put a few quarters in those machines if I wasn't so damn worried about Brooke."

"I tried it once, on a riverboat on the Mississippi. Lyle and I..." She halted. She didn't have the easy way of talking about a deceased loved one that some people did. "Lyle and I went on a vacation once," she said, and felt a weight lift, "and we set aside a hundred dollars to gamble with."

"And?"

"We lost every penny."

"Live and learn, I guess." He was scooping up rice with a fork, mixing in the vegetables, chewing, swallowing. She couldn't take her eyes off his Adam's apple.

"Ouch," he said.

"What? Oh, your lip."

"This spicy stuff hurts like the devil."

"You should have called the police about that incident, you know."

"I *am* the police, Ms. Winslow, may I remind you?"

"You may."

The air in the room seemed to vibrate with the kind of taut stillness present before a rainstorm in summer. The preface that told you what was coming.

"Pardon?" she said, realizing he'd said something.

"I said, oh, nothing."

"No, tell me."

"Well, maybe you can talk to Brooke, you know, if she'll talk to you. Feel her out a little. She might confide in you. She sure won't confide in me."

"I'll try. Girls that age are touchy."

"Girls any age are touchy."

"Have you dated since your divorce?" she asked carefully.

"Not really. I've been too busy."

"Two of a kind," she mused.

The meal was finished. Empty cardboard containers littered the table. She expected him to rise and say, "See you in the morning," or "Well, I better go now. It's getting late." But he didn't. He sat there, looking tired but relaxed.

"How about the news?" she offered, uncomfortable with his closeness. She got up and turned the TV on, then stacked the containers and stuffed them in the bag.

"Sit down, Anne. You've had a long day, too."

"Mmm." She sat, her hands squeezed between her knees. She wasn't good at this, yet she had to admit to herself that she didn't want him to leave her alone.

She wanted—craved—his company. But at the same time she was afraid of it.

They watched the news for a while, not speaking. She wouldn't have remembered had a world war been declared. She was too aware of Mitch, his long legs stretched out in front of him, his arms folded across his chest. His brow was furrowed, and she knew he was worried about Brooke.

The nearness of a man was strange to her now. Unsettling and thrilling.

Funny, but every second of the time spent with him in the hotel room was indelibly impressing itself on her mind. She knew she would recall with acute clarity the hum of the air conditioner and the big rose-colored flowers on the green satin bedspread. The lampshade with a slight burn in it from a bulb; and the stain on the green carpet by the TV. And the air that was scented with mild disinfectant and Chinese and...Mitch.

She guessed she'd always known she liked his male scent. Such an animalistic response, but there it was. And she couldn't help wondering if it was the same with him.

The news droned on. The national headlines and then local stuff. Was he really watching TV?

She noticed that he was unconsciously touching the cut on his lip. "Does it hurt?" she ventured, her voice almost a whisper. Slowly, her cheeks hot, she reached out, touching the scabbed-over cut, marveling at her daring. This was crazy, crazy. She couldn't breathe. God, why couldn't she breathe?

His eyes met hers, and something ignited in their depths. He covered her hand with his. "No," he replied, then he drew her close and kissed her, gently, then harder, until she had no breath at all left in her lungs.

They rose, and locked together, they made their way to the bed. He repeated her name against her lips—"Anne, Anne"—and inside her mouth, and she could taste blood from the cut that had reopened. It only inflamed her more.

They shed their clothes, and she marveled, once again, at her boldness. But she wanted this man so badly.

He was muscular, with dark hair on his chest, and she couldn't get enough of the feel of his skin.

"Anne," he murmured, "are you sure? Are you...?"

She quieted his words with her lips, and when he raised his head, she said, very deliberately, holding his gaze, "No strings attached, right?"

He didn't answer but pulled her up against him, so that her breasts were crushed, and she took that for acquiescence.

He lowered his head and licked her nipples, and she moaned. It had been so long. He took his time, caressing every part of her, licking and kissing, and her body was in a struggle to escape her desire, while coveting it all the same.

Then he lifted himself above her, his face transformed, and his arms pinioned her, his body anchored hers, his hair rough, his skin satin, and he entered her, thrusting, and she cried out in ecstasy and relief at their joining.

The curve of his shoulder, the paleness of his skin, warm neck and chin, and again his mouth on hers, the sharp metallic taste of blood. His breath so quick, his heart beating against hers, his hardness inside her.

The sensation rose in her; the old remembered feelings awakened, flowered, and she threw her head back and closed her eyes and met him with equal strength on the battleground of pleasure.

The end came with a climax fierce and prolonged, hers then his, and they lay there, sweat drying on skin in the too-cold room, the neon lights of the casino blinking wild colors at the window.

I lied, she wanted to say. *I want there to be strings attached. I'm falling in love with you.* But she couldn't bring herself to tell him that—the risk was too great.

"Anne," he whispered, and his hand stroked her hair, her shoulder, while on the television screen the weatherman said, "And it's going to be another gorgeous day tomorrow, folks. A high of one hundred and two, not a cloud in the sky...."

CHAPTER TWENTY

GETTING BROOKE RELEASED from the detention center took the better part of the morning and even then, despite the call Anne's friend Matt Zwerling had made to the juvenile judge, her release wasn't a snap. The judge seemed out of sorts, and Mitch and Brooke sat there, embarrassed, as Anne stood up, introduced herself and said she was a friend of the family, then made it a point to let the judge know that Mitch was *the* James Mitchell, hero.

Mitch could have died.

Still, the judge had his say, and he gave Brooke a long, stern admonishment. "I never want to hear about this sort of behavior again, young lady. And I'll be following your activity. I don't care if you live in Timbuktu—I'll be watching."

"Yes, sir," Brooke replied softly, her lower lip quivering.

Mitch drove as they headed along the Strip toward the interstate that would take them back to Utah. Brooke slouched in the backseat, her eyes red rimmed, an occasional sob welling up in her chest.

She was miserable, her hormones raging, puberty dragging her down into a black abyss. Mitch kept eyeing his little girl in the rearview mirror, his heart sinking. He'd never seen her this bad, her clothes dirty, her nails chipped, her skin broken out, her hair hanging in ragged tangles. He was actually afraid for her, scared to death of the misery she was suffering. What if she got so low she… He shied from the thought.

Anne kept trying to cheer her up. "You want to stop for an early lunch, honey?" Or, "Would you like to catch one of those new virtual-reality shows at one of the big hotels? There's this roller coaster up on the very top of the Stratosphere…"

"No," was Brooke's only answer.

Mitch exchanged glances with Anne. He couldn't think about last night. He was far too consumed with worry over his daughter, and by the look in Anne's eyes, so was she. What a mess. What a god-awful mess, he was thinking, sitting at a traffic light, when Anne suddenly turned toward him.

"Pull into that hotel," she said.

"What?" The light turned green.

"Pull into the entrance to New York New York."

"Anne, I don't—"

"Just do it, please," she said, and he put on his directional signal, baffled.

"Okay." Anne took off her seat belt and faced Brooke. "I want you to come inside with me and no arguments, young lady." She sounded, well, angry, Mitch decided.

"Dad," Brooke said.

But Anne put up a hand. "Now, you listen here, Brooke. Your dad can't help you with this. Out of the car. I'm getting really fed up with this self-pity act. *Out.*"

Mitch said nothing. He was too bemused to speak. Brooke looked mad and defiant, but Anne's tone indicated she meant business.

"Out," she repeated. Then, when Brooke finally opened the back door and stepped into the heat, Anne told him, "We'll be about two hours. Meet us right here, okay?"

"What's going on?" he asked.

"Little Miss Brooke is about to learn how a woman shakes off depression. We'll be fine. Don't worry."

"But what am I going to do for two hours?"

"God, Mitch, go put some quarters in a slot machine. I don't know." Then she and Brooke disappeared inside the huge new hotel—New York New York.

He parked. And he tried putting a few dollars into a slot machine in the fabulous casino, but he got bored, and took a walk down the Strip to kill the time.

What in the devil was Anne up to?

Anne. The heat of the August day beat down on him and he found it hard to grasp a thought, but he remembered last night despite his sluggish mind. Oh, yeah...he remembered. It was as if he could still detect the scent of her hair, feel her soft skin. He'd always known her skin was pliant and satiny.

The memory of their lovemaking consumed him as he ducked into a casino to cool off. He'd forgotten such simple animal pleasure. Yet with Anne it had been more. There was the newness, but also a singular sense that they'd been together before, as though they were meant for each other. What a crazy thought.

Oh, yeah, the lovemaking had been good.

An hour to go, he mused, heading back toward New York New York. What was Anne doing?

And hell, what had she meant *no strings attached?* Did she think he was going to forget the whole thing, walk away cold? He knew her better than that, knew she didn't take lovemaking lightly. Even though he'd met her only a short time ago, he knew that about her. Or was he telling himself this to bolster his own ego?

Damn.

Well, obviously she was a chicken. And he guessed he couldn't blame her; she'd been burned badly once. He'd been burned, too, though not nearly as miserably, and maybe that was why he wasn't as shut down as she was.

Some of his happiness at what they'd shared was tarnished. He was falling for her—hard—and she was keeping her distance. He felt bad that she was still so troubled, so torn up about her husband's death. He wished he could do something, but that didn't seem possible—Anne wouldn't let him.

Mitch got the car from valet parking and waited near the entrance. Two hours came and went, and he drummed his fingers on the seat next to him, watching the big open entrance.

It was crowded. Taxis and limos and airport shuttles coming and going. Busloads of tourists. Where were Brooke and Anne?

Almost two and a half hours must have gone by before he spotted them heading toward the car.

He swallowed and blinked behind his mirrored sunglasses.

His daughter— Her clothes were new: a lavender patterned blouse with capped sleeves, different khaki pants, not all baggy and sloppy, brown sandals with little heels, painted toenails and fingernails. But it was her face, her hair...

Miraculously, his daughter had turned from an ugly duckling into a swan. Her hair was short, cut in some incomprehensible way to make it appear full and bouncy, and it framed her face. There were colors in it, too—blond and red streaks. Her skin seemed fresh, healthy. And she had on lipstick.

Her entire demeanor had changed. She no longer slouched and shuffled; instead, she walked briskly, with confidence, her back straight.

Holy cow. That was Brooke?

He couldn't move from his spot. The women—and Brooke sure looked as much woman as child now—climbed into the car and Anne only said, "Ready? Let's go."

But Brooke was giddy. "Well? Well, *say* something."

"I...I don't know *what* to say," he admitted.

Anne laughed then. "Amazing what a couple hours and a credit card can do, huh?"

"Do you like it?" Brooke persisted, leaning toward him, smiling shyly, expectant. *"Dad."*

"Well," he said, clearing his throat, "I guess I'm going to have to enroll you in a nunnery now. How could you do this to me?"

They both laughed, conspiratorially, but Mitch would be damned if he knew what was so funny.

He couldn't get over the transformation in his daughter. He turned onto the interstate and kept surreptitiously eyeing her in the mirror, unable to fathom the change, the self-assurance. How could this be? Was that all it took—a change of clothes and a haircut? He'd never, not in an eternity, comprehend women.

Anne and Brooke talked a lot on the drive home. They were still chatting about the dress shops at the hotel at a late lunch at a roadside café. Even nail-polish colors. Mitch was so relieved he could have grabbed Anne and crushed her with kisses. Oh, he knew Brooke's troubles weren't over, but right now he felt wonderful.

Except, of course, for the as-yet-unsolved murders in his park and this woman who'd come out here and changed everything. When he'd taken this job he'd pictured himself spending his life alone. Now, though, everything had shifted, and he had to wonder what his reaction would be when Anne got on a plane back to Washington.

"No strings attached," she'd said last night. But was she really that tough? Or, for that matter, was he?

Apparently, he realized as they neared the exit to Moab, she wasn't thinking about her toughness at all. Or him. Or last night. Now she was talking about that shard, its uniqueness.

"It really is extraordinary, isn't it?" she kept saying him.

"Yeah, sure."

"That piece of broken pottery...not to mention the fibers found on Zachery Sterner's clothes..." she reflected out loud, "they're the tip of an iceberg. But I'll bet you anything..."

"Really," he said, but she ignored him.

"...that both the student's and Paul Kasper's deaths are connected to the shard and those fibers. Unique...very old..."

"I wouldn't bet against you," he said, trying to keep his mind off her legs, the slimness of her hand as she gestured with animation.

"Oh, I do hope the tracking equipment is here."

"About the equipment," he said, suddenly sobered. "I'm going to handle it."

"What?"

"Doing the actual placement and the tracking. I've got some good men working under me, too, and..."

"Whoa, there," she interrupted. "This is *my* deal, Mitch. Don't think for a minute you can ditch the *delicate* female. Oh, no, you don't."

"What? What?" Brooke was asking from the backseat, her ears perking up.

"Never mind," Mitch said.

"I'm in on the whole thing," Anne said, determined. "And I'm not going to argue about it. Period."

He drove in silence then, while Anne briefly explained her plan to Brooke. He didn't know whether he was angry at Anne for her stubbornness or if he admired her. She had his head all twisted up. The one thing he did know was that the idea of Anne in harm's way made his gut churn.

Damn, he thought, how had she done that? And why had *he* let it happen?

JERRY STUDIED THE REPORT in his hand as he stood in the Moab post office. At last, proof that New Ruin was ancient, hundreds of years older than any known Anasazi site. The academic world was going to be turned upside down. *Oh, yes, yes!*

He eyed the date given to the tree-ring sample from the roof beam he'd sent to his friend at the lab. *200 A.D.* Scientific proof. And wait till he stuck this proof under Draco's nose. Draco, who even now was in Moab trying to manipulate him into turning over the rest of the New Ruin artifacts for a million dollars.

It wasn't enough. Not with this paper proving the dates. *Shit,* he would have Draco eating out of his hand. He might even drive him out to the site, which Draco had yet to see, really get the man salivating.

The idea came to Jerry as he drove along Main Street toward the Rivers Saloon. How to keep Draco on the hook—how to ensure Draco would pay any price Jerry asked for the artifacts. These and future ones.

A little blackmail. *Of course.*

And, Jerry realized, he could kill two birds with one stone. What if Draco was at New Ruin and somehow Jerry's nemesis, Ranger Mitchell, the friggin' *hero,* could be lured there; and what if something happened to Mitchell while Draco was present? The screws would be permanently put to Draco. Jerry would have the power, man, the power over him forever.

"Oh, beautiful," he whispered as he pulled into the parking lot, and everything fell into place.

Before joining Harv at the bar, Jerry phoned Draco at his nephew's apartment in the park. "Hey, how would you like to visit New Ruin?" he asked.

"Is it safe? I mean, do you think…"

"Of course it's safe. You wanna see it or not?"

"Yes. Yes, I do."

Jerry told him when and where to meet him in the morning and then hung up.

One fish on the hook. Now, for the other. The *hero.*

And Jerry needed Harv for that.

Over their usual shots and beers he laid out his plan. Harv listened, trying to grasp the concept of what Jerry needed him to do. Then he said, "But, Jerry, what if Mitchell isn't on his usual patrol route tomorrow? How am I gonna—"

"Hey," Jerry cut in, lighting a cigarette. "Either

Mitchell is on Devil's Lane between noon and one tomorrow, or he isn't. If he's there, you know the plan. If he isn't, well, you figure it out.''

"Gosh, I guess I'll just join you at New Ruin, then.''

"Oh, brilliant, Harv.''

"So that *is* what I should do?''

"Yes, Harv, yes. God Almighty, you got a brain in there?'' He rapped his knuckles on the side of Harv's head.

"You know,'' Harv said, ignoring Jerry, "with Mitchell, that'll be three dead.''

"Keep it down!''

"Oh, right. But, Jerry, I'm serious. This is like that curse I told you about, the King Tut tomb thing. This is real scary. What if—''

"Stow it,'' Jerry said, "and get a grip. I'm doing this *for* the Anasazi.'' And he knew right then and there that someday, someday real soon, he would have to cut Harv loose. It was a shame, but this was just too big—way too big for old Harv here.

He lit another cigarette and began contemplating.

MITCH DUSTED OFF HIS HANDS and knees and stood back up, looking around the parking lot at the Rivers Saloon. No one in sight. Thank God.

He drove out of there quickly, confident he'd set and activated the tracking device properly on the underside of Hawkins's pickup. It had almost seemed too damn easy.

CHAPTER TWENTY-ONE

HARV WASN'T the brightest guy in the world, but from a lifetime of moki poaching in the park, he was a genius when it came to the rangers' patrol routes. Heck, he knew them better than *they* did.

Jerry had briefed him at least ten times on the scheme. Drive to Devil's Lane, which was hardly a lane; rather, it was a narrow four-wheel-drive route between two rows of rock spires, essentially a short-cut to isolated regions in the Needles District. If all went well, if James Mitchell followed his self-assigned patrol route, he should pass Harv on the schedule, sometime between noon and one o'clock.

Harv got there and faked a broken-down truck at around eleven-thirty. He opened the hood, carefully severed the fan belt on the cooling system and then waited, going over and over Jerry's instructions in his head.

At 12:42 he spotted dust pluming into the clear, dry air in the distance, and then the distinctive white Bronco came into view across the valley floor.

His heart raced. *Oh, boy—oh boy.*

"Don't screw up," Jerry had said. "Don't screw up, or I'll goddamn kill you, Harv."

Mitchell spotted him and stopped, as Harv knew he would. Hell, they were the only souls alive within a twenty-mile radius. And, as Jerry had predicted, Mitchell read Harv the riot act.

"How dumb can you be?" the ranger said, peering under the hood, handling the severed fan belt, which Harv had been mindful to shred as opposed to cut. *Clever.*

"You got a permit to be in the park?" Mitchell asked on.

"Ah...no," Harv sputtered. "I was just out for a drive, see, and—"

The ranger put up a hand. "Spare me."

Then Harv went into his act, surprising even himself. Must have been his nerves, he thought, that lent authenticity to his babbling, nerves and the big drops of sweat that rolled down to his collar. "I'm—I'm *glad* this happened," he sputtered. "I'm really glad. I can't take it anymore. Jerry, man, he's gone nuts. And there's this place, this incredible place that we found... That's how it all started. You wouldn't believe it, Mitchell. It's amazing. We call it New Ruin, but everything's gone wrong since we found it. I want *out.* Maybe I could make a deal with you. What if I show you where it is? I had nothing to do with any of this... Oh, I helped, you know? But that's it. I want out. You can help me. *Will* you help me?"

He was very, very cautious not to mention the murders, and when he was done with his rambling pleas, he was bursting with pride. He deserved an Academy Award.

Mitchell was staring at him now, just staring, his face expressionless.

Uh-oh. Maybe he hadn't laid it on thick enough?

Harv began the whole litany anew, but the ranger cut him off. "I heard you the first time," he said, obviously disgusted. "Okay. Say I can put in a word for you. I'm not promising anything. But then, Harv, you haven't given me anything. How about for starters you tell me where this Anasazi site is."

"No, no, if Jerry... It's not that far, though, and Jerry isn't due there till late today. If I show you, well, you could say you stumbled across it."

"Like the student? Like Zachary Sterner?" Mitchell said in a steely voice.

"I don't know nothing about that. I only dig up the pots. That's all I do. But I'll show you New Ruin. You won't believe it. It's going to change history. I'll take you—"

"All right," Mitchell interrupted, although his tone was wary, and he was eyeing Harv suspiciously.

Then he went for his radio.

"What're you doing?" Harv felt panic rise.

"I'm going to let dispatch know."

"Oh...no, man, no. You can't tell anyone about me taking you there. Jerry will find out. He'll kill me. No. I'll show you, but you can't tell a soul I did."

Mitchell needed a lot of convincing, and plainly he was doubtful, but in the end he nodded, his curiosity getting the best of him. Just the way Jerry had said it would.

Harv puffed up with pride. He, not Jerry, had set the bait and hooked the big fish.

MITCH PARKED in the spot Harv indicated. "This is where Jerry and I always park," Harv said, and Mitch wondered about that. If Harvey were setting a trap— which he could easily be doing—then Jerry's truck had to be nearby. It wasn't, and there couldn't be many places to park in this canyon, so maybe Harv was on the up-and-up.

As if reading Mitch's thoughts, Harv said, ''Jerry's not gonna be here for hours, like I told you, but let's get going. Hey. Maybe you ought to leave that gun in the car, though.''

''Why, Harvey?''

''Well, I hate the things, you know? And there's no reason to carry one here.''

''All the same,'' Mitch said, ''I'll bring it along.''

Which he did. And he was damn glad each time it bumped against his hip on the steep climb through a cut in the rock. He didn't trust Harv as far as he could throw him.

How many times, Mitch wondered, had he driven by this cut and never seen it or even suspected it existed? Amazing. But then, Canyonlands hid thousands of secrets.

Despite his reservations about not letting Martha know his whereabouts, he had to admit he was pretty damn excited. New Ruin. This was the missing piece to the puzzle. This was the motivation for the murders. And Jerry Hawkins was at the center of it all. Of course.

Keep your cool, he reminded himself.

He followed Harvey and tried to stay alert. For all he knew there was no Anasazi ruin up ahead. This could be an ambush. He wouldn't put anything past Jerry Hawkins.

On the other hand, maybe Harvey was telling the truth. Mitch had always considered him a crook and a liar, but a murderer? Harv had never fit the psychological profile; Jerry fit *that* bill. So maybe this was on the level. And that meant the ruin really was up ahead. Mitch wouldn't lie to himself—the thought of its existence sent a thrill through him.

He was musing about the shard and those fibers and about Anne—yes, Anne—and her tracking device and about a hundred other things, when Harvey stopped short.

He pointed. "There."

Mitch looked up. He wasn't sure. It was so unusual, so *advanced*. But then the reality of the ruin washed like a hot tidal wave over him and for an instant he was dumbfounded as he took in the intricately constructed walls, the heavy T beams and broken ladders, the huge maze of rooms on the valley floor and up the canyon wall. He couldn't even begin to imagine what the ruin would look like when he climbed up into it.

"Wait till you see the whole thing," Harv was saying at his side. "Come on, let's go up. What do you think so far?"

"Well," Mitch said, "it's...wow."

"Yeah." Harv smiled, nodding for Mitch to lead the way. "Me and Jerry were pretty shocked, too. It sure is beautiful."

Mitch, despite his excitement, did not ascend the ladder first. He followed Harv. There must have been thirty rungs, and climbing was murder on his leg. Something about the tendons still needing to stretch out. Still, he made it up right behind Harv, his brain telling him to stay sharp, not to get sucked into the flow of excitement. *Caution. Exercise caution.*

And that was his exact self-counsel as he stepped off the last rung and saw them standing right in front of him: Jerry Hawkins and David Draco. *Draco?*

Here? Mitch thought in the same flash of time as he reached for his side arm.

Shit, went through his mind. But then, he'd been dumb enough to fall for it. Duped by good ol' Harv.

ANNE DROVE to the Visitor Center taking deep breaths, telling herself she was worked up because a glitch occurred while the satellite was being retasked, and no one was sure when the job would be done.

Yes. Okay. She was on pins and needles. And a lot of it was due to the screwup with the tracking equipment, but some of it, she knew, was due to the prospect of seeing Mitch again. Just *seeing* him, looking into those clear blue eyes, remembering those hands on her, the feel of his hard male body pressed to her, *in* her. Had she really done *that*?

Mitch wasn't there, however, when she walked in with the bad news about the satellite. She waved at Martha and rounded the counter that separated the tourists from the staff and still didn't see him in his office.

He was running late, she surmised, on his patrol route. She'd have to wait, then; or maybe she'd go over to the staff housing and wait there. Check on Brooke.

She turned to Martha. "Will you tell Mitch I'm going to—" But she stopped short. "You look worried. Is something…?"

"He hasn't checked in."

"Well, is that unusual?"

Martha nodded.

"Maybe it's just his radio," Anne offered, denying the sudden thump of her heart.

"Maybe," Martha said doubtfully.

Anne told herself the whole way over to Mitch's apartment that he was a tough guy and could handle himself. Sure. Look how he'd saved the vice president's life. Taken that bullet. *Sure*. He just had a bum battery in his radio and he was running a little late. That was it.

She found Brooke working herself into a tizzy. "I thought you were Dad. He's supposed to drive me up to Moab." Brooke put on her best pout.

"Oh, he's probably running a bit behind schedule. Your hair looks great, by the way. I'm such a klutz with a hair blower. Maybe you could—"

"Anne," Brooke said, "you're, well, like pale. Is something...?"

"Oh, no-no-no. I'm just a little annoyed. Remember that satellite tracking stuff I was talking about in the car? Well, there's been a delay getting it going."

"Oh," the girl said.

They started dinner together, and Anne noticed that they were both glancing too often at the kitchen clock while they fixed a salad and a casserole. Finally, she couldn't stand it anymore.

"I'm going to phone Martha," she said too cheerfully. "See what's up."

"Want me to call?"

"No, no, I've got it. Just slice up that tomato, will you?"

She reached Martha, who'd stayed late at the center. But there was still no word from Mitch.

"Look," Anne said, her back to Brooke as she walked toward the living room, "I think you better send out a search party."

"That's impossible."

''What? What do you mean 'impossible'? This is Mitch we're talking about here, and—''

''Not enough daylight left.''

''There's plenty of goddamn daylight. I insist you—''

''Hey,'' Martha said, ''don't you think I'm worried, too? But I can't send out a search party till morning. By the time they gathered and split up the routes it'd be pitch-black out and it isn't done. *Ever.*''

''Well, I don't give a hoot about procedure, Martha. I'll authorize it. Call Sheriff Warner, too, and let's get going on this.''

''I can't. You don't understand. Rescue ops can't be held at night, Anne. They don't work. And by daylight the men would be so exhausted they couldn't do the job anyway. All I can do is start the ball rolling now.''

Anne bit her lower lip. She'd known something was going to happen. She'd just *known.* ''There has to be a way,'' she insisted. ''We can't sit here and—''

''Listen,'' Martha broke in. ''I love that guy. If there was anything...''

''Well, damn it all, so do...'' She'd almost said, *so do I.* Almost. And she knew, abruptly and without the slightest doubt, that she did love Mitch. With all her heart and soul. And now, dear God in heaven, now he might be... She couldn't face that. *No,* her mind screamed, *no.*

''Martha,'' she whispered, her heart knocking furiously against her ribs, ''are you sure. I mean, isn't there anything...?''

''Not until daybreak.''

''Oh, God,'' Anne breathed.

''Exactly,'' Martha said.

"You'll call...if Mitch should show up or..."

"I'll be here all night. Will you stay with Brooke?"

"Of course, of course."

But when she was off the phone she realized how hard that was going to be. Brooke was no child. She had to be told her father might be in danger, or worse. Anne wouldn't tell her that, no way, but Brooke would guess.

Anne took a long deep breath and turned around to face Mitch's child. Oh, God, this was too hard. And what if Mitch really was... *Don't even think it,* she told herself fiercely.

"What?" Brooke said when she saw Anne's expression.

Anne took another breath. "Come here," she said, "and let's sit for a minute. We need to talk, kiddo."

"Oh, no," Brooke said, "oh, no." And Anne realized the girl already knew.

CHAPTER TWENTY-TWO

THREE AGAINST ONE were definitely bad odds. Mitch raised his hand from his holster slowly, so they could see the movement. *Do not overtly threaten a perpetrator.* "Well, well, nice to see you again, Jerry." He nodded to Draco. "And you, too, *David*."

No wonder Draco had found out who he and Anne were. He'd had a direct line to Jerry. He studied the three men, carefully, coolly, and still couldn't see a weapon. *Good.* And then, despite his precarious position, he took a quick look around. The ruin was astounding.

"So this is it," he said, placing his gaze back on the man. "This was worth two lives."

"You're damn right," Jerry snapped.

"*Jerry,*" Draco warned. Then to Mitch, "Amazing, isn't it? The carbon dating came back at 200 A.D. And the tree-ring dating confirmed it. Do you realize what this means?"

"Vaguely," Mitch replied, "but obviously not the way you do."

"This place existed five hundred years before the Basket Makers crawled out of their underground pits and built the first stone house! This is completely new, completely unique. A thousand years before the height of Anasazi culture, and they were making pottery as good as any in history." Draco stared at him. "And no one knows about it but us."

"Zachary Sterner found it," Mitch said. "And Paul Kasper."

"Unfortunate," Draco said, shaking his head. "I never meant for—"

"Oh, shut up, Draco," Jerry hissed.

Mitch couldn't help noticing the stone houses, so well preserved, clustered at the base of the rock wall, climbing up it. An open kiva nearby, a pile of dusty shards, some pots. Clothing, bones, tattered textiles, yucca-fiber sandals.

Yucca fibers. Of course. The stuff found on Sterner's shorts. The shard. The black shard.

"These people," he said, "were very advanced, I take it."

"Advanced? My God, unbelievably advanced," Draco replied.

"Did they happen to do black-on-black pots with raised figures?"

"Goddamn it, how do you know that?" Jerry asked.

"I found a potsherd when I came across the Sterner boy's body. He had it in his pocket."

"The little sneak," Jerry snarled.

"It's safe with a Justice Department agent right now, gentlemen, don't worry."

"So that's what she is," Jerry said. "I figured FBI."

"The shard won't mean anything," Draco said, "unless it's tied to this place."

"And it won't be," Jerry put in.

"Can I take a look?" Mitch asked, playing for

time. Could he get away and use his radio in the Bronco?

"Sure, be my guest," Jerry said.

But all three men followed him, up the ladders they'd made to reach the topmost rooms; through perfectly preserved dwellings; past petroglyphs of fanciful animals, of men hunting, of birds and graceful plants, of the hunchbacked figure that Indians two thousand years later would call Kokopelli.

"Beautiful, isn't it?" Draco offered, as if they were best friends on a pleasant Sunday outing in the park.

They came out on top of the pueblo, and Mitch could see the faint outlines on the valley floor of square, irrigated fields. Above, the sky was brilliant blue against the ragged edge of the mesa top.

His brain was moving at lightning speed. They wouldn't, couldn't, let him live after he'd seen this. Hawkins definitely had this planned out. But maybe he could still take Hawkins by surprise—Harvey wasn't a killer and neither was David Draco, but Jerry...

The tracking device. Was it working yet? Could Anne track him? Or would Jerry be long gone from here before it started sending signals?

Either way, Mitch knew, he'd have to make a move and soon. He still couldn't see that anyone had a gun, and hell, he could hardly shoot an unarmed man. Even Jerry. They didn't know that, though.

He was near the edge of the cliff, the three men directly behind him. *Now,* he thought, get the drop on them. If he had to shoot one in the leg he'd do it, he was thinking, hesitating for a heartbeat too long.

They jumped him so fast he had no time to react, no time to draw his gun. He struggled with the Hawkins men, while Draco yelled in the background. He almost got the upper hand, when Jerry slipped and went down. But he recovered as swiftly as a striking snake, and the next thing Mitch knew, Harvey had an arm around his neck and Mitch was off balance, choking, locked in combat, struggling too close to the cliff edge, too close—

Next something happened that Mitch would never comprehend. Jerry stood back for a moment then lunged, catching Mitch and Harv unawares, and Mitch felt himself lose his equilibrium, dragged by Harv, the two of them scrabbling, their bodies propelled out over the edge into nothingness. And Mitch was falling, falling, and his last coherent thought was *what a stupid way to die.*

JERRY STOOD at the lip of the roof, staring down at the bodies. His breath came fast, his chest heaved with effort and a cold sweat slicked his skin. Harvey lay broken, blood puddling beneath his head. Mitchell was unmoving, obviously lifeless.

"Oh, my God," David was saying over and over, his voice cracking. "Oh, my God—oh, my God."

"Shut up," Jerry told him dully.

David turned to Jerry, a stricken look in his eyes, his face pallid. He tried to speak, but nothing emerged. He gagged.

"Come on, Draco, we're outta here."

"Jerry...Harv? Shouldn't we...?"

"They're dead." He drew in a breath and stepped back from the edge. "Too bad about Harv, but what the heck? It'll look like he was the bad guy all along when they find the two of them."

"You didn't...you didn't have to. You shouldn't have...There must have been another way."

"There was no other way, believe me. We're safe now. Time for Chick to *discover* New Ruin."

"Oh, my God—oh, my God..."

"Let's get the hell out of here, *Mr*. Draco."

They climbed down the ladders, descending through the rooms that people had lived in nearly two millennia ago.

Although Jerry's words had been bold, now his knees were rubbery. Killing Harv had been a necessary evil, but it didn't sit well. As he moved downward through the pueblo, past the petroglyphs, he felt the weight of unearthly surveillance. He'd done it because he'd had to, he wanted to tell the spirits. They'd understand, wouldn't they?

Or maybe Harv's fear of a curse wasn't so far wrong.

ANNE REACHED the Attorney General at a cocktail party late that afternoon—evening in Washington— and pulled no punches.

"Sorry to bother you, ma'am," she said briskly, "but I have a federal agent in danger on this operation, and I can't wait any longer for the satellite to be retasked. If you could make a call over to the Pentagon..."

"Done," the woman said.

Anne thanked her, and then she uttered the words that had been bubbling up in her chest for some time now. "And, Madame Attorney General, I am tendering my resignation as of the termination of this operation. You'll have a letter shortly."

"Excuse me, Agent Winslow?"

"You heard me. I quit." Then she hung up.

Her hands were shaking, her mouth dry; she didn't know if it was due to her rash decision to quit or to Mitch's disappearance.

"Will you be able to find my dad now?" Brooke asked.

"I hope so. I sure do hope so." She looked at Brooke, saw the fear in the girl's eyes. "I'll find him. I promise."

What she couldn't guarantee was that she'd find the girl's father alive.

MITCH HEARD A MOAN. Who was making that noise? Where...? He forced his eyes open, saw the dust-dry sandy soil, the rock wall, the shadows gliding across it. It was late. Anne would be worried. Brooke...

He struggled to move, and pain exploded through his body. Then he realized who and where the sound was coming from: *him*.

Memory came back in flashes. The men jumping him, his gun useless, Harvey choking him. He tried to roll over, to get to his feet, but agony made him feel faint. So he lay there, breathing slowly, shallowly.

He was alive.

He managed to move, curling his body, then pushing himself up on his hands. Head hanging, breath coming in huge gulps, he stayed that way until he could pull his legs under him and attempted to sit. Hot knives pierced his ankle. Worse than the gunshot. He sank back, panting, and then he saw Harvey. Eyes still open, sand stuck to the dry film in them, a pool of black blood spread like a dark halo beneath his head. He was stone-cold dead.

Jerry. Jerry Hawkins had pushed them both off the edge. Yes. Craning his neck, Mitch looked up to the rooftop. How far had they fallen—thirty feet, forty?

He examined his injuries as best he could. His head ached; his shoulder and ribs and hip were bruised, maybe cracked. His ankle—broken for sure. Scrapes and lacerations. A concussion…likely.

No one knew where he was.

Could he get to his Bronco? It was, what? A half mile away. An easy walk. A stroll. But not in the shape he was in.

He felt the shadow of the bird's wings before he saw it, gliding above him. The harbinger of death in this dry country. He swallowed.

He had to get into the shade before tomorrow's sun parched him, killed him, if his injuries didn't do him in first. He had nothing, no food, no water, no blankets, no radio—all were in his Bronco. Unreachable.

The sun was setting. It was dusk on the canyon floor. No one would search for him tonight. He had to last until tomorrow. He had to. He knew, without questioning, that Anne would look for him with every resource she had.

Brooke. Just when she'd been so happy, a changed girl. She'd been through so much—her parents divorced, a new baby brother and stepfather, and now her father missing. Poor kid.

He had to make the effort. He dragged himself a few inches, his broken ankle shrieking at the movement. Toward the front of the pueblo, along the ancient stone walls. Then a few more inches. His head ached, and he thought he heard voices, but it was only the newly arrived magpies, clucking and murmuring approval of their find.

He must have passed out again, because when he was next aware it was dark out. He dug his fingers in the hard ground and pulled himself forward. He had to get to his Bronco, he kept thinking, kept telling himself. The radio. Water. He had to get there or he'd never see Brooke or Anne again.

ANNE WAS CURLED UP on Mitch's couch. It was very late, but she couldn't sleep. She stayed there, waiting, Brooke asleep next to her. Thank heavens Brooke had finally drifted off, because Anne couldn't bear the reproach, the naked fright in the girl's eyes.

She watched the hands of the clock on the wall crawl around. Her eyes were scratchy, but her heart kept pounding in her chest. The dread, the tearing anxiety, the awful anticipation of loss—they were all too familiar.

Where was Mitch? she cried silently.

She'd waited for hours for the call to come from Washington informing her the satellite was retasked and the tracking device operational. And she was going out of her mind. She'd been there before, and she'd been crawling up out of the abyss, up to the sunlight, to life. All because of Mitch.

And now she was going to lose him, too.

There was nothing to do but sit and wait. The call would come soon, but even if they could track Jerry's truck, he might not lead them to Mitch. And the search would not start till dawn.

Frustration gnawed at her with sharp teeth, then she got angry—an all-too-familiar mental reversal. She would *not* lose Mitch. She'd track Jerry's truck, and Mitch would be there, and he'd be all right. He'd be alive.

Damn you, she thought. *Damn you, Mitch. You better come back to me!*

The phone rang at four-thirty in the morning.

"It's done," the attorney general said. "I'm patching you through to the Pentagon, Agent Winslow. Your password to log into their system is alpha-zulu. Good luck."

From that moment on the race was against time. Anne phoned Martha and told her to log her computer into the Pentagon, go to operational satellite and use the password. "Brooke and I will be over in five minutes. And let's tell the search team we have a go."

By the time the search party, mostly rangers and a few volunteers, arrived, Anne and Martha had already spread huge grid maps out on the counters and floors of the Visitor Center and Martha's computer was logged into the Pentagon's tracking system, her screen filled with grid lines and a bright green blip— the tracking device on Hawkins's truck—which was blinking but stationary in Moab.

But not for long.

As soon as the sky over Canyonlands turned from black to opalescent pastels, the green blip began to move from Moab toward the Needles District. They were all anxious, hunched over the maps, drawing lines as Martha called out grid coordinates from her screen.

About an hour into the operation, Joe Staghorn noted that Hawkins was driving into the park on the southernmost route, but that told them nothing substantial.

So they watched the screen and marked the maps carefully. For what seemed like hours. Brooke made coffee—at least three pots—and Anne tried to stay patient. It was hard, though, so very hard. She would stake her life on Hawkins knowing exactly where Mitch was. *Oh, yes.* And she was sitting here doing nothing.

The sun was blazing in the morning sky when Lonnie crouched next to Anne and followed the line she'd been drawing. "It looks as if... Well, I can't be sure, but..."

"What?" Anne pressed. "Just say it."

"Well, I think he's heading to Chick's Red Canyon dig."

"Of course," Anne whispered. Draco. Chick Draco. She'd known he was involved all along. "Call the sheriff and get him out there right away," she said, trying to sound confident.

But the question still hung heavily in the air: would that green blip on Martha's screen lead them to Mitch?

CHAPTER TWENTY-THREE

THE SUN AWAKENED MITCH. Its slanted rays came over the jagged rim of the mesa and reached him where he lay huddled in the pueblo. He opened his eyes and tried to sit up, but he was dizzy. Dizzy from a concussion and lack of water. He peered around; everything looked so different in daylight. And he saw the place where he'd first fallen and how far he'd crawled last night.

Not very goddamn far.

Well, it was morning. He'd lived through the night, and they'd begin searching for him today. Maybe they already were.

His breath rasped in his throat, and he knew he had to get out of the sun. It would suck from him whatever moisture his body still hoarded.

The voices came to him again, and for a moment he thought it must be the ancient denizens of New Ruin going about their lives, chattering and calling to one another. Kids, mothers, the men starting out to hunt. But he realized it couldn't be the Anasazi—must be the ravens and magpies that were circling.

It occurred to him that there was a stream in the valley floor. He'd noticed it yesterday. But it was far, too far. God, he was thirsty.

He pulled himself along the base of a crumbled wall toward the shade, every muscle screaming, his ankle throbbing. The ground was rough beneath him, scraping at his skin. It was covered with potsherds, broken pots discarded two thousand years ago from the rooms above.

He stopped to rest, panting, his mouth dry, muscles cramping from dehydration, then he crawled on toward the shade.

They'd find him. Today. Soon. He just had to hold on. He started inching along the ground, and one last coherent question struck him: How long would it take for his stripped, sun-bleached bones to become part of the ancient debris that littered this ground?

BY THE TIME Anne reached the Red Canyon dig she was mentally exhausted and sick with fear. Logic and all her training and experience told her that if Hawkins was involved in Mitch's disappearance, then Mitch was already dead. There simply was no other conclusion to draw. But her heart stubbornly refused to accept the obvious. He couldn't be dead. She'd know it, sense it. He *couldn't* be. To hell with the odds. Miracles happened every day. He was alive. Alive.

The sheriff's helicopter had been there for an hour when Joe Staghorn pulled into the parking area near the dig, Anne riding in the passenger seat. Maybe, she prayed, maybe Warner had already extracted the information from Jerry Hawkins. Maybe...

Hawkins was leaning against his pickup, smoking a cigarette, a lazy grin on his face. He was insane, Anne realized when she looked into his eyes. He'd gone completely mad. He'd never talk. Never. And Mitch...

Chick Draco was there, too, sitting on a camp chair,

his hands clasped in his lap, his head down, his shoulders bowed. Did he know anything? Anne suddenly wanted to rip the information from them, to force them to talk.

Sheriff Warner took her aside. "Hawkins has a story, all right, but I'm not sure..."

"I'll interview him," she said. "And Chick?"

The sheriff only shrugged.

Rage and sick fear battled inside Anne, swelled in her. As she approached Hawkins, she wanted to crush his cigarette in his face. She fought for control.

"I'd like any information you have on the disappearance of Ranger Mitchell," she said coldly.

"I told the sheriff already."

"Tell *me*."

"Well, like I said, I saw Mitchell in the park, and I explained to him where Harv was."

"Harvey. Your cousin."

"Yeah, Harv. I left him up at this place he discovered. A ruin that he went nuts over. I thought Mitchell better see it."

"When was this?"

"Oh, late yesterday afternoon."

"And Mitch went up to this place, this ruin?"

"Yeah, I told him where it was. Then I went home."

"Where's Harvey now?"

Jerry shrugged insouciantly.

Anne felt rage boil up inside her. He was lying; she knew he was lying.

She spun around to Joe Staghorn. "Let me see your gun, Ranger," she said, her stomach churning.

"Gladly." Staghorn smiled, unsnapped his holster and handed her his revolver.

"Hey," the sheriff was saying, but he backed off when Anne fired a look at him.

She lifted the gun and pointed it at Hawkins. "Where is Mitchell, you son of a..."

"Whoa," Hawkins said, straightening, the grin fading. "Careful with that thing. You don't want to shoot anybody."

"Don't I? I've got nothing to lose, Hawkins. Don't goddamn underestimate me."

"Listen," Hawkins began, but they were interrupted by Chick.

"Stop," he said, his voice breaking, "no more violence. Oh, God."

Anne whirled on him. "You better tell me what you know, Chick."

"Yes, yes. He...Jerry...he came this morning and he told me about this place, New Ruin. This fabulous place. He was going to take me there. He gave me a map, but then the sheriff got here." He looked up, wringing his hands, his face tortured. "And he said Mitch was missing, and I thought...I kept thinking. Two murders, Mitch missing...that ruin... Oh, God."

She looked back at Jerry. His face was sullen now, one eye shut as cigarette smoke drifted up.

"You're under arrest, Hawkins," she snapped.

"Hey. Hold on. I told you, it was Harv."

"Don't give me that crap," she said. "I don't buy it, and I'll guarantee a federal judge will issue a search warrant now and we'll have the murder weapon." She glared at him, at the sudden sweat that had popped out on his upper lip. "You kept the gun, didn't you, Hawkins? It's written all over your face."

He was silent.

"You thought you were so smart." She turned to

a sheriff's deputy. "I want him placed under arrest.
No bail. For now we'll call it accessory to crimes
committed on federal lands. I'm sure we'll be raising
the ante, though, to murder."

Two murders, she thought, and then there was
Mitch. But she couldn't contemplate that. No. Mitch
was okay. He had to be okay.

The deputy snapped handcuffs on Jerry's wrists
and gave him a shove toward a waiting vehicle, all
the while reading him his Miranda rights.

Chick cleared his throat. "I have the map," he
said, still visibly shaken. "I think we can find this
ruin."

"We'll take the chopper," Warner put in, but Anne
was already hurrying toward it.

It turned out to be the longest ride of her life, the
whole way her body and heart and brain shuddered
with the vibration of the helicopter. Warner spent
most of the time on the radio, first to Martha at the
Visitor Center and then to the search party members,
who were somewhere below and behind them, following in four-wheel-drive vehicles. Anne spoke only
once, and that was to Brooke, who was waiting at the
center with Martha.

"We're on our way in the helicopter to your dad
right now," she said, her lips dry, her heart so heavy
it felt like a stone in her chest.

"Is he all right?"

"We'll know in a bit, honey."

"Will you radio us?"

So brave. "Yes, Brooke, immediately. It'll be
fine."

But would it? Logic tried to intrude, but she ban-
ished it. *Be alive, damn it. Be alive, Mitch.* He

couldn't leave her alone. Never again. And he couldn't leave Brooke. If there was a way, any way at all, Mitch had survived this…

A headset on, Chick sat next to the pilot. He read the map, pointed and directed the pilot to a landing spot on the valley floor. The chopper settled there, kicking up dust. Anne was out before the rotors had even drooped toward the ground.

"It's still—" Chick twisted the map and pointed "—a half mile up this cut."

"Let's go," Anne said tightly, breathless already, unaware of the pained looks Chick and Warner exchanged as the sheriff grabbed the litter and medical kit and Chick remembered the water.

The first clue that they were on the right track was Mitch's Bronco parked on the route a few hundred yards from where the helicopter had landed. "Oh, God," she said, panting, and she practically ran the entire way up the narrow cut, Warner and Draco barely keeping pace.

"Ravens," Warner finally said behind her.

She looked up to see birds rise into a wedge of sky, as if someone had flapped his arms to scatter them.

"That's not good," he added.

She didn't dare ask what he meant. They rounded a shoulder of rock and there was the ruin. She heard Chick gasp, but it didn't mean a thing. Nothing would until she found Mitch. The neat, square rooms with T-shaped doorways and the tiers of dwellings rising on the cliffside were merely a meaningless backdrop to this drama.

"I don't see anybody," the sheriff said, setting down the litter, catching his breath.

"He could be anywhere," she panted. "In one of those rooms…"

She didn't wait for the two men. She raced through maze after maze of rooms. She stumbled often. Over crumbled walls and fallen rock. Cutting herself, getting up, not even dusting off, searching, searching.

"Mitch! Mitch!" she cried until her voice was raspy.

Up two ladders. Through another jumble of rooms. Down. Half falling off the last rungs. Searching and crying out. Sobbing now.

Once, she spotted Chick Draco below. *Damn it*. He wasn't even searching! He was on his hands and knees, examining an object, his face filled with wonder. *Oh, God,* she thought. *Oh, God*. "Mitch!" she cried.

And then she saw something.

She stopped in her tracks, panting. Over there. Fifty, sixty yards away. Something out of place. Against the wall of the pueblo. A huddled pile of rags? Gray rags…

A uniform. An arm. Outstretched.

"Mitch," formed on her lips. Then louder. *"Mitch! Sheriff…Draco, over here, over here."* Then she was running, tripping, scrabbling over rocks. *Be alive, be alive*.

She reached him and collapsed next to his body, her heart hammering. "Oh, God, Mitch," she wept, and she touched his back.

He stirred under her hand. At first she thought it was her imagination, but then his arm moved and he turned a little, and she saw his face, dried blood streaking his forehead, and his eyes opened, bleary, trying to focus.

"Mitch." Her voice filled with fervent thanks.

"Anne," he whispered through cracked lips. "I knew it, knew…"

"Sh, it's okay." She stroked his forehead. "Can you tell me where you're hurt? I've got men here. We'll get you out. Mitch. Oh, my God, you're going to be fine."

"Hawkins pushed us…fell. Think my ankle's broken."

Hawkins. "'Us'? Mitch…"

"Harvey. He's dead. Back there."

"What?"

Then Warner and Chick were there with the equipment and water, but Mitch wanted to finish. "Jerry."

"Jerry killed his cousin?" Warner said as he opened the litter and set it next to Mitch.

"Yeah. Pushed him. David Draco was here, too. Gotta arrest them. Jerry and David."

"Well, I'll be." The sheriff gawked.

"And you witnessed it," Anne said. "My God." She held the water bottle to his lips.

Mitch. Drinking water. Alive. The tears came again and she felt Chick's hand on her shoulder.

Carrying Mitch down from the ruin and back to the chopper was brutal labor. He was deadweight, had fallen unconscious soon after he'd taken the water. Warner and the pilot did what they could to make him comfortable. He was alive. Yes. But for how long? Getting him to Moab was crucial.

The chopper lifted off, leaving Warner and Chick to await the search party and to radio in to Martha and Brooke to tell them to drive to the hospital in Moab. But Anne couldn't think about any of that now. She simply kept her fingers on the pulse in his neck, because she couldn't hear anything in the helicopter.

Don't you dare die on me, Mitch.

An emergency team awaited them at Allen Memorial Hospital. They whisked Mitch away so swiftly she couldn't say much to him. He opened his eyes when she murmured, "We're here," and he tried to smile, squeezed her hand, and then he was on a gurney being wheeled inside. She stood there on the helipad, the rotors of the chopper still turning slowly, winding down, as her heart also wound down. She felt lost and alone and empty. What if they'd gotten to him too late?

She knew she should check in by radio with the sheriff, find out about Harvey Hawkins, see if the rescue team had found his body yet. And then the FBI in Phoenix would need to issue an arrest warrant for David Draco. Accessory before and after the fact. Murder one. Not to mention the theft of artifacts from federal lands.

A lot to be done. But not until she got word on Mitch. She prayed word would come before Brooke arrived.

It didn't, though. Anne was sitting, her heart still beating too quickly, on a vinyl couch in a waiting room when Brooke and Martha rushed in.

"How is he?" Brooke cried.

"He's going to be fine," Anne said, pushing herself up, and Brooke ran into her arms and burst into tears.

Martha's eyes met Anne's over the girl's head. Questioning.

"He's banged up and he probably has a broken

ankle, but he'll be fine,'' she said, holding Brooke. She prayed she was right.

The three of them sat in the waiting room, and Anne told them what had happened.

''You mean that man pushed my dad off the pueblo roof?'' Brooke asked.

''Him and Harvey.''

''His own cousin,'' Martha said.

''He'll get convicted this time,'' Anne said. ''There's an eyewitness.''

''Yes, my dad.''

An hour later Chick Draco burst into the waiting room, his eyes wild behind his glasses, his fine hair standing up in wisps on his head.

''Oh, Anne, there you are!'' he gasped. ''I got here as fast as I could. How…how is he?''

''We don't know yet,'' she replied. ''They're working on him now.''

''I've been out of my mind with worry, and then it took so long for the search party to get back so I could get my truck, and nobody knew anything…'' Chick drew the back of his wrist across his forehead, wiping away sweat.

''I think he looked worse than he actually was. His ankle is broken, but the doctor was mostly concerned about dehydration,'' Anne said.

''Yes, of course, dehydration. I warn my students about it all the time. This climate…deceptive, dangerous.'' Chick drew in a lungful of air and let it out. ''I was afraid I'd get here and find…oh, God, that Mitch was…''

''He's going to be fine,'' Brooke said staunchly.

''You're right, yes, certainly, he'll be just fine.'' Chick sank into a plastic chair across from the three women. He put his head into his hands. "So many people dead," he muttered. "Needless, useless. I feel so terribly, terribly guilty. My own uncle. I should have—" he raised his head, devastated "—I should have known. All these years, all those incredible artifacts he had in his gallery. Me, of all people, fooled just like his customers. I believed him. I can't forgive myself."

"It's not your fault, Chick," Anne said softly. "And we never would have found Mitch at all if it hadn't been for you. You saved his life."

"But I still can't forgive myself."

"You couldn't have known," Martha added.

Chick shook his head, closing his eyes. "Uncle David," he whispered.

"You can help prosecute him," Anne said. "If you feel that you can do it. Be an expert witness, something like that."

"I could. I might do that. I have to do *something*."

"And New Ruin," she went on, "you have an opportunity there. Study it, set up the site for others to come in. Protect it."

"Yes," he said. "It's an unbelievable find. New Ruin will need protection."

Anne wished Chick the best in his nasty affairs; he was a true innocent, caught in the middle of the conflict only because he was related to one of the criminals. She supposed his guilt was natural, if unwarranted.

"It wasn't your fault," she repeated. "Remember that."

"I'm not mad at you, Mr. Draco," Brooke said. "You didn't make any of this happen."

"Brooke, honey, that helps—really it does. I appreciate it.'' He looked at Anne. ''Do you know how long it'll be before they're done with Mitch?''

''Quite awhile, I think. You don't have to wait. We'll call the Visitor Center the minute we hear anything.''

''They want me to report to park headquarters here in Moab. Maybe I'll go on over there now.'' Indecision tinged his voice.

''Sure, go on. You can't do a thing here.''

''I'll call, though. I'm a wreck over this, total wreck. I should phone my wife. Yes, I better do that first. She must be worried, too,'' he said distractedly, pushing his glasses up.

''Sure, go on, phone Ellen,'' Anne said.

''Yes, I will. Thank you all for being so understanding. It helps a lot.'' He shook his head again. ''Uncle David, I can't believe it.'' And then he wandered away, his tall frame loose-jointed, his shoulders bent. Mumbling to himself.

''The absentminded professor,'' Martha said, sighing.

''Amen to that,'' Anne replied.

As the hours crawled by like tortoises, Anne fought drowsiness. She ate something Martha got in the cafeteria, couldn't remember what it was a minute later. Realized she was terribly thirsty when she drank a soft drink down.

She rested her head on the back of the couch, Brooke on one side of her, Martha on the other. Anne felt Brooke reach for her hand, and she grasped the girl's fingers and hung on, and they waited like that. Finally, the doctor pushed his way through the doors, and they all sat up as if stung. Anne struggled to her feet. She was afraid to ask, afraid…

But he was smiling.

"My dad?" Brooke said in a little voice.

"Your dad is just fine. He's dehydrated and has some serious bruising, and we put his ankle in a cast, young lady, but in a month he'll be just like new."

"Just like new," Anne repeated, and never knew that she was crying and laughing at the same time.

IN SEPTEMBER THE WEEKEND dawned bright and clear. Mornings were cool, so cool you needed a jacket, but by noon the sun heated the land. A few trees, mostly the cottonwoods in the riverbeds, were turning golden.

Mitch, Anne and Brooke started out from Moab early, drove across the park to the now-familiar winding canyon that led to New Ruin. They parked, got out of the Bronco, hoisted backpacks and began the trek to the pueblo.

It was off-limits to the public, a gate put up, wire fencing, signs. But Mitch had the key to the padlock. New Ruin was soon going to be overrun by archaeologists and anthropologists; *National Geographic,* the University of Colorado, of Montana and several other entities had applied for excavating permits, and he'd wanted to see the ruins once more before it became the center of a maelstrom.

They climbed to the highest terrace and settled themselves on a low wall built of perfectly fitted sandstone blocks. The entire valley stretched before them.

"How's your ankle?" Anne asked.

"Fine."

"You sure, Dad?" Brooke wanted to know.

"Hey," he said, "you've been babying me since I broke it. Enough."

Anne sighed and looked around, drawing in a breath of the cool dry air. "Beautiful. The whole month I was back in Washington I kept thinking about New Ruin. Now here I am."

"Yes," Mitch said.

"What do you think of the house Dad rented in Moab?" Brooke asked.

"Very nice."

"See, Dad," Brooke said. "And I started school. I'm a freshman."

A freshman. Anne had to smile at the pride with which Brooke spoke.

She began to unpack their lunches then, busying herself, wondering if she hadn't been crazy to come back, to let go of her lease on her apartment, store all her stuff at her sister's—including Yoda. Maybe she'd read too much into the few things she and Mitch had said while he was in the hospital. Maybe...

"So, *Dad,*" Brooke was saying, "ask her."

"Brooke, now's not..."

"Ask me what?" Anne took a long drink of water, then shaded her eyes and glanced at Mitch. He was so damn handsome, the autumn light dancing in his hair, golden on his skin.

"Dad." Brooke again.

"Hey," Anne said, "what gives?"

Mitch turned to his daughter. "Weren't you going to check out that kiva, honey? The one down on the lower terrace?"

"Oh, like hint, hint?" Brooke grinned wickedly.

"Some privacy, please?" He shot her a stern look.

"Okay, okay, I'm dying to check out this kiva, Anne, so I'll see you in a while."

"What about lunch?"

"Forget that for now," Mitch said.

They watched Brooke cross a maze of rooms and then disappear down a ladder.

"Um," Anne said, wondering, at a loss. For all practical purposes, she'd ended her life in the East. She knew she was going to settle here—nearby, anyway. Beyond that? Well, she didn't know. In the hospital Mitch—on painkillers, she recalled in alarm—had said something about her living with him. Said he needed her. He loved her. He'd said those things, but...

She'd left Moab only two days after he was admitted to the hospital. She may have quit her job, but myriad loose ends remained to tie up in the government's case against Jerry Hawkins and David Draco, including running more lab tests and attending to depositions. Their separate trials wouldn't even get under way for another six months at the earliest.

Yet none of that mattered at this moment. What mattered was her life, her *new* life. But she wouldn't lie to herself. She was scared to death.

Mitch drank some water and cleared his throat, staring straight ahead. "So," he said.

"Well," she began, smiling a too-bright smile. "Ah, what was Brooke getting at?"

"Uh, we did some talking while you were gone," he answered casually.

"Mmm."

"And... Damn, Anne, I think I better just come out and say it."

"That would be good." Her tone was neutral, but her heart was stuck in her throat.

"We—Brooke and I, that is—well, we want you to move into the new house with us."

"Oh."

"Damn," he said again. "That's not exactly it. I, well, I want to marry you, Anne, and Brooke is all for it, too. I know it's a lot to think about, and you don't have to answer right now..."

"Yes," she breathed.

"Yes?"

"Absolutely. But it's got to be me and my cat. We're a set."

"Your cat. Right. Of course." He turned to her suddenly. "You did say yes?"

"Uh-huh." Joy blossomed in her. "I know that I love you. I love you and Brooke and this place. Especially right here. There's no curse, you know, as the papers and TV are saying. It's not cursed at all."

"No, it's not."

"It's magic, Mitch. For me, for us, it is. If it hadn't been for New Ruin..."

"You two never would have met," Brooke said, her voice startling them.

Mitch took Anne's hand. "And how long have *you* been listening?"

"Long enough," Brooke said. She sat down next to them, and Mitch put his arm around Brooke's shoulders and Anne's and drew both his girls to his sides.

"You know," he said, gazing out across the land, "this isn't half-bad."

Return to the charm of the Regency era with

GEORGETTE HEYER,

creator of the modern Regency genre.

Enjoy six romantic collector's editions with forewords by some of today's bestselling romance authors,

**Nora Roberts, Mary Jo Putney,
Jo Beverley, Mary Balogh,
Theresa Medeiros and Kasey Michaels.**

Frederica
On sale February 2000

The Nonesuch
On sale March 2000

The Convenient Marriage
On sale April 2000

Cousin Kate
On sale May 2000

The Talisman Ring
On sale June 2000

The Corinthian
On sale July 2000

Available at your favorite retail outlet.

HARLEQUIN®
Makes any time special ™

Visit us at www.romance.net   PHGHGEN

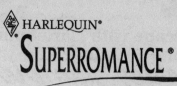

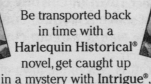

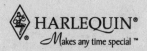

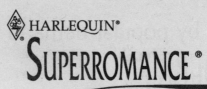

Welcome to cowboy country!

MONTANA LEGACY by **Roxanne Rustand**
(Superromance #895)
Minneapolis cop Kate Rawlins has her own reasons
for wanting to sell her inheritance—half of the
Lone Tree Ranch, Montana. Then she meets
co-owner Seth Hayward and suddenly splitting the property
doesn't seem like a good idea....
On sale February 2000

COWBOY COME HOME by **Eve Gaddy**
(Superromance #903)
After years on the saddle circuit, champion bronco
rider Jake Rollins returns home—determined to find
out whether his ex-lover's daughter is *his* child.
On sale March 2000

Available at your favorite retail outlet.

Visit us at www.romance.net

HSRRANCH